# The Merkaba Mystery

IVA KENAZ

Copyright © 2017 Iva Kenaz

www.ivakenaz.com

First Edition

All rights reserved. No part of this publication may be reproduced, stored in a retrieval system, or transmitted, in any form or by any means, electronic, mechanical, photocopying, recording or otherwise, without the prior permission from the publisher and author. For information, write to: ivakenaz@gmail.com

Identifiers: ISBN: 1545457638 (paperback)
B0716W2HZL (eBook)


Author: Iva Kenaz
Editor: Jenny Papworth
Cover Design: Gunnar Tryggvason
Book Design: Iva Kenaz

# Contents

| | | |
|---|---|---|
| 0 | THE FOOL | 15 |
| I. | THE MAGICIAN | 29 |
| II. | THE HIGH PRIESTESS | 42 |
| III. | THE EMPRESS | 54 |
| IV. | THE EMPEROR | 70 |
| V. | THE HIEROPHANT | 86 |
| VI. | THE LOVERS | 100 |
| VII. | THE CHARIOT | 116 |
| VIII. | JUSTICE | 130 |
| IX. | THE HERMIT | 142 |
| X. | WHEEL OF FORTUNE | 163 |
| XI. | STRENGTH | 179 |
| XII. | THE HANGED MAN | 194 |
| XIII. | DEATH | 205 |
| XIV. | TEMPERANCE | 217 |
| XV. | THE DEVIL | 234 |

| XVI. | THE TOWER | 246 |
| XVII. | THE STAR | 261 |
| XVIII. | THE MOON | 270 |
| XIX. | THE SUN | 288 |
| XX. | JUDGEMENT | 303 |
| XXI. | THE WORLD | 315 |

*This novel is dedicated to my hometown, Praha.*

# How the Story Came to be

It all began with a dream in which I ambled across an unfamiliar looking Prague, watching as buildings were being torn down. I felt a strong bond with one of the houses and begged the workers not to demolish it, claiming that it was my home. After I woke up, I researched some old paintings and photographs, wondering whether I would find the street I dreamt about. Finally, I did. It was the Narrow Lane, located in the old Jewish Town, also called Josefov or the Fifth District, in Prague.

From that point on, I had similar and even more vivid dreams of places, which I later found on old maps and paintings. It all seemed to be linked to a Prague before its fatal renovation, which happened between the years 1896 and 1903 and mainly affected the Jewish Town. I found this an interesting historical period, when the old ways met the new, and technical developments were taking over the world. I felt inspired to write a novel set at the turn of the century in Prague, but didn't quite have a story.

Around that time, I began to have even more intense and regular dreams about a Prague which looked more beautiful and colourful than the one I knew. It was a fantasy version of the city. I found it curious, since according to legend, Prague is a threshold to other realms. In fact, Prague's local name *Praha* is derived from the word *práh*, which translates as *threshold*.

Gustav Meyrink, a visionary author who described Prague's renovation in his novel *Golem*, wrote that he felt as though the city truly was a threshold to other realms. He also spoke about a group called 'Seven Brothers' which supposedly established towns on inter-dimensional thresholds, and that the members came from Allahabad, India. Allahabad used to be called *Prayaga* or *Prayag*, which bears a definite similarity to Praha or Prague, and means *meeting place* or *place of the confluences* in Hindi. The city was built on a confluence of three rivers, but who knows whether there was a deeper meaning to that title.

In regard to the legend, Meyrink also mentioned a mysterious Masonic lodge, the Sat Bhai. Curiously, the name translates to 'seven brothers' in Hindi, and in one of their texts, Prague is referred to as *Pryaya*.

Before I began writing a story inspired by the above-mentioned dreams and legends, I studied various philosophies on spirit travel or *the threshold passing*. I also delved into teachings such as the Kabbalah and Sacred Geometry, and became intrigued by the idea of the Merkaba - the divine chariot or throne from Ezekiel's vision in the Bible, also called the light body.

I felt guided to base the text on the Tarot's Major Arcana as I consider the trumps to be the secret keys to the Merkaba and the Tarot symbolism is naturally present in most stories anyway. I divided the novel into twenty-two chapters, based on the Tarot archetypes, starting with zero, the Fool.

As I was writing with the Tarot's Major Arcana symbolism in mind, I began to deeper understand the correlations between the Merkaba, the Tarot, and the Tree of Life. This book therefore blends fiction with research and contemplation on these esoteric themes, which remain utterly fascinating to me.

"I don't know any other city like Prague. It makes someone who lives there, and who aligns with it spiritually, magically lured and tempted to visit the locations of its unsettling past. It seems as if the dead woo us, the living, to visit the places they used to reside in, whilst whispering that Prague's name is no coincidence, and that it has a threshold much thinner than in other parts of the country.
Then, we find ourselves wandering under some influence, hearing or seeing things that we have not known before, and imbibing a feeling, which stays with us until old age. A feeling as though we had, somehow, crossed over a threshold."

*Invisible Prague,* Gustav Meyrink

# Chapter 0

## The Fool

*Memories from Prague (locally Praha), August 1896*

Remember. That was the first word which entered my mind when I regained consciousness. The emotions that followed were a blend of relief and fear, then anger sneaked in, and finally, there was love for someone who remained a nameless, faceless phantom.

The soft whiff of the pine-scented breeze awakened me to my surroundings. I opened my eyes and found myself standing waist deep in moonlit water. Before me was a confluence of two teal-blue rivers. I felt a smooth, warm rock beneath my feet, and as I looked down, I saw a large, round-shaped stone radiating white light through the ripples. On its surface, a symbol was engraved. It resembled two six-pointed stars on top of each other. I sensed that it was communicating to me, but something disturbed the connection with it; a tall, male figure wearing a long cloak stood on the shore. I felt indifferent to the stranger, although slightly intimidated, as I couldn't see his face in the darkness beneath his hood. He watched me for a moment then walked away, and I was left alone with the glittering water and the ancient trees.

It was then that I realised I knew nothing about my past. I only guessed that I had some history. I didn't recognise the place I found myself in, yet in some ways, it seemed familiar. I gazed back down at the stone and found that its light had vanished.

Once I had calmed my sea of emotions, I focused on my body. In one hand, I held a grey scarf made into a bag with a few objects wrapped inside, in the other, a letter. I made for the shore, but underestimated the current and the silt-covered stones. They made me slip, and sink deeper into the water. I managed to hold onto the scarf bag, but couldn't catch the letter. It was carried away, and disappeared along with my understanding of who I was, where I was and why.

There was only one thing I was certain about: I had a mission to pursue, which was connected to the certain someone I loved and a certain city he went to. I felt compelled to follow the stream, hoping it would guide me to a place where I could find some answers.

That's how I ended up in the middle of Prague. Like the countryside, I both did and didn't recognise it. I was lost in its beguiling atmosphere; the dry, powder-like air, and the crowds of overdressed people who ventured through the ancient stone labyrinth along with me.

As I passed the city walls, the looks and whispers

that had been following me intensified. People were eyeing me, some just confused and pitying, others glaring in outraged disbelief. I wondered if it was because I was dressed differently. The local women wore long dresses too, but these were cinched in tightly at the waist, which accentuated the cascades of their full, layered skirts. They also wore their hair tight at the neck, sometimes decorated with hats or flower clips. I, on the other hand, had wild, black hair, and wore a purple, flowing gown decorated with a simple white, oval-shaped brooch.

I wandered around in despair, hoping for at least one memory to drag me from this strange feeling of oblivion. Soon I found myself in a large open space, a square with a memorial decorated with winged statues and a dominant female figure on top. The buildings were colourful, some grand, some simple, and some with two windows spanning the frontage.

Suddenly, I heard barking behind me, and turned around to face a scruffy stray dog. He was barking at me, as if he wanted me to follow him. Since he seemed to know his way round the city, and I longed for some guidance, I decided to take his lead. The dog headed for a large corner building, and slipped into a tiny lane that led us towards an ochre-coloured church, which seemed almost red in the encroaching dusk. Its round transept loomed over us as we headed to a street called Maiselova. The street sign was in two different languages, one of which I could actually read, which comforted me a little.

I didn't know if the stray dog was the right guide, but I stuck with him, even though he seemed to be taking me into a less illustrious part of the city. The streets were shabby and the buildings were covered with old layers of dust and mould. The dog's agile pace kept my hopes high as we entered the melancholic Jáchymova Lane. The space was very narrow. It looked as if the buildings leaned in towards each other, seeking solace in the gloom of their shadows. I observed the layers of repainted façades, with many colour tones hiding beneath the most recent one. The rooftops were adorned with variously sized, crooked chimneys, and the windows were scratched and soiled.

Untraceable whispers surrounded me as I marvelled at the lane's atmosphere. It made me wonder if it was the buildings that I was hearing; whether they were exchanging news on what had happened here and how the people were feeling. It was terrifying really, how alive they seemed, as opposed to me – a lost fool whose only comfort was a stray dog.

From this confined space, we walked into a small clearing with a green water pump with a picturesque lantern attached to it. The dog turned left into a street called Narrow. The name made no sense to me because it was wider than those I had passed before, and far livelier as well. It seemed to be a market street, as there were many shops, crammed with all kinds of goods from clothes to books and kitchen supplies. The shopkeepers hovered around the entrances, wooing in potential customers. I was grateful for all the hustle and bustle as it made me stand out less. Undecided about where to go from here, I looked around for the dog, but there was no sign of him. He must have disappeared into one of the shops, or maybe he'd returned home.

With this thought, my eyes fell upon a building at the street's end and widened in awe. I recognised it as my home. It had two storeys, four windows in each, and its white, rather clean façade contrasted starkly to the dark, tower-like building next to it. Only one thing seemed to be missing from how I remembered it – a tall pine tree growing by its entrance.

I approached it with a sense of bewilderment,

quickly followed by a blur of memories that danced across my mind, flirting with me from afar, alluring but ungraspable. The more I tried to hold onto them, the more distant they became.

I was standing opposite the building when I heard a male voice calling out to me:

"Hello, lovely! Come on inside! There are many things that you might like in here!"

I turned to see where the voice was coming from, and spotted a middle-aged, roughened shopkeeper, who stood among four other men who grinned at me. The way they were scrutinising me seemed almost belligerent.

I was timid, and cautious of the locals. For some reason, I had a feeling that I couldn't trust anybody. However, that was until I met *her*. She was wearing bright, splendid clothing, and an extravagant red flower in her thick, grey bun. She looked like a young girl despite her ripe age, and although I was certain I had never met her before, she was the only one who had struck me as trustworthy so far. Perhaps that was down to her friendliness, or maybe it was because she was waving at me from the entrance to a house that I regarded as my home.

I approached her, hoping for answers, and she pulled me inside her shop right away, gentle but insistent.

"Come on, dear, have a seat. I'm just going to close the shop and I'll be right with you."

She acted as if we had been friends for ages, which made me believe that I had come to the right place. A little more relaxed, I sat on one of the chairs, and watched as she bustled through the shop, bringing some clothes that were hanging from the door shutters inside, then carefully closing the door and waving at a few customers.

"Come tomorrow, ladies! We're closing for today."

Through the humble shopfront, I spotted the stray dog again. He glanced at me and ran off, either seeking a new mission, or perhaps giving me a sign that he had brought me to the right place. I smiled to myself, silently thanking him.

Then I took in the shop's atmosphere, surprised that the interior didn't seem as familiar as the building itself. There were many goods inside: piles of shoes, clothes, hats, old books, and boxes brimming with herbs, vegetables and fruit. What a strange combination of things to sell in one shop, I thought to myself. The woman's skirt whizzed past me as she reached for a burgundy overcoat and handed it to me.

"It tends to be chilly in here despite the heat outside."

I accepted it with a thankful nod as she went on:

"Thank God for these stone shelters, eh? In the summertime, they remain cool and in the winter, they keep the heat in. I'm so glad to be finished for the day. Can you imagine how many people argued with me about the price of these new coats? Aren't they beautiful?"

She touched the fabric carefully, then rattled on:

"Why do people assume that my merchandise is low-grade? I keep telling everyone that my shop is different from all the others on this street. You'll find no junk here, only carefully picked antiques, and plants lovingly cultivated in my own backyard."

I had to wait for her to catch her breath before asking:

"I'm sorry to interrupt, but do we know each other?"

She finally stopped talking, and turned to me with a surprised expression on her face.

"I don't think so."

"Oh," I exhaled, disappointed. "I thought, since you invited me inside…"

"Well, I had to save you from the men outside," she explained, "as they were staring at you like vultures. What are you doing out in such a dress anyway? Is it a nightgown?"

I frowned a bit, confused by the question.

"Don't get me wrong, it's lovely," she felt the material and nodded approvingly, "divine, really, but... did something happen to you, dear?" She grasped my hands to show care and support, but without waiting for my reply, she continued: "Or... Oh... Are you one of the midnight ladies?"

"Midnight ladies?" I shook my head, more baffled than before.

"Sounds better that way, doesn't it?" she said with a smile, and nudged me, assuming I knew what she was talking about. Then she waved her hand chirpily.

"I don't care if you are one, and if you're not, then I'm sorry to have offended you. See, this quarter is full of questionable businesses these days. It's certainly not what it used to be. Not that I don't respect the work of the midnight ladies... What a hardship!" She paused to look at me. "I'm sorry, I talk too much, don't I? Would you like some chicory? Or some real coffee? I might have a bit left upstairs."

Yet again, I had no idea what she was talking about, or what coffee or chicory was. I was just happy to understand the language she spoke.

Before I could recover, she hurried me to the back door, and into a draughty hallway that smelled of rotten wood. As she had warned, it was chilly inside, so I snuggled into the borrowed overcoat.

We stepped onto a creaky old staircase and, as we made our way to the first floor, a young man appeared on the basement steps below us. I could only see his back, and the dark curls that grazed the collar of his brown jacket, but I was certain I knew him. I was inexplicably drawn to his rather short, but strongly-built figure, and to the way he moved. I froze, wondering why my heart hammered at the sight of this stranger. He approached the door to the backyard without noticing us, deep in thought.

"If you are here to repair the chimney, I'd recommend you go up the stairs instead!" cried the woman, but he didn't even bother to turn in our direction.

"Some people can be so rude," she complained to herself and continued on up the stairs. My eyes remained on the door that had closed behind him, and for some reason I felt anxious about his departure. I had a feeling that he was important to me somehow. I wanted to call out his name and, although it was on the tip of my tongue, it faded away. I was deliberating over whether to follow the woman or him. Finally, I decided on him, but lost my footing, stumbled, and rolled all the way down the stairs. After I hit the ground, there was nothing for a while, nothing but a dark canvas upon which a white ovoid was drawn, shimmering on the path ahead.

☆

I woke up lying on a divan next to a dark green wall. I was in a small living room with midnight blue and brown carpentry, and a large fireplace. Though everything was quite decrepit, it gave off a cosy, warm feeling.

The word *remember* possessed my mind again, but unlike last time, I recollected at least something in the present – how I came to be in that humble, two-room apartment. I could hear male and female voices saying goodbye in the hallway, then the entrance door as it creaked and closed. I turned to see who was approaching.

"Don't be alarmed, dear," said the woman I had

met before, "it was just the neighbour. That scoundrel is too loud, I know..."

"Is your neighbour the man we saw before my fall?" I asked, hopefully.

"No, that must have been a random vagabond, there are many here in the Fifth District these days."

She headed for the kitchen. I rested my back against the wall, tired and disappointed. I pictured the man, wondering whether I would ever see him again.

The woman soon reappeared holding a tray with a large pot, two cups, and a bowl of sweets. "I don't think much of his type, but he brought you inside, so I should be grateful."

She sat beside me and felt my forehead for fever. "How are you feeling?" she asked, genuinely concerned. I touched my crown. It ached a bit, but other than that, I seemed to be fine.

"I'm all right, thank you."

"There were no bruises, you were lucky," she said and poured me some of the dark, nut-scented drink. "I was so worried when I saw you fall down that wretched staircase. It's decided. We need to have it fixed."

I sipped on the bitter, aromatic drink, savouring its warmth.

"We haven't introduced ourselves," she said. "I'm Vilma."

"I would love to introduce myself as well, Vilma, but I can't remember my name." My admission surprised her.

"What do you mean?"

I shrugged my shoulders. "I don't know who I am or where I come from. I regained consciousness in the confluence of two rivers, and followed their path all the way to this city.

"Everything seemed odd at first, and made no sense until I saw this house. That was the only thing I recognised. It sounds very strange, I know, and I can't explain it."

She stared at me over the rim of her cup, her eyes gentle, empathic.

"You truly remember nothing? Not even your parents? Family? Hometown?"

I shook my head.

"Something must have happened," she considered. "Do you recall any trauma?"

I shook my head again. Vilma's brows furrowed in confusion, and after a pensive moment, she went on, "Well, at least it explains the wardrobe."

She smiled, and I couldn't help but smile back, and she gave me a determined look. "We'll figure it out, don't worry. So, the only thing you recognise is this building?"

I was about to nod when I remembered the enigmatic stranger.

"Actually, the man we saw before I fell... I'm certain that I know him from somewhere."

"Really? Then it's a pity that he left so abruptly, and didn't even look our way. I wonder what he was doing here in the first place. Could it be that he was looking for you?"

She took a sip from her tiny cup then stirred it with a spoon.

"I don't want to impose, Vilma, I just don't know what to do, or where to go from here," I said, feeling guilty about burdening her with my misfortune.

"Don't you worry about that," she reassured me. "Can you imagine how dull my life is? Down in the shop every day, listening to all that gossip, haggling, inane chit chat. I would be happy to help you. It could even be an adventure."

I was relieved to hear that she cared about what had happened to me. My heart filled with gratitude at the thought of finding a friend, after being hounded by disdain, frowns and leers all day.

"Now, let me think…" said Vilma. "If we don't stumble upon the man you recognised again, we must decide how to help you on our own.

"Of course, one option would be to go to the authorities, but I worry about that. Goodness knows where they would send you. They don't welcome anything out of the ordinary.

"No. I'm not going to risk having you end up in a mental hospital somewhere. You know what? We could consult my friend Dora tomorrow. She's a psychic."

For some reason, I knew the word *psychic*, and it sounded positive to me.

"Most people are sceptical about the esoteric arts, as there are many charlatans among us, but she has proven to be extraordinarily talented. I'm certain she wouldn't regard this as a coincidence – that of all the houses, you recognised only this one.

"I'm too old not to follow signs of destiny, especially when they are so blatant. I think I'm meant to help you, and you are welcome to stay."

I grasped her hand gratefully. "Thank you, Vilma. From the little or nothing that I know about myself, you have made me remember that I too don't believe in coincidences." We smiled at each other, making a silent pact.

I asked her about the city then, particularly the part we found ourselves in. She said it was a Jewish ghetto, also called the Fifth District, or *Josefov* after Josef II whose reign was the Golden Age for the Jewish people.

"Throughout history, the locals have suffered many hardships," she told me, "and now it's the town itself that faces destruction.

"After many years of procrastinating, they have approved the regeneration of this quarter, and the expropriation law has been announced. I prayed that it wouldn't come to this, that the leaders of this city would choose to restore rather than destroy it, but this quarter's fate seemed to have been sealed long ago.

"Of course, living conditions have been tragic after all the floods and epidemics. Sickness and crime are commonplace in the Fifth District, but amidst it all, the area has magic. Since the Middle Ages, this has been one of the most important spiritual centres of Prague. Great mystics resided here.

"In a way, it used to be a town within a town. The western Jews settled by the Old New Synagogue, the eastern Jews by Old School Street. Some say that the magic will remain underground, and imbue the new streets with its power regardless.

"That's the only thing that keeps me calm – that despite the fall of the crown, the roots will be preserved. Ancient mysteries will continue to seep through the stone, whispering to those who still listen."

I liked the poetic way she spoke. It reminded me of someone.

"But what will you do when they begin to tear these streets down?" I wondered aloud.

"Well, most owners and tenants will be moved out. Some already have been. In fact, not many Jewish people live here anymore. Most of the residents are the destitute lower classes, dubious traders and criminals.

"This street should be preserved for a few years longer, but I have already found myself a new place to live. It's in the New World quarter. Nicely symbolic, eh?" She winked at me. "It's a beautiful green area, close to the castle complex, and has good access to the countryside. I'll certainly miss the Fifth District, though. After all, I have lived here since I was about your age, and have Jewish roots, just like this place."

The hint at my age intrigued me. I wandered over

to the dusty mirror by the main door and stood before it. I was in my mid-twenties. My hair was coal black, eyes olive green, skin pale, and lips chapped. I touched them, uncomfortable with the image.

Vilma noticed and reached for a tiny bag, tugging out a small jar. She handed it to me and I found a yellowish cream that smelled familiar. I patted it on my lips and tasted it. It reminded me of honey.

"Are you all right?" asked Vilma, and rubbed my arm with a mother's care.

"Yes… I just didn't know what I looked like."

"Well, you look beautiful," she said and began drawing my messy hair up into a bun similar to hers. "Once we wash you and get you changed, you will look like a doll."

A doll. I couldn't decide whether or not the word meant something to me. Vilma decorated my hair with one of her flower clips and smiled at our reflection.

✡

Although the latrines were shared, a bath was something that each tenant had to sort out on her own. Vilma told me that hygiene was a common problem in the more crowded parts of the city, particularly in the Fifth District, which still had a medieval urban design, and therefore lacked a modern sewerage system.

Vilma owned an old tin bath that she kept in the shop, and used it once a week to bathe in. That day, however, she made an exception. She poured me some hot water from a large pot she kept on the stove, and since she planned to bathe later herself, I only stayed in for a short time, so that she could enjoy the warm water as well. She loaded the bath with small cotton sacks filled with lavender.

"This should soothe your spirit after such a hard day," she said, and threw in a few more. "I'll miss that lavender garden. There's a larger one near to the house I'm relocating to, and I plan to rent a garden in the fields near Prague as well, but it's not the same. A part of the heart always remains in the area you grew up in. Despite the dark shadows of this quarter, the lavender always thrived, as did I."

I could sense how deep Vilma's emotional connection to the house and the quarter was, but I didn't want to pry, assuming it would only make her sadder. Instead, I enjoyed the hot water and how light it made my body feel.

Falling asleep was easy after the bath and the long, exhausting day. I dreamt about standing in the river beneath a dawning sky. I felt the sun's halo expand and shine over me, infusing me with its divine light. Then, a distant memory of a familiar female voice came to me. I heard her whisper the words: *Don't let them take your magic.*

# Chapter I

## The Magician

Deep in the night, I was woken up by distant giggles. I opened my eyes in the candlelit room, and discovered that Vilma's bed was empty. The noises seemed to come from the hallway. My gaze shifted to the big old clock. It was one in the morning.

I crept to the door and looked through the keyhole. Vilma's neighbour, the man who had supposedly helped her bring me upstairs after my fall, seemed tipsy. He was struggling to find the right key to his house, while supporting an equally drunk young woman. He was slender yet sturdy, and his hair was almost white despite his young age. He kept hushing the merry girl beside him, who kept giggling.

She was dressed in a tight corset with a deep cleavage and a skirt that was scooped up towards the back. I liked the dress, but wondered how it could be comfortable. I looked after them even once they had disappeared inside, curious about their relationship.

"Strange..." Vilma's voice shattered the silence that filled the room once the door had closed behind them. I swivelled round, and noticed her standing by the kitchen window, concealed behind a set of heavy velvet drapes.

"Better stay where you are, dear," she said as the floorboards creaked beneath my feet.

"What's the matter?" I asked anxiously, sensing trouble.

"There's this cloaked man standing by our house; the same one who followed me on my way to the river. I thought I had chased him off at one point, but he must have followed me home."

"What were you doing by the river so late?"

"I performed a ritual, asking the Vltava river goddess to help you find a way back home. I thought the man was a gendarme, but since when has it been illegal to pour herbs and flowers into the water?"

She tried to see through the darkness. "I'm trying to catch sight of his face. You know what's strange? Back there in the streets, I could swear it looked as though he had no face at all."

A man without a face. I imagined it and shuddered. Despite Vilma's warning, I crept closer to her in order to steal a peek, when she exclaimed:

"Oh no! That damn drunk must have left the door open!"

She turned to me, fear dancing in her eyes. "Do you think he's after you?"

I shuddered at the thought. Vilma grasped my hand, and searched the room for a hiding place. Finally, she decided to wrap me in the velvet drapes. Before she let go, she whispered:

"Try not to make a sound," then she held her breath, and tiptoed to the door. I peeked through the holes in the drapes, watching Vilma as she bent over to spy through the keyhole.

After a moment of tense silence, she flinched away. There was a sudden knock at the door. She froze, not sure what to do. Then we heard the neighbour's voice, distant yet audible.

"Can I help you, sir?"

He was so articulate that I presumed he wasn't so drunk after all. I couldn't hear the response properly, just a deep murmur, but the neighbour's voice was even fiercer when he said:

"The girl left before dusk. Now would you be so kind as to let us rest at this ungodly hour?"

Again, just a hushed reply from the intruder, then the door closed and all became silent. Vilma peeked through the keyhole again to make sure that the cloaked man had truly left. Judging by her relieved expression, he had. She straightened her back with one hand on her hips, the other resting on her chest.

"Thank God," she exhaled, and hurried to meet me in the kitchen. Together, we peered through the scratched window. The cloaked man walked away at a brisk pace without turning back, and the night swallowed him just as it had brought him – out of and into nowhere.

"Did you see his face this time?" I wondered aloud, my heart still hammering. She turned to me, and her baffled eyes locked with mine.

"No. Either the hood conceals it too well, or he really has no face."

I crossed my arms as a chill swept through me.

"He asked about me, didn't he? His voice was so deep and hushed that I couldn't hear…"

Vilma nodded.

"He asked for a young woman with black hair and green eyes. Though I usually can't stand that young fiend next door, I feel like praising the heavens for having him here right now."

I gave her a weak smile. Vilma noticed my

distress, and comforted me.

"Don't worry, it will be all right. I won't let that cloaked bastard hurt you."

"Wouldn't you rather see me go?"

I dreaded the idea of leaving, but had to ask. I reckoned that I might have been in some trouble, and the last thing I wanted was to put the nicest person I had met in danger. Vilma, however, was almost offended.

"Have you lost your mind, girl?" She looked straight at me. "We have a deal, remember?"

☆

The anxiety and fear which had built up wouldn't let me rest that night. I tried to figure out why the faceless man was after me. Vilma mentioned that some trauma might have caused my memory loss, and I couldn't stop imagining what might have happened.

I reached for the scarf bag I came with, hoping that the objects inside would make more sense than before. There was a deck of cards entitled *Tarot*, a golden cup, a small woodland wand and a white pebble with a five-pointed star engraved on it. Suddenly the word *magic* came to my mind. Having no idea what it meant, I simply began to study the objects more carefully, particularly the individual cards. The pictures seemed symbolic, and resonated with me, but triggered no memory.

Vilma's light snore disturbed my reverie. I watched her placid face, thinking about what I should do. She was so kind, and her willingness to help me was so touching, but I couldn't avoid the fact that by staying at her lodging, I might involve her in whatever adversity I was facing.

After a few more brooding, sleepless hours, I

finally decided that I should leave, and try to find the young man with the dark curls. I hesitated about explaining this to Vilma first, but knew that she would persuade me to stay. I had to go before she woke up. Although the vision of the faceless man terrified me, causing someone like Vilma trouble was even more of a worry.

With a heavy heart, I collected the clothes she had prepared for me and got dressed. I peeked in the mirror on the wall, just to check the fit. The dark blue top pulled in my waist, even though I had laced it rather loosely, and the flowing green skirts complimented the embroidered bodice.

I wavered over taking the hat that Vilma suggested I wore, as it was quite frivolous, decorated with paper leaves and velvet roses. However, it was large enough to conceal my face, so I decided to put it on. The brim curved into a figure-of-eight shape around my head. It reminded me of something, but the memory faded away.

I was set to leave, so I turned to Vilma, silently thanking her, and wishing her a good life. Worried that I would give in to hesitation again, I headed straight to the main door, and pulled down the doorknob in a slow, careful motion. I left without waking her.

As I began to descend the stairs, a figure loomed over me from above. I turned, relieved to see that it wasn't Vilma or the faceless man, but the neighbour. He stood there with his arms crossed and a challenging expression on his face. I watched him, bemused, as he set out to join me on the stairs.

I remained on the same spot, too intrigued to walk away. He had the kind of unique, soulful presence that commanded your attention right away. Initially, he struck me as younger than I was, however, on closer inspection, I supposed that he was older, probably in his late twenties.

"You wouldn't want to wander around the Fifth District at night dressed like that. Particularly if you're alone."

His eyes shifted to my cleavage. I blushed, suddenly self-conscious about my new dress, wondering why it was just as inappropriate as the previous one.

"Besides, judging by your appearance, you're evidently not from around here, which makes you even more vulnerable."

I didn't know whether to take that as a compliment or an insult, so I frowned a bit, just in case. He looked doubtful as he leaned against the wall.

"Though I don't know Vilma that well, I have the pleasure of being acquainted with her stubbornness," he said, "and I'm certain she would find you sooner or later."

"I can't stay," I said, finally breaking my silence. "Goodnight."

Without further ado, I set off downstairs.

"But who else should help you than family when you're in trouble?"

I stopped halfway down, and turned to him.

"You're Vilma's niece, right?" he assured himself, surprised by my reaction. I realised that Vilma had had to explain my visit somehow, so I went along with her story.

"Let me guess," he mused, enjoying my attention, "you came here for a holiday, and things went a bit wrong?"

I tilted my head, wondering where his thoughts would lead from here.

"Or you ran away from home?"

I didn't react, unable to exclude that option. He didn't seem to mind my silence, and went on speaking.

"I can relate to that. Though I never left home, I

tend to escape it whenever I can. Since my parents moved away to their country mansion in Moravia, I've been managing their properties here in the city, enjoying the solitude and freedom. At least the bit that I'm allowed."

He paused for a moment, his attention drifting. Then he recovered, and fiddled with the key he had been holding.

"Which part of the country are you from?" he asked with an eager look from beneath his brows.

The question made me recall something about myself and I didn't want to lie. I sensed that it was key to my personality, and probably also brought about the trouble I had found myself in, so I responded as honestly as I could.

"I can't say."

"Can't say, can't stay," he teased, as his lips curled into a contagious smile. I couldn't help but return it.

"Why don't you come back up?" he suggested. "Let's talk this through before you take any drastic steps."

I wavered. "Don't you have a visitor?" I asked. As he raised his eyebrow, I realised that he couldn't have known about my spying on him. Luckily, he saved me from the embarrassment with an apt reply:

"I do now."

✡

"Would you like some wine?"

I nodded as I soaked up the atmosphere of the neighbour's apartment. It was larger than Vilma's, but just as dark and dilapidated. The man motioned to a simple table with four chairs, and gestured for me to sit down while he reached for two beautifully carved tin cups. He disappeared in the kitchenette for a moment and returned with the wine.

It was sweet and tasted of ripe cherries, mushrooms and a pinch of caramel. Its aroma evoked a certain mood, and that mood began to open up a memory. However, before the memory was fully formed, the man interrupted:

"Did you have any idea where to go from here?"

I shook my head, unwilling to share the truth with him. I had decided to trust only Vilma, and planned to keep it that way.

"I bet you didn't think it through."

"I'm afraid I don't follow…"

"Well, you were trying to protect Vilma from that cloaked man, am I right?"

I shrugged, unwilling to admit or deny it. His finger traced the decoration on the tin cup whilst he speculated some more on my situation.

"You know, Vilma is already involved, whether you stay or go. If he's after you, then he will surely return here."

"Have you seen his face?" I asked with more courage, for which I had the wine to thank.

"No, he didn't turn my way. I found it strange… Then again, the whole situation was quite odd."

"Vilma didn't see his face either, and," I hesitated before I continued speaking, "she said it looked like he didn't have a face at all."

He seemed disconcerted at first, but chased the worries away with a grin.

"That sounds like Vilma. She's one dramatic lady."

"What do you mean by that?"

"Nothing bad. I like and respect her," he said, drowning the comment in another gulp of wine. Then, he gave me a deep, intent look. It made me nervous, so I focused on the bookshelves behind him instead. The conversation ran dry for a moment. I pretended to be interested in his many ornaments, and wondered what he was after.

The silence in which every inhalation seemed deafening was interrupted by the synchronous sound of church bells, and clocks striking four. I could no longer stand the tension. I turned back to him and, without giving in to his penetrating stare, commented on the pendant hanging from his neck. It had the same figure-of-eight shape as my hat.

"What does it represent?"

He clutched at the pendant, and to my relief, his eyes finally moved away from me.

"I was told eternity. My mother gave it to me for my eighteenth birthday. She said it's a good luck charm, meant to keep your soul in harmony."

The mention of his mother reminded me that I didn't even remember my parents, or anyone I could consider close. It gave me a bitter sense of hopelessness.

"That's nice," I said, my voice unintentionally forlorn. I cleared my throat and added: "Your mother must be nice."

He had noticed my gloom, and attempted to distract me.

"Would you like another glass of wine?"

I shook my head.

"Are you sure? You seem like you could use more."

"No, really. I know my boundaries," I surprised myself with the unexpected insight. I supposed it was another subconscious memory.

"I have no reason to doubt that," replied the man. "In fact, I believe you have more boundaries than anyone I have ever met."

Judging by the mischief in his eyes, he was just teasing me.

"So? Have I succeeded in persuading you to stay yet?"

"You have succeeded in confusing me even more, and in making me question your intentions. Why do you care about my situation or what happens to me?" I challenged him, but he took it well.

"In truth, it's because of Vilma. I worry that she would be very upset with me had I told her that I let you go. It would make her despise me even more."

"Despise is a strong word, isn't it?"

He shook his head, smirking.

"I think it's accurate, actually. I would like us to be friends, but she keeps giving me that glare." He paused for a moment. "Then again, I respect it. At least she's honest."

I wondered why Vilma disliked him, as he had seemed decent to me so far.

"Have you done anything to her?"

"Not that I'm aware of. I was hoping you could tell me. You also seem wary of me, so…"

He fingered through his shoulder-length, pale hair, and lay back in his chair, giving me a look.

"Well, Vilma only mentioned you," I explained, "but I tend to be wary anyway. It's nothing personal."

He smiled.

"I'm glad to hear that. I thought it was because of my late night visits. This apartment is like my private sanctuary, and I admit that I tend to go a bit wild here. I thought maybe Vilma disliked that. Although, when I come to think of it, she might understand. Judging from her lack of husband and black clothing, I dare to say she's also a bachelorette."

He gave me a questioning look.

"You're quite observant," I said, silently wishing he could read me as well as Vilma.

"I just like to study people," he replied, and as though hearing my thoughts, he remarked: "And I have a feeling that your story is something extraordinary."

"Why so?"

"You look like someone with a mission."

"Really? What kind of a mission?"

"The kind that can't be explained."

That notion ignited my spirit. I yearned to know what my mission was, and wished that someone could help me figure it out. Lost in my thoughts, I hadn't even noticed him leave the room, and so it startled me when I found him standing over me, much closer than before.

"Whether you pursue your mission here or elsewhere," he said, "I think you should have this."

He placed a brown leather case into my hand. It was heavy, so I assumed it contained something made of metal.

"Also, it might help you with the uninvited guests."

I opened the case and found a small polished dagger with a neat leather handle. The gift alarmed rather than consoled me. From the little I knew about myself, I was certain that I disliked weapons, particularly the idea of using them.

"I don't think I need this, thank you for the goodwill."

I was about to hand it back to him, but he wrapped his hands around mine and insisted:

"Please keep it, for my own peace of mind."

The pleading eyes and warm touch made me waver. The man truly had a way with words. He was persuasive, but in an unobtrusive way, and thus made me weigh up my options. The image of me being alone out there without knowing anything and anyone again terrified me to the core. Perhaps he was right. It would be better to stay and make sure that Vilma was safe from the faceless man. I could always flee later, after all.

"I should go."

I stood up, holding the dagger and the scarf bag that I had been fiddling with the whole night. His insightful eyes narrowed a bit. He knew that I was weighing up his advice.

Once I stepped out of his apartment, I hesitated one last time – should I set off down the staircase or return to Vilma's? As my feet reached the stairs, I turned to him. To my surprise, he said nothing more. He simply smiled to himself, and disappeared behind his door, as if he knew what I had decided to do.

☆

I managed to fall asleep again in the early hours of the morning, and dreamt of being a girl, about five years old, standing alone in the Narrow Lane. All the buildings except for the one I was waiting next to were different from those in Prague. Most façades were painted snow-white and had colourful stained glass decorating the front doors and windows.

Then, a beautiful middle-aged woman dressed in a long, dark green cape stepped out of the only familiar house. Her eyes were sea blue, and her voluminous grey hair dwarfed the rest of her. I recognised her as my second mother, a woman who took me under her wing after my parents died of the plague epidemic. I called her Atarah.

"So what do you think? Do you like our new home?" she asked, waving at me to join her. I nodded, glad to finally move into the so-called Magic Quarter, the last place in the city where magic was kept alive, though illegally. Before we crossed the threshold, she stopped me, and said:

"I'm about to show you a precious secret now. If you decide to follow our heritage, it will too become a part of your life's mission and purpose."

"And if I decide otherwise?"

"Then so be it," she said with a wink. "I would never force you into anything, child, you already know that."

She guided me into the building.

"One should learn to connect the bridge between the heart and the mind. That's what crowns you with eternity, and makes you the master of your own life rather than a slave of someone else's."

We fell into step with each other as we entered the building, ready to start our new life.

Then, suddenly, the calm image faded into another scene. I was older, about eleven years old, and there was an uproar. People were screaming, trying to escape, fighting with the city guards. Most were being taken away, including Atarah and I. We were separated from one another, taken to different places. However, our souls remained united in a solemn promise. I might have cried outwardly, but inwardly I knew that our bond was stronger than their law.

# Chapter II

## The Priestess

I had a feeling that Vilma suspected my attempt to flee, but like me, she decided not to speak of it. Instead, we focused on visiting her friend, the psychic. Vilma dressed me into the bodice I wore the previous night, and helped me fix it properly at the back. She also adorned my cleavage with a soft scarf. I understood then, that it wasn't complete without it, and was very revealing on its own. In an effort to blend in, I endured its discomfort, occasionally pulling on the laces when no one was looking.

In the early morning light, the city seemed even grimmer than before. I watched the dust motes dancing in the shafts of sunlight, sparkling like a sea of tiny stars as I walked through it. The buildings in the Fifth District were mainly golden brown and ochre, but some were painted brick red or even green. As opposed to the evening scents of dust and rot, it smelled of flowers and fruit at this time of day, as the twisting streets were crammed with market stalls and merchants selling fresh garden produce.

It saddened me to imagine that these charming, secluded lanes would be demolished. Vilma claimed that many could still be preserved if the city planners had not been lazy and driven by greed. The plan was, she explained, to replace the chaotic medieval labyrinth with a Parisian-style boulevard.

"The heads of the city need regenerating themselves, not the town," she complained, as she strolled round the corner and headed northwest towards an old stone bridge. The city was both homely and foreign to me. The more I saw, the stronger I felt that something was missing, particularly by the river.

"Could it be that there were wider, lower bridges made of wood here before? And more islands?" I asked as I watched the water's surface.

"Well, there are three islands further to the left and a larger one closer to

Vyšehrad," said Vilma. "Also, there's a big island over there to the right. The wider, lower bridges made of wood don't sound like Prague, though… Why do you ask? Have you remembered something?"

"Not really. I have just had a few glimpses or impressions."

"Aha, then why don't you try to imagine it in more detail?" she suggested.

I took her advice, but the images vanished as soon as I focused on them.

"Now it feels distant and hazy, like a dream," I said, disappointed at my vain attempt.

"Maybe it was a vision of another city?"

"Maybe," I said, yet had a gut feeling that it was Prague, only different somehow.

The hills ahead seemed familiar as well, but I kept

thinking that there should be mountains there instead, and an imposing rock further in the distance, topped with some kind of sculpture. It perplexed me, and my head hurt with the effort to visualise it properly.

"It will be all right," said Vilma, "just continue to sense and feel the place, intuition is the key to everything anyway."

After we had passed the bridge, Vilma guided me to a building complex called *By the Keys*. I had an inkling that the title was important, and that I was going to unlock something there.

The psychic lived in the smallest house in the complex. It had only two windows on the first floor and a single dormer one above. Vilma said that the whole wall of buildings would also be demolished during the regeneration. I couldn't imagine why, as it seemed to be in good condition, but Vilma explained that many houses, even those outside the Fifth District, would fall simply because of the city's modernisation.

"And these particular town jewels will be replaced by the modern, electric tramways," she said as we entered the courtyard passage.

The news made me value the architecture around me even more, and appreciate its unique spirit concealed within the stone. Since I had entered Prague, I had become enthralled by the idea that the buildings had souls. I couldn't help but wonder if, over the centuries of bearing silent witness to all that happened within or without their walls, they preserved the events as memories, and the memories eventually formed their spirits. If that were true, then would I, a person with no memories whatsoever, be less soulful than them?

We climbed the stairs to the floor with the two windows, and found a middle-aged woman wearing a light-grey dress on the threshold to an apartment.

She had straw-brown hair, deep sibylline eyes, and the sort of presence that wins you over right away. She introduced herself as Dora and didn't seem to mind me not sharing my name, as though she expected it. Judging by her kind manners and the soft, slow way of expressing herself, she struck me as a soul with a rich inner world, who opens up to only the lucky few.

While they discussed my case, I looked around the small, cosy apartment decorated with simple furniture and too many books, tins, boxes and candles to count. What struck me most was a large symbol painting on the wall – circles connected with tubes, which formed something like a ladder. I knew I had seen it before, but like my vision of Prague, the memory was incomplete.

"Please sit down, ladies," said Dora with a nod in my direction. "I can sense that your spirit would like to share something."

Without further ado, she reached for one of the wooden boxes on the nearest shelf, and took out a card deck. It was wrapped in a black cloth with objects embroidered on it: a cup, a wand and a five-pointed star. It reminded me of the objects in my scarf bag so, astounded, I asked:

"What do these depictions represent?"

"I embroidered this last winter," replied Dora. "It represents Tarot's Minor Arcana."

*Tarot*. The same card deck I had found in my scarf bag along with the objects. I stared at her questioningly, so she went on:

"See, the Tarot consists of the Major Arcana, also regarded as the trump cards, and the Minor Arcana. The Minor Arcana is divided into four suits, and each represents one of the four basic elements and the cardinal directions."

I was captivated by the information, so I began to guess:

"The cup is for water, right? And the wand is for starting a fire, I suppose? But what about the five-pointed star?"

"The pentagram has been used as a symbol of the material world, therefore it symbolises the earth element," she explained.

"And where is the sword?" asked Vilma. "That's what represents the air element in the Tarot, right?"

Dora flashed her a playful smile.

"It does, but I figured that this scarf could also symbolise the air element."

Vilma returned the smile and nodded. "That's clever."

"And what about the Major Arcana?" I enquired. "What element does that represent, if any?"

"Well, in my opinion, it's the fifth element, the one that is both the centre and the whole."

I felt that the words concealed a wisdom I already knew. It almost reached my consciousness, but like the other recollections, it just faded away. I scowled, irritated by my mind's lack of co-operation.

"And these cards, could they help me?" I asked, eager to be guided by something or someone.

Dora wavered. "I can't promise you that. For some people it works, mainly for those who are willing to work on themselves. These cards are like keys – they help us open the doors to our psyche, but what we do once we unlock them is beyond their reach."

"Fair enough," I said, willing to try anything at that moment.

"So, I have your consent? Should we begin?"

I nodded with a nervous glance at Vilma, who seemed even more excited than I was. Dora felt the deck in her palms, closed her eyes, and asked her spirit guides for protection and psychic clarity. After the prayer, she shuffled the cards and handed them to me.

"Pull out ten cards, please."

Though I was uneasy, all doubts left me once I pulled the first one out. I placed it on the table, and began pulling nine more. As Dora turned the cards over, her hand froze, brows creased, and eyes squinting. Without turning to me, she said softly:

"Would you take out ten more cards, please?"

As soon as I had placed ten more beside the previous row of ten, Dora impatiently flipped them over, and drew her breath in astonishment.

"Two more," she said in a mere whisper. I pulled out two more cards and placed them on the bottom while putting the remaining ones aside.

Dora revealed the last two images with shaky hands, and then locked her eyes with mine in disbelief. We all remained quiet for a while, stuck in a moment of uncertainty. Dora turned slowly to Vilma who, as I had I noticed, was just as overwhelmed.

"What could this mean?" she breathed.

I looked back at the pictures, not understanding. All I saw were figures and symbols that seemed half-familiar.

"Have you shuffled them properly?" asked Vilma.

Dora nodded with her eyes fixed on the twenty-two cards. Both women were shifting their gaze in awe between the cards and me.

"This is the complete set of the Major Arcana," explained Dora. "You have picked the cards in numerical order."

Though I had found it an interesting process, I didn't understand what was so unusual about it.

"But there's something even more fascinating going on here," continued Dora. "You are the woman from the prophecy."

Dora's sage eyes focused on Vilma, encouraging her to explain what she meant.

"Oh yes!" exclaimed Vilma, "the dream

prophecy?"

Dora nodded, and looked back at me.

"A few weeks ago, I was visited by one of my spirit guides in a dream. She told me that a young woman would soon come to me, seeking help and guidance. She said that I was to help her recall the reason why she was in Prague. However, she stressed that her past should remain a secret, concealed from everyone including me. I asked how I would recognise her, and she said that she would pull out the Major Arcana, card by card, from zero to twenty-one."

"Did she say anything else?" I asked.

"Just that she should go to the Golden Lane," answered Dora thoughtfully, "that it would be a crucial place for her... a place that would help her remember."

"Could it be connected to the lane's legends?" suggested Vilma.

"What legends?" I wondered.

"Invisible houses, spirits, alchemists..." she jabbered. The words sounded just as puzzling as everything else they talked about.

"Maybe I'm not that woman," I said, "or what if it's all just a coincidence?"

"Forget about coincidences," said Dora with a kind authority, and grasped my hands in hers. "Tell me how you feel about what I have just shared with you."

I searched her face and then my pounding heart, completely confused. I knew that something within me was trying to give me an answer, but I still felt too blocked to receive it.

"I don't... I just can't."

I looked away, disappointed. Dora let go of my hands, and deliberated. After a moment of silence, Vilma stood up and said:

"I can't stand this, ladies. Let's not procrastinate

any further. We should just go to the Golden Lane, and find out how we feel when we're there."

Without waiting for a response, she headed to the door. Dora and I hesitated, but finally nodded in silent agreement.

☆

The Golden Lane was charming despite its dishevelled façades and its mouldy smell, which overpowered even the soapy aroma from the washing that hung between the buildings. The poverty and ancient charm reminded me of the Fifth District, but I didn't recognise any of the tiny houses. Some had only a ground floor, and two or three windows, and their chimneys reached higher than the castle wall behind. I looked them over one by one, concentrating on my impressions of them, hoping to recall at least something important.

We caught the attention of a few locals, who probably wondered what was causing us to linger there, interrupting their midday peace.

"This lane is unfamiliar to you, isn't it?" guessed Vilma.

I nodded, a bit disheartened.

"I suppose I'm not the woman from the prophecy."

"Unless there's another Golden Lane in the city," speculated Dora.

Vilma resolutely shook her head.

"I know this city by heart. There's no other Golden Lane."

Since the street lacked any privacy, it came as no surprise when a curious face peeked out from one of the houses. It was a charismatic elderly man. His sky blue eyes watched us through a pair of round glasses and as he leaned closer, his long beard fell down from the window like a dusty curtain.

"Excuse me, ladies, could you please move this chit chat elsewhere? Not only is this woman's voice terribly loud and squeaky," with that he nodded at Vilma, who glowered at him, "but you're also blocking the only source of light I have."

"Pardon us, sir!" exclaimed Vilma in an even more high-pitched tone, and then, turning to us, said, "Let's go, girls, I had no idea that an angry gnome guarded this street."

She dragged us away, fuming. The elderly man muttered something to himself, and then called after us:

"Just for your information, there *is* another Golden Lane!"

We stopped and turned to him, Dora and I intrigued, Vilma distrustful. The elderly man gave her a mischievous smirk, and said:

"Not that I wanted to eavesdrop, but I had no choice. If you really knew this city by heart, madam, you would know that one of the streets down in the Fifth District used to be called *Golden* before it was renamed *Narrow*."

Vilma's face turned scarlet.

"Nonsense. I would know that. I live in the Narrow Lane." she said, her voice an octave higher still.

"You don't say!" the man called out, and let out a boisterous laugh. Even after he had closed the window, we could still hear him chortle. Dora and Vilma exchanged looks. Dora was amused like me, but Vilma was still as vexed as ever.

"I hope you don't trust him! she said, hands on her hips.

Dora weighed it up.

"You have to admit that it would make sense. That the girl would intuitively come to the right place."

She turned to me then, her sage eyes studying me.

"Dear girl, I wish I knew what lay behind that comely face of yours."

"I have an old map at home," said Vilma obstinately, "I can prove the damn gnome wrong."

She hurried off towards the crooked passageway at the end of the lane. Dora and I exchanged a smile, and quietly followed her to the large stone stairs that led back to the Lesser Town.

As we ambled down the avenue towards the riverbank, I had another one of my visions. In my mind, the streets were different to how they appeared now. The façades were snow white, the ground tidy, almost polished, and above the entrances hung stained glass art, framed in complicated, black iron arrangements. The noon sun shone through the varicoloured glass shards, casting reflections on the buildings opposite.

The sight was so mesmerising that I had to stop and close my eyes. I willed myself to remember it in more detail. For a moment it worked. I knew that if I walked down the street, I would find more such corners with stained glass art and assorted cafés.

I told Vilma and Dora about the vision, and while they were intrigued, it made no sense to them. They had never heard of such streets. Nevertheless, I had a feeling that it was a recollection rather than a fantasy, and began to feel homesick for a place that seemingly didn't exist.

✡

To our surprise, the old map of Prague really did list the street that Vilma lived in under the name *Golden Lane*. Vilma felt a bit embarrassed and upset that the elderly man was right. I, on the other hand, was grateful for the assurance that Dora's prophecy was meant for me. Even though it was just a part of her dream, I felt validated by it. It also strengthened my belief that the house I recognised as home was the right place to be. However, the message that my mission in Prague should remain a secret made me feel bitterly alone.

As I reflected on my situation, I overheard a noise coming from the hallway. Curiosity led me to look through the peephole. A girl wearing a bedraggled dress emerged from the neighbour's apartment and hurried down the stairs. For some reason, it unsettled me, and as I pulled back from the door, I noticed Vilma's scrutinising eyes. That woman is dangerously perceptive, I thought to myself, as I watched her head for the kitchen.

"No matter which street you were meant to visit," she said, while starting a fire in the wood stove, "there must be a reason behind it. Perhaps we should ask Dora to hypnotise you."

"What does *hypnotise* mean?"

"It's a modern technique during which your mind reaches a dream-like, unconscious state. Then, questions are asked, and answers noted down. You may have powerful visions during hypnosis, some of which vanish once you wake up. It's a very effective and safe method, but it doesn't work for everyone. And we would have to be very careful because if the prophecy is correct…"

She didn't finish the sentence. Something caught her attention. She pulled the curtain aside and peered down on the street. Sensing trouble, I stood up from the map and joined her.

"Is he back?"

Vilma turned to me and nodded.

We spent the evening inside, hiding from the faceless stranger who didn't seem to tire from the long hours of wandering up and down the street. I had trouble falling asleep that night. I couldn't rest knowing that this intimidating man was after me. After Vilma dozed off, I retreated to the kitchen with the Tarot card deck she had lent me. It was a bit different from Dora's and mine. The pictures were more up to date and colourful. Each one depicted situations and symbols that seemed profound in a subtle yet powerful way. I took in the mood of each card, and sensed that I used to be familiar with the stories they held.

I felt that on the whole, the trumps represented a journey that was omnipresent, and could be altered and relived many times and in many ways. I did not know where the thought had come from, I simply let it flow through my consciousness, enjoying its companionship.

The candles died out shortly after the church bells struck five, and so I crept over to the window to check on my stalker. To my relief, he was gone, and I began to understand why. Presumably, he showed up in the evenings and disappeared before dawn because he didn't want to be recognised. That would also explain the concealed face.

To be certain, I scanned the street once again, and paused at the sight of the crescent moon that broke through the fluffy clouds. Its silvery light fell upon the crooked roofs, shabby dormer windows and distorted chimneys. The enchanting sight pacified me, and in the serenity of the moment, I recalled Atarah's voice, uttering the word *Merkaba*.

# Chapter III

## The Empress

"I remembered something last night," I said to Vilma whilst preparing the table for breakfast. "It was a word. Merkaba. Do you know what it means?"

Vilma mulled it over.

"I have heard it somewhere before… It's from the Kabbalah, I think. Does that ring any bells?"

I shook my head.

"It's an ancient Jewish mysticism," she explained. "I have never had the patience to delve deeper into its teachings, as I know from my grandfather that it could take many lifetimes to master it. I hoped that the Tarot itself would be enough."

She paused, realising something. "Actually, there's a compelling correlation here," she said. "Some say that the Kabbalah's wisdom has been preserved in the Tarot."

Vilma's words caught my attention, and made me

forget about the delicious scent of fresh bread and steaming black tea on the tray she carried over.

"See, the Tarot was actually a card game before it became a fortune telling tool. 'A mystery concealed in something ordinary' my grandfather called it. It's definitely a wise way to store secrets, eh? In the olden days, it was a necessity, though. Esotericism wasn't as popular as it is nowadays so it had to be practised in secrecy. However, via the card game, everyone was given the chance to decode the symbols for themselves."

She reached for a glass of apricot marmalade and nodded at me to have some. I did so only to be polite, as my appetite for knowledge overpowered that for food.

"Where could I find more information about the Kabbalah?"

"Well, the Kabbalistic texts are not commonly accessible. The Jewish mystics treasure their heritage. You would have to be one of them to learn more. Kabbalah's concept is to find the path yourself, guided by signs and symbols. That's what I have always admired about the Jewish philosophy – it supports free will and personal growth. And you have to work to obtain the knowledge."

She took a sip of the strong tea, and continued speaking:

"I respect such religions over those which impose themselves on others. It's better if they slam the door in your face than if they manipulate you. Mystery and faith are to be lived not preached. Don't you agree?"

I thought about what she said, and suddenly remembered something that Atarah told me once:

*If someone gave you the rules to the game you have been playing right away, you would miss the most exciting part – the details. Sometimes it's all about the details, they make the whole more meaningful. So trust me, it's better to figure things out for yourself.*

With these words in mind, I nodded in agreement. Vilma gave me a smile, and went on:

"You know what? We should ask Dora about the Merkaba. She also comes from a Jewish background but unlike my family, both her father and grandfather were illustrious mystics."

"So she also used to live here in the Fifth District?"

"Yes, they used to live on Maiselova Street," said Vilma, her face veiled with nostalgia. "Who would think that both the building she grew up in and the building she moved to a few years ago would end up being among the first ones to be torn down? I swear that once I hear the first stones tumble it will be the end for me. I don't want to see this area after its fall. As soon as it begins, I'm gone."

The stubborn tone in her voice struck a chord. It reminded me of someone I used to know well.

"Why did she move away from here in the first place?" I enquired.

"Her family relocated when the quarter began to die, as did mine. Only, stubbornly, I stayed."

With these words, Vilma's eyes filled with tears. I searched her face, trying to understand why, whether it was because of the impending regeneration or some other memory. No matter what the reason was, I reached for her hands to console her.

"Maybe there's a reason for all this, a reason which we can't see yet?"

She squeezed my hand tight, nodding.

"That's what I keep telling myself," she said, wiping her cheeks with her apron. "I know that trade will eventually blossom in the New World area as well. I shall sell more herbs and potions, like I always wanted, no more of that old mishmash…"

The thought of Vilma's moving made me consider

whether I would be a burden.

"I promise that I'll leave as soon as I figure out what brought me here. You have so much to take care of now, and…"

"And you want to let me cope with it on my own?"

Vilma finished the sentence for me, lightening the mood. It made me chuckle, but I couldn't help myself from saying:

"I really don't want to trouble you, Vilma…"

"Oh, stop with that," she interrupted, and poured me some more tea. "Letting you stay with me is not just a kindness. I also need help. I'm not growing any younger, as you can see."

She stroked my face, and I gave her a grateful smile. No matter what happened from then on, I could sense that we were at the dawn of a wonderful friendship.

☆

On the way back to Dora's place, we passed a medieval tower gate* upon which the following sentence was depicted in big, black letters:

*Prague is a mother to the kind, but a stepmother to the ill. May this be a warning to wicked minds, as only people of goodwill are welcome here.*

I asked Vilma about it, and she told me that Prague was regarded as a mother to its citizens.

"Prague's energy is very feminine, both in its bright and dark sides," she told me. "Some even say that the city's specific atmosphere repels those who aren't supposed to be here, and attracts those who tune into its mysteries."

I was intrigued by the idea, and wondered how

men felt in such environs. Vilma just smiled at the question without responding, but she shared it with Dora later on. We assumed she would turn philosophical, and she didn't let us down.

"It's not about gender as such if you consider the idea that our psyche has both a feminine and a masculine side," she said. "This world is made of dualities. Therefore, it does not matter whether you are born as a man or a woman; it goes beyond that. The city has always attracted thinkers, artists and mystics, because it has a sensitive, gentle spirit. However, that is why evil likes to sneak into its corners as well. It enjoys tampering with such energies."

"Speaking of mystics... Do you have some Kabbalistic texts we could look at?" asked Vilma, her eyes already busy searching the bookshelves. Dora quickly joined her.

"Of course I do. You are welcome to borrow them. May I ask what you're looking for?"

"The term *Merkaba*. Does it ring a bell?"

"Merkaba? Hmm... Something tells me that it could be connected to the Tanakh. Look over there."

Dora pointed to the corner shelf, and as Vilma headed for it, Dora gestured to me to help her prepare some refreshments. Before we had returned with a tray of fruit, a carafe and some glasses, Vilma had already found a few interesting texts. She brought over three leather-bound books and laid them out on the table. Dora offered us some water spiced with lavender florets, and reached for the biggest book.

"I know I've heard the word before, but I just can't remember where," she said whilst leafing through it.

"I have a similar feeling," Vilma chimed in. "It's probably one of those things that you hear about, and remember only the meaning, not the title or the reference."

Unhappy with their futile search, Dora brought over some old notebooks and documents that she had stored in a hand-painted wooden box. I looked at the pages as she flipped through them. The alphabet was unfamiliar to me, but there were symbols that I knew I had seen before. It was mainly the five-pointed and six-pointed stars that they called pentagrams and hexagrams.

Dora explained that the old prints could only be found in Hebrew or German, the common language of the Austro-Hungarian Empire, which the country was a part of. That explained why some streets were still signposted in both Czech and German. Dora believed that Czech would finally become the official language in the coming years, because of what her card readings had predicted, and that there were many big national changes to come.

Exploring the assorted books lulled me, perhaps too much, due to the sleepless night. Dora noticed my exhaustion, and encouraged me to lie down on the divan to have some rest.

"Perhaps now would be a good time to do the hypnosis," suggested Vilma, partly as a joke, but I was taken with the idea.

"Yes, I would love to try it! If you think it wise, Dora."

"We can try it, but if you become anxious, we shall stop right away," she stressed. I had no reason to disagree, so I nodded.

The method was to align my mind with my subconscious. At first, Dora prayed to her spirit guides for divine protection, and to her favourite goddess, Hathor who, as she explained, shields us from evil spirits as well as dark phantoms created by our imagination.

"She attracts only love, which is her main attribute." Dora explained. She also said that Hathor was a part of the riddle behind the word *Tarot*, along with four more words. Together they delivered a message: *Rota Taro Orat Tora Ator*, which could be translated to: *The wheel of Tarot speaks the law of Ator*, in other words, Hathor. I was fascinated with the message, and wanted to know more, but Dora encouraged me to rest my rational mind, and focus inwards before the hypnosis.

She asked me to relax, concentrate on my breath, and move my attention from my head to my heart. Once I felt serene, Dora began to speak in a calm, monotonous rhythm. She was guiding me to imagine that I was walking through the woods, delving deeper and deeper, searching for a sacred well that represented my soul.

My imagination coloured the scene with such detail that I soon became one with it. I sensed that I was expanding, reaching far beyond my physical body, feeling light as a feather yet large as a giant bird spreading its wings. Instead of ascending to the heaven, however, I found myself descending into the well. Its depth was calling out to me, wooing me to dive into the seemingly impenetrable darkness.

After I eased myself into the void, Dora's guidance became just a part of the whole experience. I began to realise that my descent had its reasons, and waited for what was to come with open arms.

The first thing I saw with my inner sight was a familiar, pre-dawn wood. The air was still crisp, but judging by the sweet scents, and the blooming snowdrops, it was early springtime. I trod the grassy path that led home, listening to the choirs of crowing and hooting birds. I knew the woodland hollows by heart, and wasn't afraid of their depth.

Between the sprouting branches, I beheld a city that lay nestled between the hills ahead. Some of the buildings were tall and tower-like in shape, while other were large and palace-like. Despite the different sizes, though, they were all crammed closely together.

I also saw many bridges spreading across the riverbanks, connecting the islands with the land. They were very low, their stones almost touching the surging water. The windows sparkled in the darkness, mingling with the stars above.

I recognised that distant settlement. Like the woods, it was once my home. I followed the vista to the shore. On my way, I leaped in the air and floated above the ground, defying gravity. I tried to soar even higher, and dance in the air, but I wasn't as agile as I wanted to be. I knew I needed to work on my skills.

Clumsy yet determined, I floated all the way to a circular mud and straw hut with a thatched, moss-covered roof. The main door, guarded by two tall birches on either side, was painted dark blue, and the back door, which was connected to a smaller, simpler shed, was dark green.

The stained-glass windows depicted a symbol I recognised as the Tree of Life. I was on my way inside, when I noticed Atarah heading to the riverbank followed by a boy of my own age - about twelve. In the murky light, I could only see his silhouette, but I knew he was someone I held close to my heart.

Without spotting me, they headed to the riverbank. It was then that I noticed a man standing in the water, gazing at the moon. He was tall and elegant, and wore a large hat. He seemed quite calm, concentrating entirely on the break of day. When I turned my attention to his chest, however, I realised that he wasn't as calm as he seemed. I was using a skill that I had been taught by Atarah which enabled me to see other people's emotions in colour. The striking, phosphorescent hues emanating from the man's heart spoke of no good.

Suddenly, he let out a frantic roar, and burst into light. A second later, he had turned into a sparkling dust which glittered on the water's surface before it blended with the ripples.

I shifted my gaze to Atarah, who had just caught a metallic disc, a weapon used only by the authorities and those such as herself – the threshold custodians. It bounced back to her after she had exterminated the man who broke the rules. I knew it was a part of her mission, but that was the first time I actually saw her kill.

The distress made me feel dizzy. I was about to faint, when someone's arms clasped me. I buried my face into his chest, imbibing the protective energy he exuded. He was my faithful rock and haven. This time he couldn't console me. I was too shocked by what I had witnessed. At that moment, I made an important life decision. I promised myself that I would never become a threshold custodian.

During my inner oath, the younger me had aligned with the present one, and pain struck my heart. I knew I had abandoned that part of myself as well as Atarah, and in a way the boy as well...

I begged to be woken from this strange delirium, and soon after, Dora's voice began guiding me back to consciousness. Once I had settled back into the here and now, I pondered whether what I had experienced was a recollection of something I lived or just a reverie. It felt real, but a part of me wished it wasn't.

"What have you seen?" asked Vilma, unable to hide her curiosity.

"Was it anything at all? You didn't say a word the whole time."

I turned to Dora, who was watching me with a peaceful authority.

"I don't know whether it was a memory," I said, still a bit disorientated.

"Would you like to tell us more about it?" said Dora with a quizzical look.

I looked at them both in silence, and after a moment of weighing it up, I shook my head. I was worried about sharing it with them. Partly because of the murder I had witnessed, and partly because of the prophecy's warning.

"Don't worry," said Dora, "it may not have been your past. Sometimes people go back to their past lives or even the lives of others which have some relevance to their present situation. It could also be connected to your ancestral memory, or simply be an archetypal story that your mind created to help you realise something.

"Whatever it was, there is only one conclusion we can draw from this hypnosis – which is what I expected – you don't want to let me in, and there is a reason. We are not meant to know where you came from or why."

I lowered my head, feeling a bit ashamed to admit that she might have been right. For some reason, deep within, I knew it would be better if I kept the memories to myself. Not that I was against them knowing, I just worried that it could put them in danger. Why, though, was beyond me.

"Your conscious self might want to try the hypnosis again, but your soul seems to prefer introversion. And the soul is what I should respect."

"I understand," I admitted with a glance at Vilma, "and I might even agree. Perhaps it could do more harm than good."

Vilma didn't respond. I could tell she was disappointed, because usually she always had something to say, and this time she kept her thoughts to herself.

"We should let the girl rest," said Dora, and turned to Vilma with a knowing smile, "so that she can think about whatever she has seen."

"Yes, let's look for the word *Merkaba* in the meantime," responded Vilma gloomily, and helped Dora move the books to the next room, giving me some privacy. I wanted to take Dora's advice, but the soporific rhythm of the pages turning and the clock ticking was more hypnotic than the hypnosis itself, and eventually I dozed off.

✡

The dream I then had was too familiar to be just an archetypal scene arising from my subconscious.

I found myself in a different version of Prague, one that seemed just as real. I stood in a square that looked similar to the Old Town square, only the buildings were more striking, and had mostly creamy white façades. Some were rather low, with only ground floors, while others rose to more than five storeys and were built in a tower-like style. There were no shops as such, and most of the goods for sale were attached to ropes which hung down from the windows or balconies. It was mainly clothes, shoes, books and decorations. I understood that they could be bought by using coins to activate a special mechanism to release them.

The local women wore long, flowing dresses, similar to the one I had worn before Vilma lent me the tight bodice and layered skirts. The men, however, were dressed similarly, although their suits seemed simpler and more comfortable. I noticed a woman in her seventies crossing the street with her feet above the ground and I understood that gravity was different here. Most, but not all, people were able to float, and a few could soar higher, using the energy of the ether to sustain the movements.

With the sun setting behind me, I crossed a street on the city's northeastern side. After a few more steps, I entered a narrow, cobblestone lane where small, one- or two-storey houses were painted with colourful frescoes. Each depicted a local deity or showed scenes from various legends, either covering the whole house or just framing the windows and doors. I knew that in that quarter, the buildings were known by the names of the patrons that they depicted.

I stopped by the house entitled *Empress Eliza* and scrutinised the fresco, carried away by a sudden nostalgia. I recognised the face and the name. She was a kind, brave empress who I looked up to. She rebelled against her ancestors, even her husband, and planned to legalise magic again. The depiction showed her sitting on a throne within a castle complex, with green hills in the background. The highest hilltop had statues of unicorns and lions on top of it. I recognised it as a memorial.

As before, I was able to soar up and explore the house artworks in more detail. I wished I could fly above the roofs, and into the countryside beyond, but I knew I wasn't experienced enough to manage this.

Suddenly, a commotion disrupted my peace. A small crowd of people ran into the lane, and someone called out:

"Clear the path! The Empress is coming! Clear the path!"

I descended, landing just above the ground, surprised by how the tranquil space had become so cramped and noisy in such a short space of time. I understood that we all had to avoid being exposed to some deadly plague. I hurried down the lane, and ended up next to a ditch that descended to the city's lower, less illustrious areas. The panicking people began to leap or climb on the walls of the ditch, as there was no time to outrun the swift pace of the procession behind us. I had no other choice but to do the same. We were all afraid because touching someone from the castle could infect us.

We crowded onto the walls, and watched as the royal family passed by. Six men carried the Empress in an open golden litter adorned with a bright red canopy. They all seemed unwell, probably infected yet still able to work.

Most people avoided the castle complex now that the infection had spread there, except for the loyal ones. Seeing the Empress so ill broke my heart. She and her three-year-old son looked frighteningly emaciated and pale. They both wore long, black gowns which only emphasized the feeble condition they were in.

I used the technique that Atarah had taught me, and scanned their hearts. I saw subtle, almost lifeless grey tones. I recognised it as the fading hues, those that spirits had when their bodies were failing.

"I heard she has grown desperate, our poor lady," said a girl sitting beside me. "Can you imagine the suffering she must be going through? She would do anything to save her child."

I focused on the Empress's face, on the pain-filled eyes that once used to sparkle.

"Some say it was because she secretly worked with magic. The Emperor has tightened the rules against it again. I heard he even used the metallic disc weapon against some people."

The people around me slowly dispersed, even the girl feeding me with the information ran off, but I was unable to.

The procession stopped by the house at the end of the ditch – a simple building with a large decoration hanging above the entrance. It was an image of twelve pentagrams made of crystal beads, which denoted the house's name, *By Twelve Stars*. It was a healing centre, which was frowned upon by most, including the royalty, due to its untraditional practices. This was the first time that the Empress, like her predecessor Empress Eliza, had officially rebelled against the law that forbade magic.

As I watched the disheartening scene, someone touched my arm and made me start. I faced the boy whose identity had remained hidden until then. I recognised him as someone I grew up with, my best friend Turi. He had sea-blue eyes that always managed to soothe my heart, and playful locks of brown hair. Back then we were only twelve, still learning about our secret mission, and deciding whether we were strong enough to take it on.

"I found it." His whisper brushed against my ear. "Come, before they see us."

Hand in hand, we hurried towards the so-called Magic Quarter, which spread beyond the northern side of the Old Square. By then, it was already locked to the public, and we had come to the city to live there in disguise. I began to feel anxious when I caught the deep worry in Turi's eyes. He kept turning, expecting someone to stop us from reaching the building... the building that Atarah and I used to live in.

As we increased our pace, the sound of our breathing started to mingle with soft, feminine voices. I clung to them, and slowly returned to the comfortable divan in Dora's apartment.

It took me some time to realise where I was, and that I would no longer remember what happened to Turi and me after that. I felt the heaviness of my body again as the dream became less tangible. The only thing left was loneliness, and a need to find the boy named Turi.

I kept my eyes closed for a while, concentrating on the uplifting emotions that engulfed my heart. Bathing in them felt comforting, although they were tinged with apprehension.

Once I had readjusted to the present, I locked eyes with Vilma who had by then noticed my distress. She hurried over to me, wondering what had upset me. As before, I didn't want to explain it. I had an inkling that I wasn't allowed to, so I simply shook my head. Luckily for me, neither Vilma nor Dora were nosy and they respected my decision.

Dora offered me some of the refreshing lavender-scented water, and Vilma brought over one of the books they had been studying.

"Maybe this will cheer you up, dear. Look, we have found a term called the *Merkava*. It's spelled a bit differently, I know, but it's very close."

She pointed at two illustrations. Each showed an image of wheels within wheels with fiery wings attached.

"The word comes from the Old Testament, the Book of Ezekiel. In medieval times, Jewish people considered this the most crucial part of the Bible."

"And what does it say?" I asked, because the names she had mentioned didn't ring any bells.

"It's a text about Ezekiel's encounter with what was later called the *Merkava*, which translates as the 'light chariot' or the 'throne of God'."

Even though I was tired and upset, I wanted to know more, and so I encouraged Vilma to elaborate.

"In the vision, Ezekiel saw God on his light throne or chariot, followed by a group of angels called the Cherubim. The Cherubim were told to guard the way to the Tree of Life in the Garden of Eden. They had six wings and four faces resembling an ox, an eagle, a lion and a man. They all had light chariots which made them move in whichever direction they desired; the 'wheels within wheels' were also called the Ophanim. Then there was a third group of angels, the so-called Seraphim, the supreme and divine light beings."

What she said sounded bizarre yet familiar. I knew I had heard about the three groups of deities before, and in particular the word *Seraphim* resonated with me. I was certain there was something more to that story. The idea piqued my interest, and made me forget about Turi for a while.

Vilma gently touched my hand, comforting me. "Don't worry, I know it's baffling, but Dora has a friend who may be able to provide us with more information. She owns mystical books which are difficult to find in libraries and bookshops. We plan to visit her and ask for her help."

I thanked them whilst repeating the words she had used in my mind - *light chariot, the throne of God, wheels within wheels, Tree of Life, Cherubim, Ophanim, Seraphim*. I had no idea what it all meant, only that it was an important key to my past.

"What do you draw from this?" I asked, more confused and intrigued than ever.

"Well, it could mean that you used to study the ancient texts," suggested Vilma, and Dora agreed.

"What if you were far into your research and uncovered some mystery? That could explain why someone's after you, and why you are so anxious about your past."

They both looked at me, their eyes clouded with a mixture of fascination and worry. I did not know what to think. I just kept repeating the words from the Book of Ezekiel.

---

*Old inscriptions from the Powder Gate in Prague

# Chapter IV

## The Emperor

Before we went on to explore the meaning of the Merkaba, Dora served us some black tea that was to help us through the tiresome, hot afternoon. The two women discussed the September weather, and how exceptionally warm it had been that year, but I had no comparison, as the only thing I remembered was that there were seasons, and anticipated some holiday connected to them.

Once we stepped out into the late afternoon sunshine, I noticed a familiar face in the distance. It was Vilma's neighbour, deep in thought, striding ahead without noticing us. He couldn't miss Vilma's unmistakable voice, though, and soon he looked up, his eyes meeting hers.

"Oh, hello!" he said, surprised. "How are you on this lovely day, ladies?" He lifted his hat and gave a nod of greeting to Vilma, Dora, then me. His eyes lingered on mine, and the smile he gave me spoke for itself. He seemed glad that I had decided to stay.

"I'm heading back to the Narrow Street. Are we by any chance going the same way?" he asked. Vilma scowled and gave a resolute 'no' at the same time as Dora gave an affable 'yes'. I could tell that he was saddened by Vilma's reaction, and so was I, which only strengthened the secret connection we had established.

"I suppose it could be yes and no. We're going to Karmelitská," said Dora, giving him an apologetic smile, though Vilma was unembarrassed and uninterested in spending more time with him.

"There's no need to explain, I just thought it would be awkward walking in the same direction without speaking to one another."

"Well, thankfully that won't be the case," said Vilma, her face creased into a frown. As if expecting this, he lifted his hat again, and bid us farewell. "I understand, I won't take up any more of your time then."

He set off, but his pace was slower than before, which made me wonder if we should still stop him. Dora must have noticed my hesitation because she called after him:

"Why don't you take our girl home, Oliver? She didn't sleep much last night and could do with some rest."

Though I was pleasantly surprised by Dora's suggestion, Vilma's eyes blazed with irritation.

"And what about the books?" she asked.

"Most of them are in German, so she wouldn't be able to read them anyway, and we shall borrow the most useful ones for further research."

Vilma was so stunned by what was going on, that she could only blurt out:

"Are you serious, Dora?"

Dora gave her a gentle, reproachful look. "I'm

sure Oliver will keep her safe."

Oliver seemed to agree with her. He offered me his arm and said, "Of course, Miss Vilma. It will give me the greatest pleasure." He emphasised the last word and grinned at Vilma. She fumed, readying herself to protest, but Dora led her away before she could manage it, whispering something to her on the way.

I gazed after them, feeling slightly nervous about being left alone with him. Vilma kept turning after us, worried for me, so I waved at her with a reassuring smile.

"So, now that you know my name, isn't it fair that I learn yours?" he asked.

I hesitated, trying to make up some name. He noticed my bewilderment and took pity on me.

"All right, I understand. You prefer to remain anonymous."

He gave me a knowing wink, and offered me his arm.

"Let's make it a nice walk, what do you say?"

I accepted it, catching the whiff of his honey-scented soap as I leaned closer.

We set off, letting the heat from the cobbled streets seep up into our feet. By then, I had come to understand why walking had felt a little strange to me since my memory loss. If the visions and dreams truly were glimpses into my past, then the place I came from had different gravity. Having experienced the liberating feeling of leaping high above the ground, swirling and dancing in the air, I longed to be able to do it again. Deep within, I knew it was something I had loved, and a form of an escape from the ordinary world.

On the way, I learned that Oliver's family owned another apartment close to Dora's place, and he had been refurbishing it, planning to make it his main residence during the Fifth District regeneration.

As we crossed the old stone bridge, my eyes fell upon a memorial with a dominant statue on top, and four smaller figures below.

"Who is this a statue of?" I asked, making Oliver turn to me with an incredulous stare.

"Are you serious?"

I felt the blush in my cheeks, as I realised that it must have been someone significant, and that my question, therefore, made me look completely uneducated and stupid.

"Where exactly are you from?"

He meant it as a joke, but it made me feel even more embarrassed.

"Well, I just… don't remember certain things…"

Still a bit suspicious, he crossed his arms and reflected on what I had said.

"Hmm, and I suppose you can't elaborate?"

I nodded, hoping he would stop there.

"All right, let me remind you then." He turned to the statue with his arms spread theatrically. "This is Charles the Fourth, the most acclaimed ruler in our country's history. He was our king as well as an emperor of the Holy Roman Empire. He was also a mystic. People love to talk about that part of his life nowadays. People like Dora…" He paused, and as an afterthought added: "She's an interesting lady."

"She certainly is," I agreed, curious about whether the two knew each other well. "Has she ever done a Tarot reading for you?"

He gave a half smile, and set off again, slightly discomfited.

"She did, actually."

His admission amused me.

"Do you believe in such things?"

"Let's just say it surprised me. I'm not so keen on the occult, as you may imagine, but since it's so popular these days, I was curious."

"Why do you think it's popular?" I asked,

tentatively.

"I have no idea. I suppose people need a break from modernisation, and the chance to focus on something metaphysical instead. They are opening up to new religions and spiritual leaders. That is why so many secret groups and esoteric societies have been established. While I believe Dora is in it wholeheartedly and it comes naturally to her, I know some people just do it out of curiosity... Or worse..."

His serious face didn't suit him, so I couldn't help but ask what he meant. He wasn't keen to talk about it at first, but after a moment, he began to elaborate.

"Well, many of the so-called mystics fill other people's minds with nonsensical information, and use their knowledge as a tool to manipulate them. I rather listen to those who don't pretend to be enlightened. I don't like others preaching how things should and shouldn't be. I always try to think for myself: Why would or wouldn't something be so? If something is considered impossible, I try to think of ways it could be possible and vice versa.

"I hope you don't misunderstand me, though. I believe that there is something magical in this world, but I deem it better to find your own path to that magic."

His opinions reminded me of Vilma's, and I couldn't help but smile. I noticed then that Oliver was scrutinising me.

"Do you have a different view?"

I shook my head, then shrugged.

"I'm not sure, I'm not sure about anything... Nothing makes sense to me these days."

"Perhaps only that which you *give* sense to begins to *make* sense..."

I locked eyes with him, surprised by the wisdom that suddenly spoke through him, and wondered how to interpret it.

"I suppose Dora gave *you* a reading as well?" he

guessed.

I flashed him a mysterious smile, then nodded.

"And?"

I hesitated, wondering whether I could tell him the truth. Should I trust him?

"I would rather not speak about it," I said in the end.

He didn't seem surprised, but a bit frustrated.

"I ought to stop asking you questions, it seems more futile every time. I hope you'll at least tell me your name one day…"

"I hope so too," I replied softly.

Oliver gave me a look of genuine sympathy, and we stopped by a tall oak next to the riverbank to enjoy the view. He rested his shoulder against its bark, and took out a cigar case. He offered me one, but I refused, assuming I didn't smoke.

Once he lit the cigar, he threw the match into the water, eager to inhale. I watched him blow the smoke up in the air. His expressive, engaging profile was focused entirely on the sky. His facial features reminded me of someone I used to know. It could be Turi, I thought to myself, wondering what he looked like in his adulthood.

With the thought, my eye was caught by a young woman passing us by, wearing a fancy dress and carrying a large embroidered parasol. Her eyes lit up with curiosity at the sight of Oliver. He lifted his hat. She chuckled, and even though she quickened her pace, she stole one more glance at him over her shoulder.

Oliver smiled to himself, ostensibly used to the interest. For some reason, I felt a bit jealous, but the feeling was stopped by a quiet warning reverberating through my heart. I sensed that it might have something to do with Turi, but I brushed the thought away when Oliver approached. He offered me his arm again, and I simply couldn't resist it.

While enjoying the peaceful stroll, I had another strange vision. I saw the embankment turn into a network of small lanes and parks with tall leafy trees. The buildings were smaller, lighter; everything seemed much cleaner. The river had a different colour as well - a soft, turquoise blue. On the other side of the shore, the bank had more scattered rocks and stones, mainly white, and they joined up with a path leading to a tree-covered outcrop, the one with the unicorn-lion sculptures. Something drew me towards it, I couldn't tell what it was, though.

"I'm glad you've decided to stay."

Oliver's words woke me from the reverie. I felt a bit forlorn at first, but that special, beaming smile of his brought me back to the present.

"And don't be afraid of that caped clown. I'll keep guard," he added. The eye contact we shared felt like an unspoken pact.

☆

When we arrived at the Fifth District, Oliver invited me up to his apartment, but I excused myself. I decided to make some dinner for Vilma instead.

She returned much later than I had expected, and with an armload of notebooks and papers. Her eyes glinted when she shared the news with me:

"We found out some very interesting things about the Merkaba."

Ignoring the plates of bread, fruit and cheese I had prepared, she spread the books over the table, and began leafing through them, looking for something.

"At first, we thought we would find nothing on the subject, as besides Ezekiel's vision, there was no mention of the Merkaba anywhere. However, Dora's friend noticed something that we all missed, even though it was right in front of our eyes the whole time," she chuckled, "look!"

She showed me one of the Tarot cards. It depicted a woman holding two sticks, dancing in an oval-shaped garland.

"This card is called the World, and is the final one of the Major Arcana. Voila!"

She pointed to all the corners of the card, and only then did it begin to make sense to me. There were four winged beings guarding the figure in the centre – a human, a lion, an ox and an eagle.

"They are the Cherubim from the Merkaba passage in the book of Ezekiel. In Tarot, they stand for the four basic elements, and the lady in the middle is supposed to represent the fifth element."

I studied the beautiful images and words, intrigued and confused.

"Look here." Vilma reached for the box where she kept her own Tarot cards. "I have a different Tarot deck than Dora, the oldest print from Marseilles, but it shows the same image. Don't you find it strange? Of all things, you carried the talismans that represent the Tarot with you, and the one of the first words you remembered was the Merkaba. And now we find out that the two are actually linked."

"It is strange," I admitted as I observed the two trumps from the two different Tarot decks. I was certain that I had seen the image before, and the confusion made my head spin. I almost lost sense of the space and time I was in, almost remembering something, but my mind couldn't reach as far as my heart, and once again it slipped away. Vilma noticed my distress, and asked:

"Another memory?"

I nodded. "It's so frustrating. I know that I knew all this once before… Or at least a part of it…" I turned to her in my despair, seeking answers in her beaming eyes.

"What does it all mean, Vilma?"

"That you, my friend, were and probably still are connected to something truly fascinating."

She smiled and although I returned the smile, I found myself panicking inside. On some level, I was already aware that no matter how intriguing the truth was, it also concealed a dangerous secret.

✡

Before falling asleep that night, I visualised the Tarot trump connected with the Merkaba. I sensed that the twenty-two cards were the key to where I came from and why, and wished to unravel their secret. So I let the card symbolism float in my mind, lull my senses and my rational thoughts, and guide me deeper within.

Soon, I found myself in the fantasy version of Prague, just where I had left off. I walked beside the twelve-year-old Turi, who seemed troubled about something, but was waiting to tell me in private. We walked through the city's twisting streets, heading for our hideout.

The moon lit up the white and beige façades around us, and I realised that we were nearing the so-called Magic Quarter. Its urbanism and mood resembled the Fifth District, but it was even more decrepit. In fact, the area was locked away behind a pompous artisanal gate with leaf and flower décor. It had been abandoned after the sudden arrest of its inhabitants, including Atarah. Since then, it was forbidden to enter, but we were about to move into the house that I grew up in nevertheless. We had a mission to pursue, and although we were worried about being found, we knew that if we were careful enough, nobody would notice us. Luckily, most people were afraid to go there, including the city patrol.

The area had been in decline for decades, but in the olden days, it used to be the main artery of the city. Most of the buildings had miscellaneous magic shops and workrooms on the ground floors, and apartments above. The display cases still showed a variety of magic goods, mainly leather-bound books, candles, phials, wooden cases and symbolic objects. Everything was dusty, purposeless, waiting to be revived or destroyed. Only once we had immersed ourselves in the nostalgia of it all, Turi said:

"It hasn't been announced to the public yet, but I overheard the guards discussing it. The Emperor passed away, just an hour ago…"

I stopped walking, taken aback by the alarming news.

"Just when I hoped that our world would be changed," I mused aloud, "but there is hope still. The healing temple could help the Empress and the Prince. The magic could still save them."

"I doubt that they would be so lucky, or us," he brooded over our future. "I can feel it in the air, their fate has been sealed."

Turi and I were initiated in the ancient knowledge of magic, and we had moved back to the city to guard the so-called Merkaba device that Atarah used to be in charge of, to prevent it being used by anyone but those with pure intentions.

"Why are you being so dark, Turi?" I complained. "Just imagine that we wouldn't have to hide anymore. That magic would be legal again."

I grasped his arm tightly, leaning closer to him while gazing at the crooked rooftops and the blinking stars that spread between them.

"This area could be rebuilt to honour our ancestry, make our parents proud… Ah, wouldn't it be nice if the streets were re-populated by people keen to harvest the wisdom concealed in these stones?" I allowed myself to fantasise, but Turi just gave me a wan smile. He was always like that. He saw things darker than they truly were. I understood it, though, as he had had a much tougher life.

"Well, the possibility of magic ever being legalised is up in the stars... If the Emperor's brother takes over the throne, then this whole quarter will be torn down or rebuilt. Either way, let's enjoy it while we can..."

After a few more steps, we reached the building that looked the same in both versions of the city, the one where Atarah's old apartment was. Turi opened the shabby door and revealed a vestibule with ancient objects spread around in big piles, buried beneath loads of dirt, dust and cobwebs. I still considered it my home, even after we had started living in the riverside shed.

Turi grabbed one of the oil lamps, and lit it, signalling for me to follow him to the stairs. One part led up, but we headed down into a large cellar.

Once we reached the bottom, Turi put the lamp aside and took hold of the broom in the corner. He began sweeping the floor, looking for something, but the dust made it harder to see. After some time of coughing and cleaning, we finally found what we were looking for.

We gazed at the round-shaped stone, engraved with two hexagrams on top of each other.

"Also a Tree of Life?" he said surprised. "I thought that each Merkaba device had a different symbol."

I shrugged my shoulders. "From what I know, they are all identical."

Turi just smiled, and shook his head. "It doesn't matter."

He was impatient, keen to try something. "All right, let's do this."

He grasped my hand in his, squeezing it tight. "Are you ready?"

I nodded, equally agog yet also afraid. I followed his lead, even though it meant breaking the promise I made to Atarah – never to use the Merkaba device without her consent.

Together, we stepped onto the stone-like machine, into the centre of the symbol, and exchanged a brief, hopeful smile before we closed our eyes. We were expecting a miracle, but nothing happened. When I opened my eyes again, I saw the deep disappointment in Turi's face. Our hands were still locked together but our grip lacked its initial enthusiasm.

"So Atarah was right," I said, as the rest of our hope faded away. "It's not that easy."

"I thought the secret key to using it was just a myth," said Turi, "which they tell children to protect them from crossing over to the other side."

He lowered his head, and his hands let go of mine. I felt sorry for him, knowing how much he wanted to make the magic work.

"Maybe the key is in a simple detail," I suggested, "you know what Atarah says - *sometimes it's all about the details, they make the whole more meaningful.*"

"It must be," nodded Turi. "Remember the man Atarah exterminated by the riverside? He was about to use it by simply standing on it. I have to figure this out…"

I had expected him to be stubborn and not give up. I knew very well that he wouldn't change his mind about breaking the rules. I both loved and hated that part of him. It drew me to him, although it also had been building boundaries between us.

"Maybe we should stick to simply guarding it, to keeping it hidden from everyone, including ourselves. Atarah would tell us how to use it if she thought we were ready for it, don't you think?

Maybe it's unattainable for a reason..."

Turi was about to object, but a sound of creaks and footsteps disturbed us. We instinctively leaned closer to one another.

"The city patrol? I whispered.

Turi shrugged, and pulled me closer, hiding us both beneath the stairway. He then reached into his jacket for the metallic disc, the same weapon that Atarah owned. My hand stopped him before he managed to pull it out. My eyes locked onto his, and I spoke to him in my mind, knowing that he would understand. *You know that the weapon is to be used only in case of an emergency.*

Turi's hand paused, and rested on the rim of his coat, remaining alert just in case. We waited for whoever was coming down with bated breath, wishing we hadn't revealed the secret device. I pressed myself against Turi's chest, promising myself that I would stop supporting him in his reckless pursuits.

Then, a figure overshadowed us from above, and began descending the stairs. It was a young man, on first impressions just a regular citizen, but the very fact that he was in the Magic Quarter implied that he was after something. He spotted the stone with the engraved symbol right away, and his face lit up. He must have known about it, and it was time to see why.

I concentrated on his chest, willing myself to scan his emotions. There was a hectic, disharmonious mess instead of light rays. I saw no clear colour, not even a soft glow. It upset me, so I turned to Turi for advice, and was stunned at the sight of his hand, which had snuck back inside his coat pocket. I attempted to stop him, but the swift movement caught the man's attention. He turned to us in fright and bewilderment.

We all froze for a moment, trying to figure each

other out. Eventually, the man started after us. Turi panicked and without asking questions, he threw the weapon at him. In a split second, the man burst into white light. His body became a cloud of glittery particles. Some evaporated, others blended in with the shabby surroundings, erasing any sign of him having ever been there, as well as of our unlawful deed.

Turi caught the weapon that bounced back to him, and turned to me in shock. It was the first time he had exterminated someone in the name of his mission. I stared back at him, unable to say or do anything. I was too shaken. Up until then, I believed he would never be able to kill.

"That's what we are meant to do," he said in an apologetic tone. "His heart had ill intentions, you saw it for yourself. I have to protect what needs to be kept safe."

"Yet you can't protect it from yourself," I said with a trembling voice.

The angst that had spread through me had awakened me to the world where my body rested. I took a deep, relieved breath before I opened my eyes and stared into the dim space.

The dream made me think back to the familiar man that I had seen when I first entered the hallway of Vilma's home. I recalled it as if it were right before my eyes again – he was emerging from the cellar, his hair was dark and wavy like Turi's, the energy he exuded just as fiery. Could it have been him? The idea of Turi being a real person, and of proving that the dreams and visions were actual memories, was truly exciting.

At the sound of the bells striking three o'clock in the morning, I snuck into the hallway, and headed to the cellar. I didn't care whether it was safe or not, I had to see the subterranean space for myself, and find out whether there was a circular stone on the ground.

To my disappointment, I found out that the door was locked. I decided to wait until the morning to ask Vilma for help, and as I was heading back to the stairway, I sensed someone's presence behind me. I was afraid to turn around at first, but when I finally did, I noticed the cloaked figure I feared. His face was plunged into darkness, unreadable, daunting. I froze, too terrified to scream for help, or to run away. I simply stood there, staring at the nothingness beneath the hood of his cloak.

"You know what happens to those who become aware of such secrets," he said in a deep voice, "I won't warn you twice, girl. You'd better leave this house."

The hall turned deadly silent then. All I heard was the intense hammering in my chest. The figure leaned over the handrail, revealing his veiny, emaciated hand. It looked as though he was going to say something more, but he changed his mind. After what seemed like an eternity, he headed to the back entrance, like the young man I supposed could have been Turi. With one last foreboding glance in my direction, he closed the door behind him.

Relieved, I returned to the safety of Vilma's apartment and gave up the desire to explore whatever the cellar concealed. Although the faceless stranger had aroused my curiosity even more, he had also managed to stall me in my quest. I decided that until I knew more about the mystery surrounding me, I shouldn't tempt fate.

I tiptoed to the kitchen window, and watched him walk towards the river, moonlight shining on his path. He didn't turn around, yet I had the feeling that he was aware of me spying on him.

Unable to calm myself, I sat by the window until dawn. As I watched the night turn into a new day, I thought about Turi. I felt as though he mirrored an inextricable, innate part of me, and until I connected with it again, I wouldn't be able to rest.

# Chapter V

## The Hierophant

The next day, I told Vilma about the unnerving encounter with the faceless man, leaving out the strange dream I had had about her basement. The fact that he broke into the building terrified her, and so she made a resolute decision to move to the New World quarter as soon as possible. The new landlord was understanding and said that if we cleaned everything up ourselves, we could move in right away. Vilma's plan was to continue running her shop in the Fifth District during the day, but spend the night in her new home. She had already begun to inform people of her relocation, as she eventually wanted to move her shop as well.

I was nervous, worried that it might cause Vilma trouble, but she insisted that it was the right thing to do for her as well. Although the demolition of the Narrow Lane had been postponed until the beginning of the new century, the local conditions were growing worse. Also, there would be too much noise in the late autumn, during the first wave of the regeneration, which would cause her business to fall off anyway.

By dusk, we had finished packing all the necessities, and I went to say goodbye to Oliver. I waited a long time after knocking, and only when I turned to leave, did the door creak open, and Oliver's face peek out. He was in a dishevelled state, his pale hair all tousled.

"Good morning," he said, his voice raspy as though he had just woken up.

"Are you all right?" I asked, concerned.

"Yes, of course, no worries," he reassured me while nervously looking over his shoulder. I averted my eyes from the silhouette that had appeared behind him, but not before I noticed her curves and realised it was a young woman, wrapped in his bedsheets.

I was caught off guard and rendered speechless. The girl's inquisitive look, however, brought me back to reality and made me focus on Oliver. He gave me a penitent smile.

"Last night turned out to be quite long," he explained. "I met my friend Laura here at the Pub By Denice, and we simply couldn't stop talking. We have just returned."

He winked her way and she grinned. His honesty wasn't all that welcome just then. I tried to hide my disappointment behind an unnecessarily wide smile.

"Oh, that's… great. Don't let me interrupt, then."

I nodded a friendly goodbye to Laura, but couldn't bring myself to even glance in Oliver's direction. It wasn't just because he had spent the evening in the company of another woman again. I thought that he would stay in for the night, and keep guard as he had promised. It might have been because of his absence that the faceless man dared to break in. Then again, he had no obligation towards me, we were just strangers, after all.

I was going to leave when he called after me:

"Wait a minute neighbour, what is it you wanted?"

I turned to him, my eyes blank as I said, "I just came to say goodbye," and hurried back to Vilma's apartment, eager to leave the uncomfortable situation behind.

Vilma immediately noticed that something was wrong, because I couldn't conceal my discomfort.

"Another girl over?" she guessed. I nodded quickly, my eyes begging her not to comment on it. She seemed to understand and simply shook her head.

"Men like him never change."

I remained standing by the closed door, perplexed by my emotions. I didn't understand why the sight of the half-naked girl had fired me up inside. I felt an odd burden settle on my chest and neck just where the built-up tension was. It must have been because I was hiding my true feelings about the encounter. I knew it did not matter, though. It was better to stop anything that was about to flourish right at the start.

Vilma meanwhile offered me some strong tea, readying me for the busy day ahead. I took a gulp and winced.

"Bitter as life, darling, I know," she said with a light smile, which faded into nostalgia. I could feel that she was on the edge of telling me something about her past, but in the end, she decided not to. Instead, she focused her attention on one of the books that lay open on the table. The page showed two star symbols – a pentagram and a hexagram. Vilma traced their tips with her fingers.

"Sometimes all you meet is corners," she mused, and began to circle her finger around the image, "but then again, if you were moving in circles, you'd find no way out either." She pointed at the centre. "I suppose it's only here that you're safe. This determines what follows…"

The seriousness didn't suit her, neither did her sudden gloom. She noticed my dispirited expression and patted my cheek.

"I know. There's no time to philosophise now," she said and stood up, ready to go. Meanwhile, I focused on the symbols, and recalled something that Atarah had told me once:

*"Pentagrams and hexagrams are the base of all creation in the Tree of Life, and therefore also of the Merkaba."*

☆

Vilma's new home was located in a small, single storey building that had been standing opposite the city wall for hundreds of years. In comparison to the poor conditions in the Fifth District, it was luxurious. The toilet was shared, but only with one neighbour, and the bathroom was completely private.

The space was about the same size as Vilma's previous apartment, and it was fully furnished, so all we needed to do was to tidy up and unpack the clothes, sheets and study books that we had brought with us. The rest was to be delivered over the next few weeks.

In the morning, I started to clear the small garden attached to the house. I weeded the beds, making space for the herbs and vegetables we planned to sow. I could feel how beneficial the manual work was for me. It rested my mind, allowed me to symbolically bury my worries in the ground. I hoped that they would rot away; transform into something better.

Luckily, the faceless man hadn't shown up since

the move. I supposed that since we had left the house in the Fifth District his quest was over. I felt safer at night, glad to have left behind whatever had bound me to the building in the Narrow Lane. My curiosity, however, made me stay up later than Vilma. I couldn't stop leafing through the old books connected with the Merkaba. I longed to pinpoint what connected all the terms, words, shapes and dreams, and to find out whether my past truly concealed some big and possibly dangerous secret.

The following day, I decided to take a walk through the Petřín gardens. As I looked over the various rooftops and trees, my eyes fell upon the wrought iron tower whose peak grazed the dispersing clouds. Since the sky was clearing, I assumed that the view from up there would be nice. Vilma had given me some coins to spend, so I was able to pay the entrance fee, and climbed all the way to the top floor.

I enjoyed scanning the horizon, speculating about why the countryside beyond Prague was less familiar than the city itself. My heart called out to the landscape I had seen in my dreams, the range of forested mountains and rocks beyond the city walls. I was visualising the unicorn and lion sculptures in the northeast, ruminating on their meaning when a male voice disturbed me:

"Beautiful view, eh?"

Until that moment, I hadn't even noticed that I wasn't alone. A familiar looking elderly man with a long, grey beard stood behind me, gazing in the same direction. Once our eyes met, I realised that he was the man we met in the Golden Lane, the one Vilma called an 'angry gnome'. The memory made me silently giggle.

"Hello, sir," I said. "How is life in the upper Golden Lane?"

I gave him an apologetic smile, feeling guilty over

how Vilma had behaved towards him. He squinted, confused.

"Oh!" he exclaimed, remembering. "I didn't recognise you at first. You are that rude lady's friend."

I half-nodded. "Rude, but adorable."

He let out a brusque laugh, then greeted me with a proper handshake. "I suppose it would be polite to introduce myself. I'm Hieronymus," he said, then smiled and added, "not Bosch."

I presumed that being a local I should know who Hieronymus Bosch was, so I smiled back.

"Nice to meet you, Hieronymus," I said courteously, "but I hope you won't take offence if I don't share my name. I like to travel in disguise." I could see I had surprised him, yet he seemed to respect my decision.

"No offence taken, miss, no offence at all…" His eyes narrowed as he watched me. Then he cleared his throat and asked: "Have you found what you were looking for in the lower Golden Lane?"

"Not yet... I'm not giving up, though."

"Good for you," he said, resting his elbows upon the handrail, "I apologise for the 'high-pitched voice' remark. That wasn't tactful."

"Don't worry about it, my friend's remark wasn't tactful either."

He nodded. "Let's just leave it at that. Both remarks were untactful but quite apt, don't you think?"

We both chuckled, and looked over the landscape again, enjoying the twilight.

"Do you know why the street in the Fifth District was called Golden?"

"No, why?" I asked, intrigued.

"Legend has it that a local woman's daughter fell in love with a prince from a different world, which co-exists with ours, and his kingdom gave her so much gold that the whole street glittered. There are more legends about such realms and the thresholds which lead to them. It makes sense when you think about it."

I recalled the phrase *threshold custodian* from my dreams, but that was about it, so I wondered what he meant. He seemed glad to be the first to enlighten me, and continued speaking animatedly:

"Well, have you ever thought about the connection? The root of the city's name is *threshold*, right? *Praha*, from *práh* meaning threshold? Well, legend says that the city hides thresholds to other realms or realities, which are concealed behind the veil of our common perception."

He peeked at me from beneath his brows to gauge my reaction. I was very taken by the idea.

"Such hidden realms are a common theme in fairy tales," he elaborated further. "Take the Island of Avalon, for example, or the Shambhala, the legendary land inside the Himalayas. I suppose it comes as no surprise that Prague is also one of these places.

"In my opinion, the Celts who established the city knew about the thresholds in this area and built the city upon them in order to explore the worlds beyond those thresholds."

Most of the time I had no idea what he was talking about, but it fascinated me nonetheless.

"And where were these thresholds located?" I asked, thrilled to gather more information on the subject.

"I wish I knew," he said with a smile, "but I heard that one was supposed to be located somewhere on the shores of Vltava."

My heart pounded with the thought that I didn't even dare to finish. "Where exactly?"

I prompted him to tell me more, expecting him to confirm my foolishness in thinking there could be some connection between the legend and myself.

He shrugged.

"Somewhere by Lahovice – a village near the confluence of the Vltava and Berounka rivers. Although, it could very well just be hearsay. My theory is that one of those thresholds was also hidden beneath the mysterious fire that they found in the Lesser Town."

"What's so mysterious about it?"

"You don't know that story either?" I shook my head, yet again.

"Well, this happened not so long ago, so it can't really be considered a legend. During the reconstruction of Nebovidská Street, the workers found a hole with a bright flame that couldn't be extinguished. They left it open because they were afraid of it, and before the news could even spread across Prague, the fire died out… or so they said. Who knows if they buried it again.

"If my theory is correct, then these thresholds were aligned with the four basic elements. The fire one would be in Nebovidská, the water one in Lahovice, and there's a story of an invisible house in the lane I live in, which might be the threshold of the air element."

"What about the earth element?"

"That's a good question," he replied. "I suspect it would be the most accessible one, and therefore kept a total secret, such that even legends don't speak of it."

"But why would it be kept a secret?"

He gave me a quizzical look.

"Can you imagine how risky it would be to travel in between the worlds? It may come as a surprise to you, but I don't think that such tales are necessarily fiction. I have spent my whole life studying history, and thanks to my ancestors, who have been writing a chronicle for hundreds of years, I have come to believe that there is a fine line between legend and history.

"A dear friend of mine once said that legends are in fact the windows to understanding our history… I like that thought very much."

I nodded in agreement, thinking about sharing the news with Vilma later. I knew she would find what he had told me just as fascinating.

"Are you the new chronicle keeper then?" I asked.

He was proud to confirm it. "Yes. I write a new chapter every day if God allows."

"Your descendants are lucky," I said with admiration, "it's a gift to know one's past…"

I thought about how wonderful it would be to have something like a chronicle of my kinsfolk, and learn all that I yearned to know. Hieronymus was also lost in reverie.

"That is true, but I don't know whether my work will be appreciated. One never knows, though, perhaps my nieces and nephews will preserve it or follow in my footsteps. Unfortunately, I don't have children of my own." He gazed into the distance, nostalgia shrouding his face. I sensed that, like Vilma, he too avoided the subject of his private life.

"It's getting late," he said with a glance at his watch, "I'd better be off. Do you need company on the way home?"

"No, but I would like it."

"Very well then."

He gestured to me, letting me walk on ahead. As we made for the stairs, I began to inquire about the legend of Prague's thresholds again.

"What do you think these other realms might look like?"

From the sparkle in his eyes, I could tell that he was happy to return to that subject. He cupped his chin and pensively stroked his beard.

"Hmm… That's an interesting question. There

could be so many out there. The one place I have been researching the most, however, is the legend of the so-called Pryaya."

"Pryaya," I whispered to myself. It sounded familiar, not only because of its similarity to Prague.

"According to legend, a brotherhood of seven monks called the Sat Bhai ventured from the North Indian town of Prayag, now Allahabad, all the way to Europe, where they established cities in other dimensions. The names of these cities were always associated with the theme of thresholds, including the obvious Prague or Praha."

I had a feeling I knew exactly what he was talking about, yet didn't understand why.

"I feel like I have heard this before," I admitted, "but what exactly does the Sat Bhai stand for?"

"Nowadays, the Sat Bhai is a title of one exclusive Masonic lodge. I don't know whether there's any connection there, though. The Masonic societies are very private, closed to strangers."

I was about to ask another question and, at that point, I wasn't interested in these secret societies.

"I meant the title itself, Hieronymus. What does that stand for?"

"Ah, well, from what I know, it means *seven brothers*. I also think it may have some connection to the mighty Celtic tribe that roamed these lands hundreds of years ago, the Boii. That's where the name Bohemia comes from.

"The theory makes sense to me, as many historians think there are some striking parallels between Celtic and ancient Indian cultures. It would also strengthen the theory of Prague's mysterious origins. However, I have a feeling that the story behind the Sat Bhai is more complicated than that."

He paused for a moment, remembering something. "A few days ago, I overheard some people discussing this. A young man was very keen to hear about the story. He was called Gustav, but I don't recall the surname. He told the others that the Sat Bhai brotherhood's symbol was depicted above the entrance to a house in Opatovická Street.

"Out of curiosity, I went to look at it, and what I found was an emblem portraying a lion and a unicorn, separated by what looks like a boat and a pope's tiara above them. I still can't decipher it. The emblem is identical to the English coat of arms, not ours, as our patron and heraldic symbol is only the lion, without the unicorn."

I didn't understand most of what he had said, and so I thought back to the lion-unicorn statue from my dreams. I felt that my heart wanted to tell me something important, and my mind was eager to listen to it, but as usual, I was out of luck. Hieronymus had noticed my dreaminess and touched my arm, concerned.

"Are you all right, miss?"

I nodded, though the world seemed to be spinning all of a sudden. Like the first time I entered Vilma's house, I had that strange feeling again, a mixture of alienation and familiarity.

✡

After I parted from Hieronymus in the Lesser Town, I decided to take a longer walk around the city. I needed to refresh my mind and think some more about the amazing information he had provided me with.

I walked over the old bridge, enjoying the tingling in my hands and feet, which I experienced every time I stepped on those ancient stone blocks. Instead of admiring the view as usual, I studied the impressive statues, the fossilised custodians of the wild waters. One, in particular, piqued my interest. It was a saint called Jan Nepomucký. He held a crucifix and a feather, and his halo consisted of five hexagrams. Below him was a set of five ruby red pentagrams, their tips also decorated with hexagrams.* As I observed the familiar star symbols, a vision came to me...

I saw Turi and me at the age of fourteen. We were already living in the house I considered my original home, the one in the Fifth District, or the Magic Quarter, as we called it in that version of the city. We were hiding there, pursuing our important mission. The lodgings were simple, but we managed well enough. There was almost no furniture, just two squeaky beds and a small fireplace in the corner, surrounded by a pile of wood that we had gathered from the deep forest beyond the city. There were also a few boxes of food supplies from the House of Mercy, an organisation that, as I understood, helped citizens in need. They never asked questions, and so we could go to them without concern.

Turi had fixed a ladder to the window, in case we needed to escape. There were times when we had to sneak out and hide, mainly when the city patrol came to check the area. Turi and I were taking a risk by being there because had we been found, we would have been imprisoned.

We were used to finding all kinds of things in the dilapidated buildings, but that night, we brought home a big box filled with antique decorations. Before our country's law forbade magic, people used to decorate trees with magical symbols, mainly during the Winter Solstice. We were brought up to keep these traditions, and so we were excited to find the animal totems, crosses and whorls.

Turi suggested decorating the tall pine tree that stood right outside the house, and I was keen on the idea as well. We used a lantern to light up the darkened street, and began searching through the boxes. Eventually, we turned the activity into a game and decided that each decoration one of us was to hang would represent the other. I remember picking up a totem of a pig and hanging it on the tree branch, saying: "This is you!" Turi would take revenge by pick a totem of a goose. "Oh, really? Then this is you!"

We kept teasing each other until we almost ran out of things to hang. Then Turi pulled out the brightest and biggest decoration I had ever seen – a sparkling pentagram inscribed with an even more radiant hexagram. He climbed the ladder and placed it on top of the tree. His expression remained impish when he looked down at me, but his voice was serious and heartfelt.

"This is what you really are to me, Seraphina."

I was taken aback by how the light mood had transformed into such a special moment, which was to become an unforgettable memory. Touched, I gave him a smile, wondering how I could beat that. Finally, I leaped up in the air and soared higher, attempting to plant a kiss on his cheek. When I was just an inch from his face, though, our world was shaken, quite literally. Someone shook the ladder that Turi was standing on, and he staggered but managed to hold on to the top rung. I didn't see who the culprit was, I could only make out a male silhouette concealed in the darkness. When the big hands grasped Turi, he called out to me in shock:

"Run! Go!"

I wavered for a moment, wondering how to help him, but he was even more resolute the second time:

"Just run, damn it!"

I presumed that it was the city patrol, and therefore decided to trust Turi's judgement. I began to sprint off, then leaped up, and continued floating slightly above the ground, which allowed me to escape faster. As the streets whizzed past, I kept my mind focused on only one thought: Let Turi be safe.

With another high leap, the vision faded and I once again felt the world around me swirl. I leaned over the side of the bridge, trying to compose myself. Was I really called *Seraphina*? Could it be that my name was aligned with the Seraphim, hence the Merkaba? It made me think back to what Hieronymus had told me. If legends were as reliable as history, then the seemingly bizarre dreams and visions might in fact truly be my memories.

It took me a while to bring myself back to the present. For the first time since my appearance in the river, I felt completely alone, as though no one else could understand me, expect maybe the faceless man who had disappeared from my life as soon as I had fulfilled his wish. The odd, alienated feeling made my longing for the truth even stronger.

Suddenly, an old man approached the statue I was resting by, disturbing my train of thought. He gave me a polite nod and began lighting up the candles behind the pentagrams. It was only then that I noticed the stars were in fact lamps. I smiled at the lamplighter and left him to his work. With this newly found ray of hope, I carried on with my journey.

---

*Nowadays, the set of five red pentagrams below the statue of Jan Nepomucký are no longer there, but a few steps further on is a magic cross with five pentagrams, which legend has it fulfills the wishes of those who stroke each of the stars and place their left hand upon the cross.

# Chapter VI

## The Lovers

At last, I was no longer just a *girl*, *miss*, or as Vilma liked to call me, *dear*. I was Seraphina, and I didn't care whether it was my true name or not, as it resonated with me. I shared it with Vilma, who discovered that it really did derive from the word *Seraphim*.

One afternoon, I finally introduced myself to Oliver. I met him while he was helping Vilma bring over the rest of her belongings. She had refused his help until she had no other choice. Once he had finished bringing in all the boxes, Vilma didn't even bother to invite him in for a cup of tea. I felt bad for him, so I walked with him to the carriage.

"So, how does it feel to live here, Seraphina?" he asked, then paused. "I can't get used to that exotic name. How did your parents come up with it?" I shrugged and fed the horses some apples from

Vilma's garden.

"But to answer the previous question, I like it here. Different to the Old Town, but just as lovely."

"Why the hurry to move, though? I hope it wasn't because of the cloaked man." I smiled at his perception, but shook my head.

"How about you? Have you sorted out a new place for yourself?"

"Well, I'll keep taking care of the apartment in the Narrow Lane, as it's not due to be demolished for a few years. But I'll also be moving back to my childhood home, the apartment in Nerudova Street."

"Oh, yes, I'd forgotten that your family has so many properties around Prague."

He nodded, and stood beside me with hands in his pockets and a boyish expression on his face.

"I suppose I should be on my way."

"Of course, I wouldn't want to detain you," I said. "Thank you for helping Vilma, and if you ever feel like visiting us, I would be glad to see you."

His eyes lit up at the thought.

"I would be happy to stop by sometime, if Vilma allows it, that is."

He gave me the mischievous wink he had mastered so well, then climbed up onto the driver's seat. He patted the horses, took hold of the reins, and they slowly set off.

"Thank you again!" I called after him, wiping the horse drool from my hands onto my skirt. He gave me a nod and said:

"We thank you! For the sweets and for your kindness."

He tipped his hat and rode off round the street corner.

As I stared after him, an odd anxiety possessed me. Though Vilma was too sceptical when it came to him, she was right about one thing – he was not to be adored by a heart that yearned for love, unless that heart was bent on self-destruction.

"Good that you got rid of him," said Vilma upon my return.

"You did that, dear Vilma, you did that..." I teased. We exchanged knowing smiles, and silently agreed that whatever I felt towards him should remain unsaid.

"The world is desperately short of decent men," complained Vilma. "Though I was never lucky, I believe there's a good one for you out there."

"Maybe I'd prefer to live alone, like you."

"Trust me, you wouldn't. Being an old maid is not always easy, people tend to judge, gossip..."

"But Dora and you seem to be doing all right."

She flashed me a sceptical look. "Say that again after a year of living here and I'll give you a medal."

We began to unpack, keen to decorate the new apartment and fill it with Vilma's spirit.

"Haven't you met any other gentleman on your walks?"

"I have, actually."

The admission made her turn to me in surprise. "Really?"

"Yes, an interesting gentleman from the Golden Lane." Vilma rolled her eyes and began to unpack more furiously.

"Again, with that angry gnome of yours? That one doesn't count as a gentleman. In fact, he's even further from it than Oliver." I swallowed back a chuckle and went on:

"If you gave Hieronymus a chance you would find that he is actually a fascinating person."

"Hieronymus? What on Earth were his parents thinking?"

Not being familiar with the local names, her reaction baffled me.

"Does it sound strange to you?"

"It sounds ancient!" She shook her head,

laughing.

"I'm sorry," she patted my hand, "if the company of that old goat helps you then I'm happy for you."

I gratefully patted her hand back. "Thank you, Vilma. For everything."

"Stop thanking me, silly girl…" she paused mid-sentence, "Seraphina."

My heart swelled at the sound of the name. The effect it had on me made me curious about the person I had once been.

I had been putting it off, but it was high time I visited the place that Hieronymus had told me about, the building of the so-called Sat Bhai. I needed to find out more about Pryaya because the legend, no matter how unreal, seemed closer to what I was experiencing than any other rational explanation I had tried to come up with.

☆

I found the building with the Sat Bhai emblem quite easily, and as I contemplated its curious symbolism, I noticed a hexagram and a pentagram engraved in the massive, wooden door. Why was it, I wondered, that I kept seeing them everywhere?

Suddenly, I spotted a young man's profile behind one of the ground floor windows. His dark curls concealed most of his face, yet I was certain that I knew him from somewhere. I watched as he joined a group of people gathered in the spacious room, and my heart skipped a beat when I remembered who he reminded me of. He was the compelling stranger who had emerged from Vilma's basement the day we first met – the person my whole being called out for.

I held my breath and approached the front door, ready to knock. It was a bold gesture, I knew that very well, but I simply had to meet him. When no answer came, I knocked even harder, and caught the attention of a comely woman in her forties with striking, dark red hair. She opened the window, and stared at me, silently challenging me to explain myself.

"Hello," I said with a respectful smile, "I'm sorry to disturb you. Could I please speak to someone in the room?"

"This is a closed meeting and a closed society," she said curtly, then shut the window, and drew the drapes. I was unwilling to give up, and decided to wait the man out. I didn't care that it was going to be dark soon or that it might rain. I sensed that the man was important to me.

After a few hours of loitering by the entrance, I noticed the group beginning to disperse and most visitors were leaving the building. Their scrutiny unnerved me, but not as much as the possibility of missing my chance to talk to the mysterious man. I waited, anxious to set eyes on him, and to see his reaction to me, but he never emerged.

I was about to give up when I suddenly found myself face to face with him through the window. A mixture of love and anxiety welled up within me when I realised who the man was – Turi. There was no doubt that he had recognised me as well, and that my presence surprised him.

We stared at each other, our eyes locked like magnets. I could swear that time stopped. The world around us seemed to have vanished. There was only each other's reflections, and an inner greeting that was louder than any spoken word.

Then another man's face appeared behind him, and gave us both a confused look. I heard his muffled voice through the glass as he asked:

"Who is this?"

Turi's gentle expression shifted into a brooding one. He gave the man a shrug and drew the drapery.

I was once again cut off from whatever was going on inside, only this time I felt betrayal more than disappointment. I was angry. How dare he shut me out like that after we had just found each other? I wasn't going to back down, or allow him to get away with it so easily. I decided to keep waiting for him, for as long as it took, and so I did.

I waited until the lamps were lit in the streets and the stars spread across the sky. I tried knocking again, fiercer than before, but there was no response. Eventually, my exhaustion made me slide down on to the steps of the building. Although I willed myself not to doze off, I couldn't help it. I fell into a dreamless sleep.

When I woke up, all the windows in the building were dark. Everyone must have left. The thought of Turi passing me by, leaving me out there in the cold night made my heart ache. How could he treat me so badly after all we had been through? Could it be, I thought to myself, that he had never forgiven me for running off that fateful night, or had something worse happened between the two of us afterwards?

On my way back to Vilma's, I had the feeling that I was being followed, but each time I turned around, I just saw the empty street lit by Prague's distinct green lamps. At one point, I spied someone who I thought was Turi in the shadow of a building, but as soon as I focused on him, he disappeared around the corner. I hurried back, and searched the street, hoping in vain that he would reappear.

✡

The following day, as I passed the House at the Keys, a familiar face crossed my path. It was Oliver. He was almost startled to see me, and I caught a look of guilt on his face when he greeted me. Then he turned around to glance at a young woman who was strolling towards the Old Town. I only saw her from behind, but her graceful movement told me that she was a lady. She seemed different from the girls Oliver was usually seen with, and it was obvious that she mattered more to him. Once she had disappeared from sight, the discomfort on his face faded.

"Are you also heading home?" he asked. I nodded, resisting the urge to ask who he was gazing after, because I didn't want to pry.

"Would you perhaps like to join me for an afternoon drink at my apartment? It would be nice to show you my childhood home."

I hesitated, wondering what Vilma would think about it.

"I'd understand if you turned me down." He looked at me as though he was expecting me to admonish him.

"All right," I said at last, "but only for a moment, I wouldn't want to make Vilma worry."

"Of course, I'll make sure that you get home safely. It's just a short distance up the street, at the White Angel house."

"There? I know that building. It's very nice."

He offered me his arm and led me up my favourite street in the Lesser Town, named after a recently deceased writer, Jan Neruda. I liked it because the exuberantly decorated architecture reminded me of the street from my memories. Each one of the buildings had its own unique charm, and the names were depicted in the various frescos, reliefs, statues and other personalised signs above the entrances.

After a few more steps, we stopped beneath a beautiful white statue of an angel, the silent guardian of the building. Oliver took out his key and was unlocking the front door when I spotted a male figure out of the corner of my eye. Even before I turned to face him, I sensed it was Turi.

He was approaching us, this time without turning away or hiding. I couldn't help but lose myself in the sea-blue eyes that you could easily drown in, silently pleading him to talk to me. How I longed to find out more about what kind of people we grew up to be, and what happened to us.

He recognised me too, and I knew it wasn't just a recollection of one chance meeting through a window. His look spoke for itself. Then his eyes flickered over to Oliver, and his expression changed. As before, he became distant. They greeted each other, curtly and politely. Oliver opened the door for us, and they both gestured for me to enter first. It was an odd situation. I was standing between two men who I was attracted to, but only one of them was marked with the sign of destiny.

I walked inside and automatically headed for the stairs. Oliver motioned for me to continue, so I obeyed. Although the moment I had been waiting for was finally here, I couldn't bring myself to seize it. I didn't know what to say, or how to start a conversation with him after the strange meeting the other day. The thought of another disappointment made my knees feel weak.

So I quietly climbed the stairs, slower than usual, just to buy more time. When we reached the first floor, Turi headed for the door opposite to Oliver's. Seeing him leave me again was too much to bear. I gathered my courage and blurted out:

"Excuse me!"

With his hand on the doorknob, he turned to face me. He seemed pleasantly surprised, relieved, yet also torn, as though struggling with something. I held his gaze, and continued speaking:

"I'm quite certain that it is you, but I have to ask – you are Turi, right?" His eyes lit up, which is why I was so baffled when he said:

"I'm sorry, miss, you must have me confused with someone else."

The desire to fall into his arms and greet him as my beloved Turi was brushed away in an instant. He looked at Oliver again and finished our brisk conversation with a polite nod.

"Have a nice evening."

He disappeared behind the door, once again making me feel crestfallen. I couldn't explain why, but I had an inkling that he was afraid of something or someone, which was preventing him from talking to me.

Oliver's hand landed on my shoulder, bringing me back to the here and now with the question:

"What's going on, Seraphina? Who is Turi?"

I remained speechless, unable to explain, silenced by my confusion.

"It's all right, I don't have to know," he consoled me, and guided me inside his apartment, saying, "I've grown accustomed to the fact that your past is out of reach for me."

"I fear that it's out of my reach as well," I admitted, unable to hide my low spirits. Oliver narrowed his eyes, studying me, and I couldn't help but ask:

"Do you know that man?"

"No, but we have a common friend, Fabian."

He then guided me inside, showing me around the affluent and spacious space. I couldn't understand why he stayed in the Narrow Lane if he had such a mansion close at hand. However, his living arrangements were far from my thoughts at that moment. I had to know more about the neighbours.

"Do you know Fabian well?"

"I used to think so. We grew up together. His parents own half of this building, my parents the other half. We were best friends before he met that woman."

Without asking, he handed me some cognac and poured himself a glass as well. Although I wasn't keen on drinking the alcohol, I was impatient to hear what he had to say, and therefore accepted it without protest.

"What woman?"

"A crazy one, associated with all kinds of esoteric lodges."

I remembered he had spoken of his distrust of such societies before and supposed that she had something to do with it. Oliver expertly tasted the cognac and added:

"Strange how some people change... how their minds become clouded. As I told you before, I'm not against mysticism or spirituality as such, not even the fact that they keep their activity a secret, it's the organisation that makes me uncomfortable. A group always needs a leader and sheep... and once you become a sheep, a part of your individuality is bound to be suppressed.

"And what about the poor leader's ego?" he continued. "It must be tested greatly, don't you think? If someone considers himself or herself more enlightened than the others then that is, in my opinion, a road straight to hell."

"Do you know anything more about Fabian's lodge?" I asked without paying much attention to his theorising, desperate to know what I should do to become closer to whom I believed was Turi. "How do you go about becoming a member?" Oliver turned to me, startled.

"Are you serious?" He looked upset at first, but hid it behind a smile. "I can see that my opinion is of no value here."

"No, not at all. I agree with what you said, but... well, it's complicated."

My voice began to tremble as I found myself

caught in this trap. I couldn't explain anything without revealing more about myself.

"Is it connected to your past?"

I nodded, and took another sip of the cognac, wincing at the fire in my throat.

"I understand if you remain a closed book to me," he continued, "but I take it as my responsibility to warn you. There are many societies here in Prague, so don't pick the one with the darkest aura."

"What do you mean?"

"I might be wrong, I know nothing about that lodge, just the woman who introduced Fabian to it. It took only a few weeks and he was bound by her spell."

"Then it's her who is the problem, and not the group, right?"

Oliver hesitated. The tables seemed to have turned, and it was he who didn't want to share the truth. Without responding, he moved over to the window, his finger tracing the rim of the cognac glass. I watched his back, admiring his strong, proud posture, silently wishing he could help me.

"Would you... would you perhaps introduce me to your friend Fabian?" I spluttered.

Instead of answering, he expression became even more serious, and he beckoned me to come closer. I approached him and followed his eyes. The sight terrified me. The faceless man was back.

"He was supposed to leave me alone," I whispered, holding my breath in fear.

Oliver turned to me, concerned. "Will you ever tell me who he is?"

"I wish..."

"Do you have enemies? Do you owe money to anyone?"

I shrugged. "Not that I know of."

"I wish I could help you somehow." He paused, then asked:

"Are you sure that it wouldn't be wise to report him to the authorities?"

I remembered what Vilma had thought of that option, so I shook my head.

"I believe I can resolve this on my own, and I have a feeling that I'm on the right track now."

"Does Vilma support your decision?"

"Actually, she was the one who suggested it. She tends not to trust the authorities for some reason."

"Oh," he paused for a moment, surprised, then added: "Then it might indeed be a wise move."

His profound respect for her made me want to trust him, confide in him, but I couldn't bring myself to do so.

"Still," he said as his eyes flickered back at my pursuer, "that man is so damn eerie."

I agreed and stepped away from the window. I couldn't understand what the stranger still wanted from me after I had so obediently fulfilled his request. I hadn't even approached the Narrow Lane or the Fifth District since I received his warning. Was there some other place he wanted me to stay away from as well? I turned to Oliver, bewildered, searching his face for answers. He pulled the curtain closed and ran a thoughtful hand through his hair.

"Let's hope he leaves soon. I'll take you home then."

☆

The church bell chimed midnight and the faceless man was still haunting the street. Oliver kept checking on him, drinking coffee for a change, trying to keep his mind alert. He offered me a cup as well, but I found the taste too bitter. When I told him that I preferred chicory, he laughed and explained that chicory was coffee for poor people. It made sense because I lived with a woman who could hardly afford the chicory itself. The thought of her reminded me of the stress I had put her under. I told her that I would be home before dusk when we parted, and I was used to keeping my word.

"I'm worried about Vilma, worried that she's worried," I said. Oliver mulled something over. Then he took the last sip from the steaming cup and set it down on the windowsill.

"All right, that's enough. Let's go anyway."

I crossed my arms anxiously. After all, we didn't know what the menacing stranger was capable of.

Oliver grasped my hand to comfort me. "Don't worry. If you are with me he won't dare to try anything, and if he does he will pay. Come on now, we can't let Vilma down."

I marvelled at his unflagging efforts to win Vilma's favour. I couldn't understand why it meant so much to him, but hoped he would succeed one day.

Oliver pulled on my hand, guiding me to the door. Although I was afraid, I hoped that as he had scared off the faceless man before, he would be able to do it again.

Just as we were leaving, we heard a noise coming from the corridor and looked at each other in confusion. Oliver peeked through the keyhole, and before I had a chance to ask what was going on, he revealed the scene to me.

The entrance to the opposite apartment was filled with people. Some were leaving, others staying behind, chatting. There was only one woman amongst the group of men, the unpleasant red-haired woman who I had encountered at the Sat Bhai building in Opatovická Street. She was busy talking to a familiar, tall, dark-haired man in his mid-forties. I wondered what made them meet so late at night and searched Oliver's face for an answer. He rolled his eyes, and I guessed that it had something to do with Fabian.

The visitors were so absorbed in their conversation that they didn't even notice us until Oliver cleared his throat, and said, "Hello, Fabian."

The man who was talking to the red-haired woman turned in our direction, his expression distant, aloof.

"Oh, hello."

The two just stared at each other, and the conversation ran dry before it had even begun. I, on the other hand, wanted to learn more about the lodge, and so I dared to greet Fabian as well and said, "I hear that you are a member of an esoteric lodge…"

Fabian and all the faces around him turned to me. Silence spread through the room until Fabian broke it.

"I assume Oliver told you," he said as his eyes shifted over to Oliver and then back to me. I nodded, alarmed by everyone's shocked expressions. Without preamble, I explained:

"I think we could have common interests." My voice shook a little, which made me blush.

Fabian tilted his head, intrigued, though the way he was sizing me up seemed disdainful as well.

"What makes you think that, miss?" he enquired.

I wanted to share at least a part of the reason, but was rendered speechless. It was Turi. He had just appeared behind Fabian, and was peering at me from beneath his eyebrows, clearly upset. I was unable to read the wordless message he was trying to give me. As I opened my mouth to speak, Turi slightly shook his head, indiscernible to the others, yet very clear to me.

"Well? What kind of interests?" pressed Fabian, his voice irritated. Turi stopped me before I had even begun to reply:

"Apologies, miss, but this society is strictly for men only."

I looked at the woman standing nearby. She gave me a mocking smile then looked away as if I wasn't good enough to bother with.

"The only female companions who are welcome here are the wives of the members, or spiritualists," he elaborated further. "If you're neither, then perhaps you should find a more suitable lodge to join."

I tried to make sense of what he had said, as the cold way he spoke contradicted the warmth in his eyes. I furrowed my brow, exasperated. Fabian too was surprised by Turi's comment, but after they had exchanged a conspiratorial nod, he attempted to rid himself of me as well.

"My friend is right. Now if you have nothing more to add, please excuse us." Without turning back to me, he uttered a curt farewell: "Miss. Oliver." He then retreated into the apartment, and the rest of the guests joined him. Oliver offered me his arm, ready to continue with our plan of taking me home, but I was too shaken by Turi, who hovered by the door, apparently thinking something over. I asked him:

"Could I have a word with you in private, please?"

He gave me that warning look again.

"What good would it do? I have already told you everything you need to know," he answered evasively. His distant behaviour didn't worry me anymore, I read the truth in his eyes – it was all just a façade. I grasped his arm in despair, and whispered:

"I beg you. I have some important things to discuss with you."

"This is not a good time," he insisted, as his eyes deliberately flickered towards Fabian. He silently pleaded with me to obey him and I began to understand why. He was trying to protect me from those people. As nobody, including Oliver, was paying any attention to us at that moment, he said in a soft tone: "I'll find you later, Seraphina."

I froze, and before I was able to respond, he was gone from my sight.

✡

Oliver and I were quiet on the way home; both equally rattled by what had happened at the White Angel house, and nervous about my stalker, who had been following in our footsteps the whole time. I was glad about Turi's promise, but a troubling premonition had seized me ever since we parted. I wondered what he was protecting me from, whether it could be the faceless stranger or Fabian.

Although he kept flashing me inquisitive looks, Oliver kept to his promise and asked no more questions. As we neared Vilma's home in the New World, we noticed that the pursuer was nowhere to be seen.

"I'll stay here for a moment longer, make sure that he really is gone," said Oliver, and once again checked the street to make sure we were safe.

"Thank you, Oliver, for everything. Mainly for your respect of my privacy."

He responded with an amicable smile. "I should be the last to disrespect the right to that."

Sensing a double meaning, but anxious to return his kindness, I didn't seek an explanation. Instead, I smiled back, planted a friendly kiss on his cheek, and entered Vilma's haven.

Before I blew out the candle that night, I had a vision which I could finally consider a real memory – Turi and me, already adults, falling asleep side by side as though we were lovers.

# Chapter VII

## The Chariot

I sensed that my fortune had changed once I heard Turi say my name. He became the torch that shone a light into the dim past. Finally, I was certain that I came from the place of my visions and dreams. That is why I shared some of the memories I considered harmless with Vilma. However, days flew by and there was no sign of Turi. Vilma, who already knew that I had stumbled upon him, encouraged me to be patient with him, and focus on remembering my past instead.

"I have a feeling that the first word you remembered, Merkaba, is the key." Her comment brought to mind the Merkaba devices. With the thought, my eyes fell upon the wrought iron case that Vilma kept her Tarot cards in. It had a hexagram engraved on it. I took it as a confirmation, and suddenly knew what I should do next.

"I have to return to the Narrow Lane, Vilma," I affirmed.

"Why on Earth would you do that? The place is a mess, and the owner had probably rented it out by now."

"No, I meant just for a short visit."

"But I don't have the key anymore. We can't just break in."

I knew Vilma would go on describing her thoughts into detail, so I got straight to the point.

"Do you remember the dream I told you about? What Turi and I found there?"

"Yes, the large stone with the hexagrams."

I nodded, and continued speaking:

"If our past was linked to that building, then it must have been concealed there all along. Wasn't that why I saw Turi leaving the basement the day we met?"

Vilma considered the idea, as it slowly grew on her.

"Well, finding it would certainly be something, eh? And when I come to think of it, the tenants never lock the basement, and they often leave the back door open. That's probably how your Turi managed to sneak inside." She paused, her expression becoming troubled again as another thought crossed her mind. "But what about the faceless man?"

It wasn't that I didn't feel afraid of him, but my curiosity was stronger than my fear. I was ready to confront him if I had to.

"If that stone truly exists and was the reason why he chased me away from there, then it must be important. We have to learn the truth. I can't keep avoiding my past. I can't live without knowing who I was, who I am." I spoke quickly, unable to just sit there and discuss it. Vilma squeezed my hand, attempting to calm me down.

"You know that I support you wholeheartedly,

but if we go there, then we should not be alone."

"Please don't suggest waiting for Turi again."

"Actually," she paused, and a faint blush coloured her cheeks, "I was thinking of someone else..." I tilted my head, encouraging her to finish.

"You know who I mean," she muttered.

"Dora?"

Vilma rolled her eyes. "I meant a person more capable of scaring off aggressors."

"Hieronymus?"

"God! No! How could he protect us? Shake his dusty beard?"

I smiled at the comment and wondered who might be the knight she was thinking of. There was only one person left, one who was already involved anyway, and would be honoured to help the woman he, for some reason, kept trying to impress.

☆

Fortunately, Oliver didn't let us down. On the stroke of midnight, he picked us up in a carriage and drove us to the Fifth District. I hadn't been there since the demolition process had begun, and was shocked to see how deserted and lonely some of the streets were. It felt as though the bricks and stones knew what was coming, and were silently awaiting their fate.

The first wave of the quarter's regeneration was scheduled for October, in about a week's time. Twenty-three houses were to be torn down, fifteen of them near to the Old Town square, the area where the new avenue would later be built. The quarter's western part would remain untouched for a few more years, but the living conditions there had worsened rapidly. As Vilma predicted, most people had already moved out, which lowered the rents, and the quarter had become poorer than it had ever been. My heart ached at the vision of its dark future, and I empathised with all those who had tried to save its unique charm. After all, it was there that I felt closest to home.

Oliver still used the apartment in the Narrow Lane from time to time, and so we didn't have to stage a break-in or wait for the back door to be left unlocked. Holding his antique candelabra aloft, he led us down to the basement, ready to help search for the mysterious stone. I told Oliver that finding it could help me understand why I was being followed, but nothing more. I felt bad about not sharing the complete truth with him, but he didn't seem to mind. He had already become accustomed to my secretiveness, and claimed that he really just enjoyed helping us out.

We spent many fruitless hours searching the clutter of old boxes, cases, and such like. However, eventually Oliver stumbled upon something that resembled a trap door. It was secured with a sturdy lock so we began to rummage through the dusty objects on the floor, hoping to find a tool to break it. Just as we had found a hammer, we heard a noise from upstairs. It sounded like a door squeaking.

"That must be one of the tenants," whispered Vilma with a glance at Oliver. "I bet it's that old hag who wakes up so damn early. She claims to not hear anything, but I have never believed that. She slanders too much to be deaf."

Oliver and I smiled.

"Just wait here, ladies, I'll take care of it," he said, gesturing at us to stay put. He paused on the threshold to the stairs and, carefully looking around, said:

"There is no other entrance to this cellar, is there?"

"Not that I know of," shrugged Vilma, also scanning every corner.

"All right, then you should be safe down here."

He took a candle from the candelabra and proceeded to climb up to ground level. We tried not to make a sound, patiently waiting for his return. After a while, we became nervous. We heard no voices coming from upstairs, and no more squeaking of the doors or stairs either.

"What's taking him so long?" complained Vilma, shuffling about with her arms crossed. "I hope he wasn't distracted by some girl."

"Should I go up and check on him?" I asked, but Vilma was strongly against that.

"Just wait here, darling, you would be too soft with him. I'll go."

Like Oliver, she also reached for one of the candles and began to climb the stairs, muttering to herself, "I knew it. He seemed too good to be true tonight…" In no time, I heard her voice from above.

"What's with all the loitering about?"

"I thought I saw a male figure at the back door, but he disappeared."

Hearing the words, I imagined the faceless man and panicked. I was hoping that we would have more time before he showed up. I took hold of a half-broken broomstick that I found, and went on with searching the ground on my own.

At one point, I realised I couldn't hear Vilma's or Oliver's voice anymore and instead, heard steps behind me. I turned, and right where I had found the broom, there now stood the faceless man in all his glory, more terrifying than ever. I had no time to think. I simply set off and sprinted up the stairs back to the hallway. I didn't even stop to think how he could have appeared there if I had my eyes on the entrance the whole time.

Once I was back on the ground floor, I searched the hallway for Oliver and Vilma, hoping they would be within reach. Finally, I spotted them upstairs, searching a wall of antique closets that stood outside Vilma's former apartment.

I wanted to call out to them, but I had to be careful to not wake the neighbours and bring about more trouble for us. I was going to run after them when someone caught me from behind and covered my mouth. I froze in terror, and stared at the large male hand. Even if I had been ready to scream it was now too late.

The man dragged me all the way to the back entrance and outside the building. The night chill swept through my petrified body as he turned me around to face him. To my surprise, there was no hooded darkness, but familiar blue eyes, wind-burned cheeks and dark curls.

"Turi," I exhaled, slowly recovering from the shock. "Oh my, you chose a good time." A gentle smile spread across his face. Then he nodded towards the street.

"Come with me before he finds us."

For a moment, I wondered if he had been the one following me all this time, but his words brought me back to reality.

"But what about Oliver and Vilma?" I asked, worried.

"He will leave them alone. He's after us."

"Who is it?"

"I'll try to explain…"

He grabbed my trembling hand, and led me to a cabriolet-type chariot that stood beside Oliver's carriage. A placid, white horse was waiting for us, guarding the two seats beneath the folding canvas roof. Turi helped me inside the chariot, jumped in and took hold of the reins. The horse began galloping, taking us away via Carp Street, and towards the Charles Bridge. I kept looking back, worried about Vilma and Oliver.

"They don't know about the threshold, right?"

asked Turi.

"Threshold," I repeated, remembering the threshold custodian reference from my memories, as well as what Hieronymus had told me about Prague's thresholds.

Turi noticed my distress, and reassured me. "Then they will be safe. He guards the threshold."

I then realised that he must have meant the symbol-engraved stone we were looking for in the cellar.

"Is that what it is?"

"Yes, a threshold with a special device, which was created to transport the threshold custodians between the two realms. Have you not remembered it yet?"

"I did. I just could not recall the device's purpose. It begins to make sense now... so we have really come from another realm?"

He nodded. "From Pryaya, a different version of Prague, which exists outside this time and space."

"I have heard of it," I admitted. "An acquaintance told me about the legend. I wondered whether my visions were connected to it, but it seemed impossible."

"I know. If I hadn't met my local friends, I wouldn't have believed it either. This realm makes you so grounded. However, I am certain that it is true now. Ever since I saw you, the girl who I thought I had just imagined, all my doubts vanished."

His eyes locked onto mine for a moment, then shifted back to the road. As I watched him, I couldn't help but ask:

"Why haven't you approached me sooner?"

He answered with an earnest look my way. "I had to protect you."

"From the faceless man?"

He turned around to make sure we weren't being

followed before he replied, speaking in a quieter voice:

"Him as well..." he wavered, then continued, "After I noticed that you were also being followed by him, I began to look after you from a distance, in case you needed my help. When I found out that you were heading to the Fifth District tonight, I guessed what might happen. The thresholds are under his watch along with the people who know about them."

"So, there is more than one threshold?"

"There should be five in total, each one connected with one of the five basic elements. The one in the Narrow Lane is located underground, and therefore connected with the earth element. The one in Nebovidska Street was connected with the fire element, but once it was found, the device disappeared and the supernatural fire beneath it died out."

I marvelled at how the legends and theories that Hieronymus had told me about were becoming true. Like he said, they seemed to be just as reliable as history books. I shared the thought with Turi who didn't seem surprised.

"And have you heard about the legendary House at the Last Lantern?"

I shook my head, prompting him to tell me more.

"Local legend says that there's an invisible house at the end of the Golden Lane, one that exists in a subtler realm. The Pryaya legend is similar, and it also mentions that the house was, in fact, the air threshold and that there was a shifting device built inside it." He paused for a moment, thinking something over before he added: "I crossed over that threshold. I appeared in a house that, once I had come to my senses, just disappeared."

"I remember!" I exhaled, with the sudden memory of Hieronymus's story of the invisible house in his lane. "I have heard of the mysterious house before. It would connect the two Golden Lanes in Prague if they both concealed a threshold..."

"Which is the other Golden Lane?"

"The Narrow Lane used to be called Golden."

"That can't be a coincidence," he said, then asked, "which one did you use to cross over?"

"I suppose the water threshold, as I regained consciousness in the river."

"Then you must have been by our riverside home before you shifted."

"You remember that place too?"

"Of course." With those words, his face became troubled again.

"I'm sorry, Seraphina..." The apology took me by surprise.

"What for?"

"For not finding you sooner," he answered sadly. I touched his arm for comfort, which made him look me in the eye again. The tenderness in his expression was something I feared yet craved. I realised I was not ready to confront my mixed emotions, so I placed my hands back in my lap.

"And where's the fifth threshold?" I asked, curious to hear more.

"*Nowhere* but *everywhere*," he said.

"What do you mean?"

"It's the most mysterious threshold, the one that preceded all the others, and one that everyone needs to find for himself. I don't know if you remember this, but Atarah told us that the fifth element is aligned with the *one* and *all*, the godly essence that lies beyond our comprehension. Many ancient cultures considered it to be the life force, which created all the other elements and all that was, is and will be. With regard to the thresholds, the fifth one is not a mechanical device, but rather our own inherent light chariot. The one that transfers the spirit from one dimension to another."

"Merkaba," I breathed. His eyes widened in excitement.

"Yes, that! So you do recall it?"

"It was one of the first words I remembered, and I also know that we called the secret, circular stones the Merkaba devices. My friend Vilma helped me discover some references in the Kabbalah, but I haven't managed to put all the pieces together yet."

"My friends and I have been trying to find out more about it as well. That's why we sought help at the Sat Bhai lodge. They are closely linked to the legend of the Pryaya, and the secret of the thresholds."

"So the people I saw at the White Angel were not from the Sat Bhai?"

"No, you met Fabian, his wife Berta, and some people from another esoteric society. Fabian and Berta have been trying to become members of the Sat Bhai, but their efforts have so far been futile. The first time we saw each other was when the three of us were trying to find some clues. They didn't want to share anything. The Sat Bhai are closed to newcomers." He paused and turned back to me with an embarrassed expression. "I'm sorry about my behaviour back there. I didn't want my friends to know about you, because I'm not sure if I can trust them."

"Why is that?"

Turi fidgeted in his seat.

"I have come to realise that some of the esoteric societies they associate with are far from spiritual. They have all these ancient codes, but have lost the connection with them. I mean, the fact that most of the lodges don't even accept women, except for wives and spiritualists, says a lot about them, don't you think?"

I smiled without comment.

"And what about Fabian and Berta? Do they agree

with you?" I went on to ask.

"Not really. These days, I have begun to feel a bit distant from them. See, at first, they were the only source of information I had regarding my past. They told me that we have always had a common goal, to learn how the devices work. I must have found out first because otherwise I wouldn't be here. It disappointed them that I lost my memory. They didn't know that would happen. We have been trying to find the key to the riddle that I once found but lost. However, with time, I began to doubt the validity of some of the things they told me. It feels as though they care mainly about what my subconscious can reveal to them."

"That doesn't sound right," I mused, overwhelmed by a bad premonition. "How did they learn about Pryaya?"

"They claim that I had been contacting them in dreams before I crossed over, but I have a feeling that's not true... It just doesn't feel like something I would do. I think I was more of a scientist, you and Atarah were better at metaphysics."

I was so intrigued by his story that I couldn't stop asking questions.

"Did they say what you told them in these alleged dreams?"

"That's what confuses me. Many things I have recalled fit the descriptions I supposedly shared with them." He paused, then continued with a more upbeat tone. "For example, that Pryaya was a city of sorcerers and spiritual masters before the dark magic began to take over. After many years of the so-called Great Magic War, all magic was declared illegal. That is why most people in Pryaya are unaware of the thresholds and the devices built upon them. They have been kept a secret in both realms, guarded by the threshold custodians."

I thought it through as our chariot passed over the

old bridge. I knew that I used to be aware of Pryaya's history, and wished to recall more on my own.

"But enough about me," said Turi. "What do you remember, Seraphina?"

I ran through all the insights that I had experienced.

"The city, Atarah, you and me... Mainly you and me and our friendship."

With these words, I locked my eyes onto his. He lifted a brow.

"Friendship? Is that all it was to you?"

I blushed. He noticed and grinned at me. I didn't know how to answer, and though he seemed to have enjoyed watching me struggle with it, he eventually changed the subject.

"Do you recall why you came here?"

"Not really, but I have an inkling that I came for you."

The answer surprised him.

"Why do you think that?"

"I have no solid explanation, I just do," I admitted.

He became pensive, for reasons I couldn't fathom.

"Why do *you* think you crossed over?" I asked.

"I'm not sure. Fabian and Berta think that I wanted to meet them," he smiled at the answer. "But everything tends to be about them in their minds."

"And why do you think we lost our memories?" I asked. "Have you found the answer to that?"

"Not yet," he said with a thoughtful gaze ahead. For a moment, we rode in silence, lost in our strange situation. I was gathering the courage to ask about something that had been on my mind ever since I stepped into the chariot with him.

"Do you..." I hesitated before completing the sentence, feeling nervous and shy, "do you know what happened in our adulthood? I have no memories of us after our unfortunate separation."

From the look on his face, I could tell he didn't see that question coming. His face remained focused on the road, but his lips curved into a sad smile.

"I would rather you remembered that for yourself," he said. I liked the idea, but it frustrated me.

"Listen, Seraphina," he continued after a moment. "No one can know about the thresholds and the Merkaba devices, especially not those you care about. We don't know how the threshold custodians in Prague operate, they may be even tougher than those in Pryaya."

"Is the faceless man one of them?"

"Yes. He must be mainly in charge of the earth threshold, as I see him there the most."

"How strange," I ruminated. "I feel as if I have known it all along, somewhere deep inside, it only needed to be brought back to the surface."

Turi nodded. "That's how I feel each time I learn something new about Pryaya."

I finally came to understand what Atarah was guarding and why she was protecting it from people with bad intentions. Not that I would agree with her methods, but at least I was aware of what they were for.

"He seems far more sinister than Atarah, though," I said, deep in thought, "I don't recall Atarah wearing such an odd outfit."

"They only wear it in society," explained Turi. "So as not to be recognised. At least that was why I wore it. Once you put on that magic cape, your face disappears in its hood."

"You wore it? When?"

"When I began guarding the air threshold at the House at the Last Lantern."

"Is that from the time I don't remember?"

He nodded.

"I just hope you won't be disappointed when you

do remember, because it might change things for you, and I'm not sure if it will be for the better. From what I have seen, you have the chance to establish a nice life for yourself here, and I wouldn't want to be the one to spoil that."

He paused and wavered over something, probably a memory he didn't want to share. I longed to understand what he was hinting at, so I tilted my head, encouraging him to continue.

"You don't have to associate with me, Seraphina. Perhaps you would be better off forgetting all about our confusing past, and focus on your future in Prague instead. There's still time to get off this road." He glanced at me tentatively, checking my reaction.

"Don't be a fool, Turi," I said with a reassuring smile, "I'm happy on this road. I'm not giving it up for anything."

"Me too," he said softly.

We looked quickly at each other, and then focused on the blur of street lamps and stones ahead. It made me think about the hazy past and future, but also made me appreciate the present moment.

# Chapter VIII

## Justice

We reached the New World quarter shortly before sunrise. Turi already knew where I lived. He admitted that he was the one following me after my unsuccessful attempt to contact him at the Sat Bhai house.

"I'll be away for a few days," he said while patting the placid horse before him. "One of the esoteric societies has a meeting outside of Prague. Berta believes that they could have the information we need, so we shall join them."

The news disappointed me, as I had hoped that we would continue where we left off soon.

"Please promise you will come and meet me when you return," I beseeched him.

"Of course I will. Until then, try to remember more about our lives."

His smile chased away my worries. I trusted that

he wouldn't let me down anymore.

It was time to part, and I found myself vacillating over whether to shake his hand or kiss him on the cheek. He seemed to have been struggling with the same dilemma. He hesitated for a moment, then simply hugged me. It was a quick, strong embrace, and before I could recover, I found myself standing on the cobbled stones alone, watching him ride away into the break of the new day.

Touched by a familiar, creeping loneliness, I set out in the opposite direction. Even though we seemed to have re-established our bond, I felt that something else was tearing us apart. It could have been a secret unshared or unrecalled, or someone else's interference. Whatever it was, I speculated that it could be the reason why we didn't appear in Prague at the same time and in the same place. I made a promise to myself to be patient and to look forward to our next meeting with optimism.

Having been so absorbed by my meeting with Turi and all the information he had provided me with, I had almost forgotten about Vilma and Oliver. As soon as I was able to focus on the here and the now again, I hurried back home. I hoped that they were already there, and luckily found them waiting for me.

"Thank God!" exclaimed Vilma, when she spotted me in the doorway. "Dear girl, I thought I had lost you."

She embraced me, and kissed my forehead with motherly affection. I was relieved to see that they were all right, and that they were waiting for me there instead of the Fifth District. Oliver, who had been sitting at the table with a cup of coffee, watched me with a thoughtful gaze. The fact that Vilma made him coffee, a luxury she was saving for Christmas, made me hope that something good had come from our parting that night.

"I'm sorry I left you there," I said, looking intently at Vilma, "but I finally met Turi, and he wanted to speak in private."

Vilma clasped my hands.

"Really? You must tell me everything!"

I wavered and shifted my gaze to Oliver. He used that polite smile of his to hide his disappointment.

"I should let you two talk…"

I felt bad about chasing him out after all that he had done for us.

"I'm very sorry, Oliver."

He turned around, confused.

"You have nothing to be sorry about, Seraphina."

"I do, I'm sorry that you went to all that trouble… I want you to know that I'm very grateful."

"As always, it has been my pleasure," he said, and turned away from me to finish his coffee. "Too bad that we couldn't find what you were looking for." With his hand on his chest, he bowed to me, then to Vilma.

"Well, have a good day, ladies. And don't forget to sleep a few hours longer tonight."

Vilma didn't usually respond to his greetings or farewells, but this time she surprised us both with a heartfelt goodbye. She even waved after him. It was clear that she had warmed towards him, which made me feel less guilty. At least he had managed to impress her, like he wanted.

After Oliver had left, Vilma sat me down, and poured me some of the precious coffee.

"There's no use going to sleep now," she said playfully, "it's too early."

I smiled and took a sip, realising that I had begun to like the taste.

"I'm glad you don't cringe at the sight of him anymore." I said to ease the atmosphere.

"Who says that I don't? Maybe I'm just better at hiding it."

I didn't believe that, and hoped she would say more, so I waited for a moment.

"I might have altered my opinion of him a tiny little bit. We talked a lot while we were waiting for you. I found out that he didn't have an easy childhood. He had a very strict upbringing. Imagine thinking that such a lack of attention and care was normal? No wonder he is so messed up." She paused, realising something. "But let's not talk about it now. Tell me about Turi."

Since I had promised Turi and myself that I wouldn't share the truth about our origin with my friends, not even my dear Vilma, I had to find a way to explain it without letting her in on the big secret.

"I was right about him. We were friends, hopefully still are… though, we may have been even more. I wish I could tell you everything, and it's so hard to admit that… I just can't."

"Oh," breathed Vilma, disappointed.

"I hope you are not upset with me," I added quickly, "because I'm so glad you have been involved in helping me with my past, trying to help me put all the missing pieces back together. Please trust me when I say that if you knew the whole truth, it would put us both in danger."

Vilma looked into my eyes. It was the first time I had seen her speechless.

"Well," she said after a moment, "that makes me want to know even more!" We both laughed. I was relieved to see that she wasn't upset with me.

"So Dora was right, eh? Well, I'll have to respect your decision, darling. You must have a good reason to conceal the whole truth from me. I'm just glad that you are safe and have the answers you needed," she said.

"I'm not sure about that. The answers I have received raised even more questions."

She lifted her chin feistily. "Then I'll help you find

them, whether or not they remain concealed from me."

Her earnest promise touched me. It made me realise that she was a true friend. To show her how much I appreciated her, I embraced her tighter than ever. Winded or not, she had to know how much she meant to me.

✡

Ever since Turi and I had parted, I found myself in a fever of excitement. I wasn't able to concentrate on anything else but my mysterious past. I needed to find out what had brought me to Prague, and why I had such a powerful need to come after Turi.

That afternoon, I joined Vilma to do some shopping at the Havelská market square. The stalls brimmed with all kinds of goods, mainly fresh food, flowers and handicrafts. Vilma felt inspired, and was considering earning some extra money herself by selling her handmade beeswax candles and creams there the following year.

I, meanwhile, took an interest in one of Prague's painted buildings. It depicted a colourful fresco of a man with big white wings, holding a sword in one hand and golden scales in the other. I knew I had seen the figure before, though depicted slightly differently. Vilma noticed my silent fascination with the image, and remarked:

"That's the House at the Golden Scale, one of the square's special buildings."

I kept staring at it, trying to work it out. "Is this one of the local patrons?"

"Yes," said Vilma, "he's one of the seven archangels, Saint Michael."

"Archangel," I repeated, intrigued, "what does that mean?"

"They are the angels who are closest to God, hence the word *arch*."

"So they are like the Seraphim or the Cherubim?"

"Actually, archangel Michael is regarded as one of the Seraphim."

I was going to ask another question, but became speechless, as the memory of Atarah's voice echoed in my mind:

"That's why your parents gave me this picture before they passed away. They worked with the so-called Seven Rays, the seven rainbow hues of the source, or as I like to call it, the auras of the Seven Seraphim. Following in their footsteps, they thought you might like to learn from these powerful deities as well."

The words guided me to a moment in the past when Atarah gave me a drawing of seven figures. Each represented one of the seven rays that originated from and returned to the source of white light: ruby, orange, yellow, green, blue, indigo and violet.

"Like the many different colour tones, there are many more such beings in the ethereal worlds," she explained, "but these emanate straight from or go straight to the source. There are many roads to the Merkaba, and your parents followed the one that leads through colours."

As I concentrated on the surroundings, I realised that we were in the apartment that Turi and I used to live in, at the house in the Magic Quarter. The space was much tidier back then and everything was in its place. The shelves were filled with all kinds of books and magic tools including Atarah's dark magic cape that the threshold custodians wore when they needed to be in disguise. We venerated every one of those objects, though I wasn't really aware why at that point in my life.

As my gaze panned across the room, I caught my

reflection in the wrought iron mirror on the wall. I was about eleven years old.

"Whenever you are in trouble," said Atarah, "take a look at this picture, communicate to the Seven Seraphim, and let them help you."

I traced the drawing with my fingers, silently honouring the gift.

"Are they known in Prague as well?" I asked.

"Yes, they take care of that realm too, but the locals call them different names like archangels, gods, goddesses, and each of the seven has a different name depending on the culture. However, the word Seraphim is identical in both our worlds."

"Why are you giving this to me now?" I asked, as everything Atarah did had its own reason and timing. She didn't answer, and I thought I knew why. She had been acting rather mysteriously the whole day, and seemed to be preparing me for something. I knew that we were going to move soon, but guessed that there was something more to it. After a moment of hesitation, she simply said:

"Please keep it hidden from the authorities."

"I didn't think that revering deities was forbidden."

"The Seraphim are different. They have been associated with the Merkaba mystery. If they saw this drawing, they might think that you are one of us."

Atarah's placid face changed as we overheard voices, slamming doors and footsteps. She held her breath, then exhaled:

"They are here."

With these words, the main door swung open and three guards burst into our sanctuary. They captured Atarah in silence, with cold, merciless faces. Before they dragged her away from me, I tried reaching for her hands, but failed.

"This is unfair! If you only knew how precious she

is!" I called after them in despair, but the guards didn't even look at me. I wasn't important to them, they were only here to complete their task. Atarah's eyes warned me to stop.

"Remember what I told you, Seraphina," she said, "and please don't hold grudges. There is no justice without a judge, and the toughest judge is the one inside of us. Keep him on a tight lead, my dearest one."

Two of the guards took Atarah away while the third stayed behind to explain my fate to me.

"We don't banish children who practise magic. As long as they are willing to mend their ways, they are safe. You will be taken to the Establishment for Suspicious Youth now. They will provide you with all necessities, education and pastimes until the judges decide when it is safe to set you free. You may gather your belongings now, without the magic-related things, naturally."

I watched the man, holding back tears, suppressing the rising anger. He was in his late twenties, wore the scarlet uniform of Pryaya guards, and had a metal disc tucked by his waist. I already knew the purpose of that weapon, as Atarah had the same one. It was a humane execution tool. If the metal disc hit you, you would simply burst into light and vanish, leaving nothing but a small amount of sparkling dust behind. Since the Emperor and Empress had decreed that only such weapons should be used by the authorities, the world was thought to be a better place.

Magic was another story, though. Its practice was forbidden after the Great Magic War between the white and dark magicians. I was born in its aftermath, so I could only sense the impact it had had on our world. The dark magicians supposedly cast a powerful curse on the empire, and almost destroyed the whole continent. From then on, people turned their backs on magic in general, even on those practices which seemed harmless such as astrology or alchemy. Atarah once told me that the dark magicians misused even that. They began to interpret the rulers' horoscopes negatively and set them against one another. Their alchemical skills allowed them to manipulate human minds as well as bodies.

Atarah considered the desecration of the sacred teachings a disaster. She believed that everything in our world had its dark and light side, and so she suspected that turning away from the light side of magic could bring about more of the dark side.

Soon after the guard took me to the Establishment for Suspicious Youth, I learned that our beloved Magic Quarter was going to be locked away from the public, including its inhabitants. The plans were to rebuild it into another common avenue. However, these had not been finalised.

I began to understand why Atarah had decided to bury the secret Merkaba device a few days before the Magic Quarter attack. It was her responsibility as the earth threshold custodian. She hid it deep under piles of soil, carpet and other kinds of rubbish, because that was what the quarter would become – a dumping ground.

Once I had been given a room at the Establishment, I sat down and solemnly promised myself I would never forget Atarah's magic teachings, no matter what. Her warning reverberated through my heart the whole time: *Don't let them take your magic.*

I hoped that Atarah would be given the mildest punishment, which was banishment from Pryaya. She could then find shelter with her friends, the water threshold custodians. The water threshold was located in the valley beneath the highlands, where enormous rocks rise from the riverbed. On the tallest one, the unicorn-lion statues were erected as a memorial to the end of the Great Magic War. I recalled what the two animals represented then – the beast and the prey united in peace. Unicorns used to live among us, but after the war, they died out. Atarah said that their spirits could not handle the darkness in our world, so their souls had to leave.

Anyway, the woodland was now a place where society's outcasts lived. Some said that it was contaminated with evil, that the spirits of witches and necromancers roamed the forested hollows; but Atarah thought that this was just one of the many fear-mongering tales that were meant to scare people away.

"There's great power in that area, one which heals, not harms, the spirit," she used to say. "If ever I have to flee there some day, and you for some reason stay behind, keep your eyes on the highest peak, and wait for a sign."

Luck must have been on my side, as my window faced that peak, and so I could check on it day and night.

My life at the Establishment for Suspicious Youth wasn't as bad as I had expected. We were taught to mend our ways, but were provided with all that we needed, and were encouraged to follow a path which we enjoyed. Some of the children came from the Magic Quarter too, but either pretended to not care about the way we were brought up, or really tried to start anew. I didn't blame them, we all wanted to be part of an ordinary life one way or another.

I missed Atarah every minute of the day. With her, the world was filled with surprise and wonder, but without her, it seemed to lack purpose. However, even if life became boring and grey on the surface, when alone, I prayed to the Seven Seraphim for protection and guidance.

As the weeks and months passed, I waited for a sign. I knew that Atarah was imprisoned in the tallest tower in Pryaya, the one that shone scarlet at night. I often watched the light before I went to sleep, weeping for her. I tried to remember her words of encouragement, and to keep my promise.

Nevertheless, I was upset by the law, and with the Emperor and the Empress, and decided that I would never follow their ways. To me, they were unjust and cruel, and I refused to become their property. Back then, I could not see the good in my isolation from Atarah, but with time, I realised that it gave me precious insights about what most people in Pryaya considered normality. I left behind the fairy tale for some time, and allowed myself a taste of how difficult their lives were. It made me empathise with them, and understand why they decided to live without magic.

Above all, however, my loneliness allowed me a stronger connection with the Seven Seraphim. Sometimes, they answered my questions by guiding me to read certain books or go to a place that provided me with new information. One night, I asked them to show me where I belonged in society, in order to decide which school I should apply to. They sent me a message in a dream:

I appeared in a darkened space, where the only light source was a female performer, who danced in what looked like two white tetrahedrons spinning inside a translucent globe.

The next day, the other children told me that the theatre had opened the so-called air-dancing classes for youngsters, and accepted anyone regardless of their background. I attended one of the performances to see what air-dancing really was, and I became fascinated with it. I knew I was destined to study it because the artists performed in white tetrahedrons spinning inside translucent globes. I knew that the shapes represented something crucial, that they were a riddle, but it wasn't the right time to solve it. Not yet.

During my first air-dancing class, I met a boy my age, Lavi, who later became a good friend of mine. Unlike me, he came from a well-established Pryaya family. He didn't seem to mind my Magic Quarter roots, though, and respected me as his equal.

"Just keep the dream alive, Seraphina," he used to tell me, "and trust that we shall soar higher than the others."

He must have been right, as at the end of the course we were both accepted to a long-term study program at the Air Dance Academy. I was very excited, but soon learned that the timing was all wrong. A few days before the school started, a fire was lit in the crowns of the unicorn-lion statues. I knew it was Atarah's doing, as it had never happened before.

Although I had been waiting for the sign for a year, when the moment finally came, I found myself caught between joy and regret. A part of my heart belonged to the air-dancing, but the other part to Atarah and the place she was heading to, the wild riverside woodlands.

# Chapter IX

## The Hermit

I hoped that during the days of waiting for Turi's return, I would recall more about my past, but I had no other remembrances after the one triggered by the sight of the golden scale fresco. One afternoon, I tried to connect to my subconscious using the items that I had brought with me from Pryaya – the scarf bag, the wand, the cup and the stone with the two engraved hexagrams.

Squeezing and flipping the stone in my palm, I wondered why those few objects were the only belongings I had chosen to have with me. Then I remembered that I was also holding a piece of paper when I first regained consciousness, but it fell into the water after I slipped. Could that mean, I asked myself, that I was aware of the chance of memory loss and wrote a letter to myself before I left? I wish I knew the reason for Turi and I crossing different thresholds. The thought made me remember the House at the Last Lantern that Turi talked about. I decided to visit Hieronymus, and inquire about the legend.

As I passed the cathedral and ambled along the ancient basilica, I admired the three medieval towers which enclosed the charming lane. It made me wonder whether that ethereal building was concealed in one of them. On the way, I also thought back to Dora and her prophetic dream. Could it be that I was meant to visit both Golden Lanes? From what I heard, they had been important to me in my past.

I was glad to catch Hieronymus at home, and although I had disturbed his research, he insisted that I came in for a cup of something warm. The house's interior was even tinier than it looked from the outside. Despite the cramped space, though, there was enough light because there were two grated windows on both sides of the room.

Hieronymus lived humbly, but seemed content with it. The single upholstered chair, corner bed, and few simple, wooden chests for storing clothes and food were enough for him. His work desk faced the Dear Moat, and was brimming with books, papers and old ink jars.

While I admired his cosy home, Hieronymus neared the tiny stove around which hung various pots and cups, and reached for a pot and a dark green tin from the shelf above.

"Would you mind chicory? That's all I have."

"I love chicory, thank you."

"So what brings you here, Miss Seraphina?"

"I came to ask you about the House at the Last Lantern." He looked at me, his child-like eyes open wide and sparkling.

"Oh yes," he chuckled while he placed the pot on the stove, and shoved some more branches into the fire. He then beckoned me over to his table, and offered me his armchair while seating himself on a wooden box nearby.

"That one is my favourite of all Prague legends," he said, "perhaps it is so, because I live here. I have never been lucky enough to see the house, though. Legend has it that Sunday children are the only ones who can see it, and I believe that."

"It's a pity that I don't know on which day I was born."

"I would be surprised if you did. Most people don't know, and most people don't even care. It's the same with the legends."

"And which lantern is it positioned by?" I wondered, impatient to absorb his knowledge, "the one closer to the cathedral?"

"Well, my friend, how can you tell where the first or the last lantern is?" He gave me a challenging smile, then tasted the chicory, and spiced it up with some cinnamon before he poured me a cup. "Why do you think it would be closer to the cathedral?"

"Oh, I have no idea, it was just a guess," I admitted.

"Guesses are important. Most people believe it was closer to the Dalibor Tower, but I agree with you. I have always had a feeling that it was on the other side, by Mihulka Tower. Anyway, nobody knows how the houses were numbered in the olden days." He took a sip from the steaming cup. "However," he continued after a short pause, "if the legends I told you about last time were true, and the Sat Bhai have something to do with it, then it could be deliberately misleading. Perhaps it's down in the Fifth District, where your friend used to live."

The mention of the Sat Bhai made my heart race. How I wished I could tell him what I had learned from Turi, and that we were, in fact, from the legendary place he told me about. Although I couldn't share the truth, I allowed myself to at least weigh up the possibilities with him.

"I have been thinking of the Pryaya legend a lot since our last meeting, and keep asking myself: What if the Sat Bhai didn't actually establish Prague or Pryaya? What if they only placed some kind of magical chariot upon the ancient thresholds, so that people could travel between the two worlds?"

Hieronymus peered at me thoughtfully.

"What a compelling thought," he said, slightly suspicious, as if sensing that I knew more than I let on. Luckily for us both, he respected my privacy. "Why haven't I thought of that before? Your interpretation makes more sense, because how could a few individuals, no matter how powerful, create an entire world?"

"I suppose both interpretations are possible in a world we can't understand or explain," I conceded, so as not to seem too self-assured. He nodded and took a long, pensive sip of his drink. I joined him, appreciating the warming cinnamon.

"My friend said that the invisible house could only be seen during the full moon. Is that also what you have heard?" I queried then.

"No," he exhaled, recovering from his thoughts, "that's new to me as well... It could be so." He searched my face, his imagination running wild.

"I have to admit that I have tried gazing at the lane's lanterns at different times of the day, and during different moon or yearly cycles, but nothing happened." He must have caught the disappointment in my face, as he quickly added:

"Nonetheless, the moon reaches its fullest tonight, so you could come by and try your luck. I would keep guard, make sure you are safe from prying eyes and vagabonds."

"You would do that for me?" I asked, touched by his kindness.

"Of course!" he exclaimed, "it's not every day that you meet someone with such similar interests. I value that."

"That's true," I agreed, "I'm also glad we have met, Hieronymus." My lips involuntarily smiled when I pronounced his name, because I remembered Vilma's reaction to it. I wondered what she would think of our plan, and whether or not I should tell her about it. I supposed it would do no harm if I did, and more importantly, she would never forgive me if I shared a secret with the man she considered her new enemy.

☆

After midnight, Vilma and I approached the Golden Lane. We were both a bit evasive about our motives. I claimed I was just interested in the legend, and Vilma said that she came along to protect me, even though I could tell that she was curious to meet Hieronymus again. Since he and I had become better acquainted, she was also intrigued by his knowledge.

Hieronymus was surprised to meet Vilma again, but in a good way.

"Good evening, Miss Seraphina, and…" He gave a mischievous grin, hesitating over how to address Vilma. Finally, he said:

"I don't think there are any words for describing such a peculiar creature."

"You're the one to talk, you old goat," said Vilma, hands on her hips, brows furrowed.

"I thought I was a *gnome*?" replied Hieronymus, amused rather than upset.

"Well, it seems that both descriptions fit well enough."

"In another pleasant mood, I see? Has your psychic given you a bad reading today? Or has some deity in a dream come with bad news?"

"If you don't believe in fortune-telling dreams or card readings, how come you believe in legends becoming reality?"

"Because my research suggests that legends are, in fact, reality." He tried to impress her by appearing confident and educated, which irritated my dear Vilma even more. I stood between them, wondering why the two tended to quarrel so much. As I watched them eying each other, it occurred to me that their animosity was just a way of concealing a mutual affection. They were both stubborn and too proud to admit it, though. I decided to try and bring them together with an introduction.

"Vilma, this is Hieronymus. Hieronymus, this is Vilma."

They shook each other's hands, but Vilma couldn't resist making fun of his name, which for some reason she found so comical.

"Tell me, Hieronymus, did your parents come from the Middle Ages?" He was readying himself to strike back, so I interrupted.

"Hieronymus makes a wonderful, spiced chicory. Maybe you could have a cup or two together?" I suggested. Vilma didn't respond, just lifted an eyebrow challengingly, but Hieronymus said:

"I'm sorry, lady Seraphina, but I don't think I can let this woman into my house."

"Ha, you call that a house?"

They were like children, trying to win a game of insults. I worried they would never grow tired of the teasing. I turned to Vilma with a pleading expression. She warmed up at the sight of me, and turned to Hieronymus in a friendlier manner.

"I suppose I could pay a visit to that dungeon of yours. I could use a hot drink."

"Or a strong one," suggested Hieronymus, and glanced back at me, whispering: "I may have some plum liquor at home. A glass or two might do her good."

"I can hear you!" said Vilma, who had already set off to his house, "and I can assure you that I'm not some young hussy who would be seduced by an interesting chat and a glass of liquor."

"Oh, so you do find me interesting?"

"Certainly not! Just the books you have read."

"Shush woman, you will wake up the neighbours."

"Oh, I forgot that my voice is too high-pitched for your cultivated ears." I watched them walk towards the tiny house, absorbed with their banter.

After they disappeared behind the door, I mulled over where to position myself, if closer to the Mihulka or Dalibor Tower. Though there was a beautiful lantern by the narrow corridor on the eastern side, my intuition guided me towards the western one. There, the lantern was attached to a blank wall which had a tiny roof above it, an indication that it was some sort of a house.

I sat on the stool that Hieronymus lent me, and leaned my back against the shabby, dank bricks opposite the lantern. Its bright ray reminded me of the Seraphim. I wondered about their connection with the Merkaba, as well as the Sat Bhai and the Tarot. Could it be, I thought to myself, that through the Sat Bhai brotherhood, the Seraphim brought us the Tarot, a riddle that helps to find the Merkaba? Could the cards reflect their wisdom of how to regain the great power we lost?

With this thought, the lamp's flame flickered, and didn't stop moving, although there was no breeze. The motion felt hypnotic and, as I gazed at it, I felt a soothing inner stillness. My eyelids felt heavy, but I kept promising myself not to fall asleep. I wanted to stay awake to experience a miracle, to catch at least a glimpse of the secret building. My body's fatigue overpowered my mind, though. As I hovered on the edge of sleep, I began to delve back into my past…

✡

I returned to the moment I remembered last time. I was leaving Pryaya and my air-dancing dream in search of Atarah. It was dawn, and I was cautious not to be recognised by anyone. Most of the citizens were in a hurry anyway, heading to work, school, or just shopping for the day.

Like me, some floated above the ground to achieve a greater speed. I was surprised to see a very old man who soared higher than the others. I wondered whether he used to be an air dancer, and the thought stirred regret inside me. I hoped that some day when I was older, I could apply to the Air Dance Academy again. I would have to do so under a new identity, of course, because my escape from the Establishment for Suspicious Youth meant banishment from the city society.

I paid more attention to Pryaya's technology at that moment. It seemed more advanced than in Prague. Electricity was harvested from the sun and quartz stones, and as I understood, this was not something new. In fact, it had been used for hundreds of years in our world. The transportation was mainly by trams similar to those being built in Prague, except they used a different fuel and had a white, serpent-like appearance. They connected the most significant parts of the city, not including the Magic Quarter, which had by then been officially locked away.

I remembered my home's history as well. I knew that our people shared a common belief – that the world was created by the gods and goddesses who lived in the crown of what we called the Tree of Life.

It was thought to be a complexity of realms which sprung from the same seed, and grew on one trunk, but evolved into different branches. Some were closely linked to our realm, others were further away, unreachable.

Our society had a deep respect for our roots and ancestral heritage, but this was linked mainly to the power of the mind. Despite such philosophy and our deity worship, most people had closed themselves off to other metaphysical contacts since the end of the war, except for evolving science. Atarah considered science as close to magic as one eye to another. "It has only one flaw," she used to say, "it's missing the fifth element."

As in Prague's reality, we had many countries and cultures. I recalled our world's map, and it seemed that there was only one large continental mass and a few larger islands scattered across the vast oceans. The mountains rose high above sea level in some regions.

What I found curious was that we consumed only plant-based food. The kill to survive pattern had somehow lost its meaning to us over time. Due to our science, we knew that animals were equal to us on an emotional level. Comparing this to Prague, I found myself intrigued by the difference. I wondered why I now had no trouble consuming other beings if I was not used to it. I assumed that in the density of Prague's reality, my body had just become accustomed to it. However, the recollection had altered my point of view.

And as to Pryaya's history, I remembered that it was built thousands of centuries ago as a city of the grand magicians who settled there after years of venturing from the East, the country that Prague's reality called India. Some were in touch with Prague, before the Merkaba devices became a myth.

The reason that the thresholds were concealed

from the public's eye seemed to be connected to the Great Magic War. Like most magic practices, the Merkaba devices were misused as well, and put many people in danger. Prague wasn't ready for Pryaya, and vice versa. Pryaya wasn't the only place to have thresholds to other realities, though. The thresholds seemed to be connected to the Earth's grid, the sacred geometric net that embraced the globe. Atarah called this the veins, or the fibres of the Tree of Life, and that was what I thought about on my way to the wilderness.

I left through the southern city gate, which was located by the Old Magic Castle; in Prague this was called the Vyšehrad. Beyond the gate, I looked back at my hometown. The landscape was almost identical to Prague's, except for the tall mountains ahead of me with the huge sculptures on top. In Vilma's history books, the buildings mainly echoed the Gothic, Renaissance and Baroque periods.

I admired the picturesque stone bridges which were built almost at water level, and connected the river islands. The majority of the islands had only sacred buildings. Most were stone-built, had very tall bell towers, and were decorated with various steeples. Despite the fact that there had been no religion as such since the Great Magic War, and spiritual gatherings were, like magic, forbidden, some people still went there to connect with their ancestors or deities.

I followed the well-trodden path that led up to the woodlands; the place enveloped in terrifying tales about the banished magicians and their thirst for revenge. If it weren't for Atarah, I would have probably been afraid of its dark hollows. She told me stories about strong personalities who went there to connect with nature's spirits. Two of them were her friends, the water threshold custodians.

I walked for many hours. Occasionally, I leapt up,

attempting to float above the treetops in order to get a better view, but failed due to my lack of training. I wished I could achieve technical perfection in air movement, and promised myself that I would continue practising.

As sunset approached, I reached the mountain peak with the grand, unicorn-lion sculptures. Underneath the magnificent artwork, I looked over the valleys, trying to locate Atarah's new home, but to my disappointment, there was no sign of a cottage or a house by the riverside.

I hovered above the cliff's edge, and watched the night sky reflecting on the steep, grey crags. There was nothing but wildlife surrounding me, and I panicked, thinking that I must be lost. The anxiety that had been building up inside me ever since I left my hometown collided with my lifelong fear of losing those I loved.

I sat on the moss-covered gravel, giving into my gloom, when I noticed a boy my age sitting down on the shore. He was throwing stones into the water, watching the circles grow larger and larger, until they became part of the natural flow again. My first impression of him was that he was a loner like me, and once our eyes met, it felt as if we were meant to be lonely together. I was certain that I was meant to find him, and that I had been waiting for this moment all my life. He stood up, and watched me for a while, before he called out:

"Are you Seraphina?"

"Yes!" I replied. "Do you know Atarah?"

He gestured at me to stay put, and set out on the rocky path to join me. I was surprised by how briskly he was climbing that mountain slope. It became trickier when he reached the smooth rocks, though, so I reached for his hand to help him up. The physical contact awoke a strange sensation in my body. I had never felt that way before. His eyes peered at me from beneath the tips of his dark, windbrushed curls, curious and inviting.

"Atarah told me you would come here to live with us soon," he explained. "She has been worrying about you."

"I have been worrying about her, too. It's good to know she had found a shelter here with you and your family. I have heard so much about your parents, the water threshold custodians." His face suddenly saddened. He set off without responding, then waved at me to follow him.

"I hope you won't mind my company," I asked timidly as he led me on a more comfortable track to the valley.

"I certainly won't," he turned to me, but looked through rather than at me when he said: "And as for my parents and siblings, they died a few years ago of a fever. I was the only survivor." The news struck my heart.

"That's awful. I'm so sorry…"

Although I didn't know him or his family, I empathised with his pain. I too missed my parents. It wasn't the same, as they died when I was very young, yet I understood well enough the feeling of missing someone to the core of your being. As if sensing what was on my mind, he said:

"I'm also sorry, Seraphina. Atarah told me about your parents."

I nodded, but said nothing. Like him, I still couldn't let go of the pain.

"Oh, and I'm Turi by the way," he introduced himself airily.

"Nice to meet you, Turi." We smiled at each other, lightening the atmosphere.

"So you have lived here alone since?"

"Yes, until Atarah came along. It's much nicer to have company."

"I bet. I don't understand how you could have

survived here on your own for years. Your spirit must be indomitable."

He shrugged.

"My parents taught me everything I needed to know. I simply had to pull myself together, in order to follow their heritage and mission. Someone had to keep guarding the water threshold."

"You are a threshold custodian?" I breathed, staring at him in disbelief. He nodded.

"I have never met such a young one," I added, impressed.

He seemed uncomfortable talking about the hardship of his early youth, so he changed the subject.

"How does it feel to live in the city?"

"Have you never been there?"

He shook his head. "For me, the city has always been just a colourful picture beyond the valleys. My parents feared going there, because of their background and beliefs."

"That's quite understandable. I love Pryaya, but society's rules can be quite strict, especially for people like us."

I began to tell him about Pryaya then, and we fell into step. From the first moment we spoke, I could tell that we were going to become good friends. I also knew that it would be a different relationship than the one with Lavi. I couldn't explain how or why, I simply felt it. Turi was marked with destiny.

☆

Before my arrival, Turi and Atarah had been discussing what to do about the abandoned earth threshold. Despite its clever concealment, she still felt responsible for guarding it. However, with Turi's parents gone, there were not many threshold custodians left. There was only one besides Turi and Atarah; the woman who guarded the invisible air threshold. Atarah said she rarely came out, as she had been closed in her own world for years.

Turi had volunteered to become the earth threshold custodian, because he always wanted to go on an adventure to Pryaya. He had also seen his parents use the disc weapon many times, and protecting those sacred places no matter what came naturally to him. Atarah had considered it, but deemed him too young for such a difficult task. His parents were Atarah's dear friends, so she wanted to look after him and keep him safe. She couldn't stop worrying about the earth threshold being unprotected, though.

One day, an intruder snuck into our oasis and headed for the water threshold. He knew the secret of how to use the Merkaba device, and had ill intentions towards it, which is why Atarah had to exterminate him. Due to that unfortunate event, and our different reactions to it, Atarah realised that Turi was emotionally ready for a journey to Pryaya.

Although it still wasn't safe for Atarah and I to show our faces there, I begged her to let me go with him. It wasn't just because I would miss him so much, it was also an excuse for me to learn more about air dancing.

"I don't think that would be a good idea, Seraphina," she argued with me. "We both know that you don't want to be a threshold custodian, you're too…"

"Weak?" I suggested.

"No, not at all, you are too empathetic, and that's a precious gift. However, a threshold custodian needs a bigger shield when it comes to sensitivity, and you don't have it in you to harm someone, even in an emergency."

"That's not true. I just didn't consider the people

you exterminated to be harmful. I saw the colours of their emotions, and understood that their hearts had ill intentions, but does that really mean they had to die?"

I was a bit upset with her at that moment, and dared to speak my mind, which I had never done before. Despite the fact that I revered Atarah's teachings, the threshold custodian law just seemed too cruel to me.

"You didn't consider them harmful because they didn't pose a threat to you or your loved ones... Yet," she explained. "A threshold custodian, however, has to consider everybody's safety, and the safety of all the realms in the Tree of Life." She reached for my hand, and held it comfortingly.

"I don't want you to take this the wrong way, Seraphina. You know I have always supported you in making your own decisions, and you have told me that you don't want to be a threshold custodian. Why would you change your mind now? Just because Turi chose that path? I urge you to think about this some more. This mission is not for everybody, and whoever decides to undergo it must embrace the fact that it's a lonely road."

I didn't want to hear that. Envisioning Turi alone in Pryaya made my heart ache.

"What if I wanted to go back to Pryaya for another reason?" Atarah narrowed her eyes suspiciously. I knew well enough that I couldn't lie to her, so I had to be smart, and present the plan in another way.

"See, it's not just about Turi. I long to go to the Air Dance Academy. I wouldn't apply for the courses, I would just watch the dancing classes from a distance, learn on my own."

My confession seemed to have changed Atarah's mind. She still wavered for a time, but finally allowed me to go along on the condition that I visited her frequently.

Over the following days, she began preparing us for our new life in the abandoned Magic Quarter. We had to take all necessary precautions not be caught. She prepared me for my double life by dyeing my light brown hair black, and later also performed a ritual that made my eyes sensitive for weeks, but coloured them green.

Turi was given the special threshold custodian cape – a black hood that, once it was on, hid his face completely. She also advised us not to be seen entering or leaving the Magic Quarter.

"Mainly during the day," she stressed with a warning glance at Turi, "and don't tamper with the Merkaba device. If you are meant to cross over, the key to its use will come to you."

Turi pretended that it was clear to him, even though we all knew how curious he was about the mechanisms of the ancient devices. He longed to study books on the subject, but they were all located in the House at the Last Lantern, an invisible house that hid the most mysterious threshold – the one aligned with the air element.

"Don't jeopardise everything your parents worked for," she added to stress her point.

Turi promised her that he would leave it alone. Nonetheless, ever since we moved to the Magic Quarter, he became ever more obsessed with the city beyond the threshold, Prague. During our first days there, he had even tried to cross over. Luckily, he failed, and realised that Atarah and his parents were not just making some story up to protect him, that there really was a special trick to using it. That was also the day when I witnessed Turi using the disc weapon for the first time, another shocking memory.

Afterwards, he made me promise not to tell Atarah about his attempt, and so I only informed her of the man's extermination. I hated hiding such a big secret from Atarah, but didn't have the heart to betray him either. We trusted each other, and were growing closer every day.

After the years we had spent living alone together, our friendship began to turn into something we couldn't name or understand. We never spoke about our tender feelings, though, and busied ourselves with other interests.

Turi had been collecting all kinds of books about the threshold legends and the Merkaba, which in our language translated as 'the light body'. Luckily for him, there was plenty of such literature scattered around the abandoned buildings in the Magic Quarter, so he had a lot to do besides guarding the earth threshold.

Meanwhile, I had been secretly sneaking into the Air Dance Academy, watching the classes, and learning more about this fascinating technique. My friend Lavi had become one of the best dancers at the school, but I only admired his skills from afar. I didn't know whether I could trust him or not, and didn't want to take any risks.

In the evenings, I performed what I had picked up to Turi, sometimes including my own choreography.

"You were meant to do this, Seraphina," he once told me. "I have a feeling that there is a hidden purpose in it for you, like there is one for me in this heap of ancient wisdom."

"That's different," I argued, "you have a mission, an important one."

"You have a mission too," he insisted. "Whatever you have a passion for is what you are meant to do. That's what my parents used to say."

He was wise for his age, and that's what I liked about him the most, along with his fervour. I often watched him leaf through the large, dusty books he was so keen to learn from, and longed to cuddle up beside him, but never dared. It was not easy for me to take our friendship to a new level.

I often compared my feelings for him to those I had for Lavi. I admired Lavi, but Turi was rooted in my heart deeper than anyone else. He was my best friend, and a fascinating companion who inspired me to do what my heart called out for. There was also a dark, risk-taking side to his bravery, however.

One day, Turi visited the public library in search of scientific books. He stayed there until dusk, and kept on reading on his way home. He was so absorbed that he didn't notice he was being followed. On top of that, he also forgot to wear his threshold custodian cape, and was therefore recognised immediately as a youngster roaming the forbidden area.

This was how he came to be caught during that fateful Winter Solstice evening. I relived all my worries and fears, as yet again I had to leave my hometown and seek Atarah's help.

✡

Once Atarah heard what had happened, she decided to have a quiet conversation with the Seven Seraphim in the moonlight. I already knew that the best way to connect with them was through the brightest light sources in our realm – the sun and the moon. That was how the Seraphim's colourful rays aligned best with our spirits.

After an intense prayer, we lay down on the riverbank and waited for a prophetic dream. I dreamt of a tiny house that seemed to be transparent, as though made of clouds. An iron lantern was attached to it, and its light was going on and off, off and on. The image then changed into another blinking light, a lamp inside a large performance hall. I recognised the place. It was in the Air Dance Academy. Like the lantern, it was turning on and off,

off and on.

Later, Atarah and I sat down in the shed to share our insights. Atarah told me that she had received guidance from her friend, the air threshold custodian.

"Her light body was dazzling, like a star. She has activated her Merkaba, and left to explore the other realms."

"You mean she died," I said, knowing that Atarah often tended to speak in riddles.

"That's another way to put it, yes," she said. "Some activate their Merkaba and wish to remain, while others are so taken with its potential, that they decide to travel elsewhere."

"Did she tell you how she did it?"

"No, and I wouldn't want her to do that. Each person has to figure it out on her own. It's a mystery, but more importantly, a journey. A journey within. We may only receive hints or clues to resolve parts of its wonder. It's the same with the Merkaba devices at the thresholds – quick enlightenment tends to do more harm than good. Wise may easily become unwise."

"Were you not at least a bit curious to learn how she did it?" I asked. Atarah resolutely shook her head.

"I respect the fact that I'm not ready. I have some ideas, I have learned the geometry behind it, and found out how the Merkaba devices work, but I suppose I'm not ready for more. Anyway, we should focus on the important news she delivered instead. She said that, due to lack of evidence, Turi would be released from prison in a few weeks. They plan to cast him out of the city, and when he comes home to us, I'm going to put her suggestion to him."

"What suggestion?" I asked.

She paused, gave me a nervous look, and explained: "Turi could become the new air threshold custodian at the House at the Last Lantern. He could finally have access to all the amazing literature he had always been so keen on."

Though I knew Turi would love the idea, I didn't want to be separated from him again.

"But what about the earth threshold?" I argued. "Doesn't that one need to be guarded too?"

"The earth threshold will soon be buried beneath rubble, that's what she said. The long-discussed renovation has been set into motion. Our Magic Quarter will soon become an avenue with rows of new townhouses and apartment buildings."

"Can they really do that? I thought it had a profound historical value." I asked, remembering why it had been left alone ever since the Great Magic War.

"Of course, but they don't care anymore. The monarchy knows well enough why we keep coming back. The quarter is a paradise for magical research. Please try to understand it, Seraphina. The authorities will keep an eye on Turi from now on. The House at the Last Lantern will be the only safe place for him."

"He would be safe here with us, too."

She gave me a reproachful smile.

"We both know that Turi would love to be there, though. The house is the library of our ancestors."

I agreed, but couldn't stop myself from sulking.

"What prophecy have the Seraphim given to you?" Atarah then asked, trying to change the subject. Reluctantly, I told her about the dream I'd had.

"That's wonderful, Seraphina!" she exclaimed as soon as I had finished speaking. "It seems that you won't be far from Turi after all." She began to elaborate on her thoughts, sagely deciphering the dream's message.

"You were guided to the *lights of your lives*,

represented by the lantern and the lamp. As Turi begins a new life at the House at the Last Lantern, you are meant to return to the Air Dance Academy, just as you have always wanted."

"Do you really think I'm ready?" I asked, excitedly.

Atarah shrugged.

"You should ask yourself that."

"But what if someone recognises me?"

"Don't worry, you have grown so much in these past five years, and you have a different eye and hair colour now. And if someone like Lavi still recognises you, you'll just have to keep him quiet." I mulled the idea over, liking the sound of it.

"Then it's not all that bad, I suppose."

"Not bad at all… and you don't have to worry about your relationship with Turi. Your souls will be in harmony as long as you support each other's light."

I hoped she was right, because I felt drawn towards Turi like a moth to a flame. I followed him without considering that it might burn me to ashes.

# Chapter X

## Wheel of Fortune

Still in the same dream memory, I found myself in the centre of Pryaya. I was already an adult, around the age of twenty, and was ambling over the grand, central bridge. On the way, I passed the newly rebuilt Magic Quarter, as well as the street with the magnificent stained glass art that I remembered from before.

Then I reached a square which reminded me of the Small Square in Prague. It was a place with tall, white buildings where clothes were hung from the walls with such fine strings that it seemed as though the items floated in the air. The shops was quite different in this reality. Indoor shops were uncommon, and goods were usually just strung from buildings or trees. If you wanted to buy something, you had to insert coins into a small object that functioned both as a lock and a coin bank, and then the goods dropped down, ready to be taken. That was the day I bought myself the sheer, purple dress that I had been wearing when I appeared in Prague.

Later on, I reached a single-storey building with a deep red façade that stood at the end of a wide road, on a small, busy square. It used to be a healing centre, but had become a memorial; a tribute to those who had died during the plague epidemic, including my own dear parents. I walked into the dark vaulted space, and scanned the portraits of the countless victims. My parents' faces weren't among them. They were mainly children and important society figures. Too many had died during that plague, there was not enough space to honour them all.

I visited almost daily, to place flowers beneath the dark grey iron lantern, and hold silent conversations with my parents. It wasn't the only reason I kept coming back, though, a part of me always hoped to meet Turi there. This was because in a less distinct reality, the wall with the lantern concealed the invisible House at the Last Lantern, also known as the air threshold. Turi moved there when we turned fifteen, and I hadn't seen him since.

The only connection we had was the unlit candle in the lantern. Someone replaced it every morning, and waited for me to come and light it. I had a feeling that it was Turi.

☆

A year later, I moved back to the Magic Quarter, and the house I grew up in. It was the only original house left, and had been rebuilt instead of torn down. Although the earth threshold was buried beneath a load of stone, and I never became a threshold custodian as I had promised myself, Atarah and I both felt that it would be good if I stayed close by. After all, the Merkaba device wasn't deactivated, only hidden away.

I established good relations with the neighbours, particularly the man who eventually bought up the whole building, my old friend Lavi's father. The fact that Lavi had been keeping my identity and past hidden from everyone for all those years made me trust him. I considered him a close friend and we had been spending most of our free time together. Even though I sensed that Lavi had begun to develop romantic feelings for me, I wasn't able to return them, as my heart still belonged to Turi.

Naturally, sometimes I toyed with the idea of being with Lavi, but it never felt right. I should never have allowed myself to kiss him on the lips. I should have known that he could mistake it as a promise, or even the so-called 'coalescence', Pryaya's equivalent of marriage.

✡

At the age of twenty-two, I graduated from the Air Dance Academy, and soon afterwards had my first professional performance at the academy's theatre hall. I danced with deep emotion, enjoying the opportunity to finally present my skill to an audience. By then, I could reach higher than most other dancers, and was able to swirl all the way to the ceiling. Each time I did, I was rewarded with a loud applause.

I was dressed in an especially bright, alabaster white gown that shone on the darkened stage along with many tiny lamps, which represented a starry sky. At one point during the show, I floated off stage and above the audience. As I gracefully twirled up and down, I began to pay more attention to the people beneath me, which turned out to be a fatal mistake. To my disbelief, I caught sight of the face that I missed so much. Turi was there, right below me. He was all grown up and changed, but as captivating as I remembered him to be. I froze, hovering above him. His gentle smile encouraged me to dance on, though I was already seized with panic. I attempted to spiral higher and regain my composure, but lost my balance instead, and fell into the audience. Some two confused men managed to catch me, and before I knew it, a big commotion followed. Embarrassment met with despair when I realised that I could no longer see Turi. My eyes searched longingly for him in the crowd of people who blocked my view.

I tried to rise, but the pain in my ankle wouldn't let me. I moaned, more from the irritation that the pain itself. Lavi took care of me from then on, telling me to go with him, so that my understudy could take over the performance. As much as I dreaded it, I had to obey.

Soon after, I overheard someone mention that the director considered me too nervous and inexperienced to perform in front of a crowd, which worried me. It was my dream to perform at the local air dance theatres, and I didn't want to jeopardise this. Another worry was, however, that I would lose track of Turi again. Perhaps he was still in hiding, I thought to myself, maybe he just came to see me perform because he couldn't come closer than that?

Lavi consoled me, and went to fetch me some medicine. I waited for him in the dressing room with my ankle bound tightly, but my mind wandering free. I thought back to the moment before my public humiliation. Turi seemed touched, and looked so worried when I lost my balance. I doubted that he had wanted me to notice him.

As I sat there, with an empty wine glass in my hand, I couldn't stop imagining Turi's face. Though he had changed a lot in appearance, and probably also in spirit since we had parted, some things remained the same. For instance, the sea blue eyes, the sincere smile and the enigmatic aura surrounding him. I supposed that I was doomed to miss him forever, and gave a sigh when suddenly, a vision of him manifested right before me.

I stood up, unbalanced but undeterred. We said nothing, caught in the long-awaited reunion. I willed myself to see the colours of his emotions, and to my relief, he emanated a harmonious blend of lush green and teal blue. It translated as joy and nostalgia.

After a moment's hesitation, he approached me, and embraced me in a tight, bear-like hug.

"I'm so sorry... You were not supposed to see me. Had I known that you would fly so high, and so far off the stage, I would have stayed in the corner somewhere..." I smiled shyly, unused to his presence. I had become so accustomed to only meeting him in my mind and dreams, that the physical contact seemed almost surreal. Once he let go of me, he checked my ankle.

"How are you feeling?"

"I should be all right in a few days," I responded, my voice shaky as well. "This is not the first time I have sprained my ankle."

He gazed at me, shaking his head.

"I still can't believe what I saw. I'm so proud of you, Seraphina. You are an incredible dancer."

The look on his face reminded me of the one he gave me when comparing me to the star. It was filled with admiration and love.

"I just hope they will let me perform again," I said with a worried smile.

"Of course they will. You are a star."

There. Another reminder of the moment that I both cherished and feared, because it preceded our fateful separation. In my delicate mood, I couldn't decide whether he meant to start where we left off, or explain why he hadn't visited me during the seven years we had been living apart. What I feared was that I had disappointed him when I left him in the hands of the authorities. He and Atarah both reassured me it was for the best, but I couldn't absolve myself so easily.

"I'm no star," I said with a wry smile, "I'm just someone who can soar high, but can't seem capable of staying in the air very long…"

"Ah," he groaned, "I feel terrible for making you fall."

"Don't. I should have been more professional, ready for anything, even ghosts from my past."

He clasped my hand. "I really thought I would just watch the performance and leave."

I couldn't believe that he had said that.

"Leave? Again? I don't understand it, Turi. I have been visiting the air threshold almost daily, hoping to find you, but it was as though you had vanished along with the house…"

"That was the idea," he explained and, after a short pause, added, "I'm sorry for not keeping in touch with you. You can't imagine how much I have hated it."

I gathered the courage to ask the question that had been on my lips ever since we parted. "Are you still angry with me?"

He gave me a confused look. "Why would I *ever* be angry with *you*?"

"For abandoning you back then…" The wobble in my voice made me falter.

"Oh Seraphina," he said with a smile, "I asked you to do it, don't you remember? I wanted you to run, return to Atarah and warn her."

"But I shouldn't have listened to you. I wanted to stay. I should have stayed."

He shook his head determinedly. "No. You did

the right thing. Besides, it's not as if anything terrible happened to me. You know that. I believe there were reasons. I was glad to move to the House at the Last Lantern. It was a dream come true.

"And, I have been visiting you, but keeping my distance, or coming to you in my threshold custodian disguise. I considered it better for both of us. I was waiting for the right time, and hoped that you would remain patient, as I did."

"But you could have given me a sign or send me a letter."

"I wanted you to enjoy your freedom, Seraphina. You chose a different path, unburdened by our heritage. You were excited about going to the academy, about living on your own in the city, and you have been doing so well. I visited your workshops sometimes, in my disguise, and watched you dance, like I used to when we were younger."

I couldn't remain upset with him when I felt his emotion, and although I knew the answer already, I still had to ask:

"Was it really you who changed the candle every morning?"

He nodded.

"I always waited for you to come and light it. I could see you, but you couldn't see me. That's how that house works…"

"How unfair!" I couldn't help but smile. He smiled too.

"I still don't understand why you enjoy being there. I can't imagine myself living in such seclusion."

Turi poured me some more wine and fixed himself a glass too. Then, he leaned back in the chair opposite me, and began to explain.

"I have loved every second of it. I was meant to be there, to study all the ancient books. I have been trying to figure out how the Merkaba devices work, and in the house, I have access to everything I need. Of course, expect for..." He fixed his eyes on mine. He was about to say something more, and I had an inkling what it was, but he changed his mind. I suppose he didn't want to upset me, or be too direct. After all, we hadn't seen each other for seven years. People change, their feelings as well. I wanted to tell him that for me, nothing had changed, but couldn't bring myself to. Instead, I asked him:

"And have you succeeded? In figuring out how the devices work, I mean."

"Not just yet, but I think I'm on the right path now... It took me years to put certain things together, come to certain conclusions. There is no doubt that the key to all the Merkaba devices is the Merkaba itself, but to come to understand the Merkaba scientifically is a true challenge."

"Have you managed it?" I whispered, intrigued.

"No. The more I study it the more impossible it seems. Nonetheless, I found out how the Merkaba looks and moves."

"Can you tell me?"

"Perhaps another time." He was weighing something up. "Until then, this image speaks for itself..."

He reached into his pocket, and pulled out the Wheel of Fortune card, one of the Tarot trumps. It depicted three wheels within wheels, in a hexagonal shape. Each of the image corners showed one face of the four-faced Cherubim, the guardians of the elements. I didn't understand the connection, and gave him a confused look.

"Meditate on it later, when you're alone," he said while handing me the card. Then he repeated Atarah's phrase: "If someone gave you the rules to the game you have been playing right away, you would miss the most exciting part – the details."

I smiled, because I caught sight of the younger

Turi then. It brought back memories, impressions from our childhood. Turi must have noticed, as he gave me a tender look.

"And how are you?" he asked, quickly adding, "besides dancing and falling."

I grinned at the comment, then wavered, unsure about what to share and what to omit. As usual, I tried to sound positive.

"I'm happy. Living my dream. I love to practise and improve. I would like to be able to dance in the skies one day, like the dancers from ancient times did."

He nodded, impressed. "You always reached higher than anyone I know, and worked so hard... I believe you will succeed in that as well." I shrugged, blushed, shook my head, not knowing how to respond to such a compliment.

"And Atarah? Do you keep in touch with her?" he asked.

"I go there often, whenever I have a day off."

"Could I ask you to deliver a letter to her? I can't leave the air threshold, but desperately need her advice on something." He hesitated about whether he should tell me what it was, so I encouraged him:

"On what?"

"Well... I have managed to establish a contact with someone from Prague..."

"Really? Is that allowed?"

"Remember the secret machine contained in the air threshold? The one that allows you to communicate with the threshold custodian on the other side?" I nodded, wanting to hear more.

"So this person from Prague is also a threshold custodian?"

"Yes. It's a woman, about fifteen years older, more knowledgeable."

"Now I know why you never come out," I said, partly in jest, partly from disappointment. The mysterious smile that crossed his face was like an arrow straight to my heart. Was he in love with that woman? He must have admired her at least. The silly, jealous thought made me ask:

"And this machine, does it transmit images as well? Can you actually see her?"

"No, we can only hear each other."

I felt relieved to hear that. Just then, a knock on the door disturbed us. Turi briskly threw on his cape, and hid behind the large wardrobe next to the entrance. He nodded in encouragement, so I called out:

"Yes?"

Lavi opened the door, timidly looking around. "Are you alone? I thought I heard you talking."

"Oh," I tried to seem relaxed. "I was just talking to myself, or rather, complaining to myself."

He smiled, proud to announce:

"No need for that. The choreographers confirmed that you are out of trouble. They all agree that you are too precious to be let go. They believe you were just nervous and that it will improve with time."

I sighed with relief.

"That's wonderful news, Lavi, thank you!" As he leaned in for a kiss, I shifted my gaze to Turi. I couldn't gauge his reaction, as he was concealed in the magic cape, however, his emotion colours changed from green blue to green red, which meant he was alarmed in some way. I planted a kiss on Lavi's cheek instead of his lips. He was taken aback, but pretended not to mind.

"Would you like me to take you home?" he asked, and before I knew it, began packing my things. I stole another glance at Turi, distressed. I couldn't stand the thought of us parting again after we had just found each other. Turi nodded to me, though, encouraging me to follow Lavi.

"All right," I said finally, "I just need to change.

Could you wait outside please?"

"Of course." He winked at me, and left with my bags. As soon as Turi took off his cape, he searched my face for answers.

"That was Lavi," I explained, "a friend of mine."

Turi narrowed his eyes a bit.

"Really? Just a friend?"

I shrugged. "Well, at one time I thought we would be more."

"So what changed your mind?" The question rendered me speechless. I couldn't tell him, not there… So, instead I asked:

"When will I see you again?"

"Soon."

"Promise me."

He smiled. "I promise."

That calmed me down. Like me, Turi didn't like to lie or pretend, he spoke the truth even if it was harsh. I gave him a tight embrace, then put on a coat and left to meet Lavi.

Straight after I closed the door, I wished I had told him what was going on in my mind. I also wished I could explain myself to Lavi, but my relationship with Turi was bound by a secret that spread beyond our ordinary lives. It concerned so much more, including things that I wasn't allowed to share with anyone, ever. I knew I should at least be honest about my feelings, though. We had been friends for such a long time, he didn't deserve to be led on, but I didn't know how to explain myself.

After Lavi and I left the Air Dance Academy, we headed down the narrow lane with beautiful, symbolic house signs – the House at the White Dove, at the Golden Key, and finally, at the Golden Wheel. The wheel began spinning in my mind, and with the image, I awoke back in Prague.

☆

What seemed like years was really only an hour. Vilma and Hieronymus came to wake me, worried for my health, as it became quite chilly during the night.

"Come on, dear, you will catch a cold if you stay here all night," said Vilma, covering me with a warm blanket. She patted my cheek. "You must have been very tired…"

I focused on her kind face then on Hieronymus's. He looked rather disappointed.

"I suppose it was hopeless," he guessed, and without waiting for my answer, he added: "It makes sense, don't you think, Miss Seraphina? Perhaps an invisible house remains invisible for a reason."

I wanted to argue with him, and tell them both about what I had experienced and recalled, but forced myself to keep it a secret, like everything else.

"Poor soul, she's still half asleep," said Vilma and turned to Hieronymus. "Come on, let's take her home."

Hieronymus was bewildered. "Am I allowed to come along?"

"You're expected to. Would you leave ladies alone in the dark city streets?"

"But I'm useless when something happens. I always freeze."

Vilma rolled her eyes, but said nothing. Unlike before, the two seemed to be on much friendlier terms.

On the way, they continued to discuss the things they had been talking about before they brought me back to consciousness, mainly Prague's history. Meanwhile, I had been trying to recall all the reawakened memories, and realised that the colourful buildings with the symbolic house signs

Lavi and I had walked past closely resembled those in Nerudova Street.

"Would it be all right if we took a little detour?" I asked my companions. They looked at me in surprise.

"Of course, where would you like to go?" asked Vilma.

"Nerudova."

Vilma was accustomed to my strange whims, but Hieronymus was taken aback by the idea.

"Why would you want to go there now, Miss Seraphina? It's not on our way…"

Vilma eyed him disapprovingly, so he put on an innocent expression, and said, "Excuse me for being so nosy, I'm just curious."

"That's all right. I dreamt about the street back there in the Golden Lane, and simply wanted to see it to bring things back," I explained. Hieronymus gave me a thoughtful nod, Vilma a conspiratorial smile. She was always happy for me when I found another piece of my past.

So, we set of to Nerudova. First, we passed Oliver's house, At the White Angel, then the house At the Golden Horseshoe, and finally, we reached the two houses which, despite their different appearances, had identical signs in Pryaya and Prague: At the Golden Key, and opposite to it, At a Golden Wheel.

I stopped to look at the wheel. In the dim light of Prague's dark green lanterns, I realised why I wanted to see it. It resembled one of the Tarot trumps, the Wheel of Fortune. I longed to find out what Turi meant when he said that I might have some insights about the Merkaba if I meditated on it, and decided to do so as soon as I was back at Vilma's.

I thanked Vilma and Hieronymus for taking me there, because it helped me recall my dream. Hieronymus wondered what the dream was and, offering him a half-truth, I said that it was complicated, and he seemed to understand.

Before we said goodbye to Hieronymus, Vilma and I caught sight of the faceless man, or as Turi called him, Prague's earth threshold custodian. He was hiding in the shadows, watching us from afar. I reckoned that he just wanted to make sure that I reached home without revealing anything about the air threshold. I wondered whether he was in charge of all the Prague thresholds, and with the thought, a realisation dawned on me. I remembered that Turi had told me the woman who contacted him at the House at the Last Lantern was an air threshold custodian too. Could it be that Berta never told him who she really was? How I wished that I could reach him. I felt so confused, and he was the only one I could talk to.

✡

After Vilma fell asleep, I snuck into the kitchen, the only other room in the apartment, in order to meditate on the Tarot. I flipped through the deck that I had brought with me from Pryaya. The twenty-two cards were well thumbed, and felt familiar in my hands. I searched for the Wheel of Fortune trump, and compared it with the one from Vilma's deck. Her version depicted a helm while mine was three wheels within wheels. They had one crucial element in common, though – movement.

The thought of movement made me recall the Tarot's anagram, which Dora had told me about: *Rota taro orat tora ator – the wheels of Tarot speak the law of Ator*.

With this peculiar riddle in mind, I also remembered what Atarah had once told me about the cards:

"Like the thresholds, the Tarot's Minor Arcana was split into four suits, which represent the four basic elements: the cups for water, the wands for fire, the swords for air, and the coins for earth. The fifth element was represented by the Major Arcana, which depicts the journey to fully engaging the light body, in other words, the Merkaba.

"The Tarot has, in both realities, been the gateway to the Merkaba mystery. Our ancestors concealed their wisdom in this simple deck of cards so that everyone would have access to it, but only those who were ready would figure it out. Just by looking at the images, something happens within us, and knowledge that we all once had begins to be reawakened.

"Many people underestimate the importance of the Merkaba, but no matter what our life's purpose or mission is, the Merkaba is the ultimate path to inner freedom. After all, how would we survive without a light body? Thanks to it, we are able to pass over to the other side after we die, and travel within the twisted branches of the Tree of Life.

"The cards were created to help us on this road to wholeness. Although for some, certain steps may be left out, or changed, the purpose of the trumps remains the same – to open one's consciousness. That is *all* they do, but they do *all* you need. As I said before, each Merkaba is unique. Whenever you dream or fantasise, you may feel it, and sense its presence. However, if you are awake to its full potential, you will be able to shift to any branch of the Tree of Life without using the Merkaba devices."

I remembered then that the subject of the Merkaba had always enthralled as well as scared me. There was a kind of holy respect surrounding it. With this in mind, I began to arrange the cards in numerical order. I studied them with more attention than before, trying to imbibe the wisdom they exuded.

The Fool on his arcane path, the Magician with his tools, the High Priestess with her sacred books, the Empress and the Emperor with their power symbols, the Hierophant with his tiara and pupils; then the confused Lovers standing under the wings of the angel, and the prince on his Chariot Throne, which again reminded me of the Merkaba.

I paused, wondering where my thoughts were taking me. I sensed that I could not take in the Tarot's vast message with the little understanding I had. It was as though I was looking at a blurry image which lacked any detail. The message was there to be grasped, but not yet. Once again, I recalled Atarah's wise words:

"Sometimes it's all about the details, they make the whole more meaningful."

To honour her, I tried to pay more attention to the details from then on. However, I was too exhausted that night, and eventually dozed off with my head resting on the table.

# Chapter XI

## Strength

Once again during the night, my spirit travelled through planes of time and space, back to my past in Pryaya. I was walking through the city, watching the sun rise from behind the mountain with the lion-unicorn statues. Since it was High Summer Day, I made for the riverbank. According to local tradition, if you dropped a flower made from dried herbs and petals into the waves, and let it drift into the sunrise, your wish would come true. Despite the recent law that forbade magic, people still kept some innocent pagan traditions alive.

When I reached the low-lying wooden bridge, which connected the two largest city islands, I dropped a fist-sized bundle made of compressed, dried petals into the water, and watched as it unfolded. It created a beautiful, large flower. The clear, light-blue waters were already filled with various other flowers, some even larger than the white stones which spread over the riverbed. I went to watch the flow of wishes every year, but my wish had never come true instantly before. That day was special, though.

I spotted a familiar silhouette in my peripheral vision, and turned to face Turi. He wore his threshold custodian cape with the hood down. He embraced me then dropped his own water flower. We never asked each other about our wishes, as we were superstitious, and believed it would bring bad luck. No words were needed. We simply watched our wishes float freely down the stream.

Later on, Turi and I walked to the House at the Last Lantern together for some privacy. On our way, I noticed Lavi in the distance, and immediately let Turi know. Since Turi didn't have his hood on when Lavi spotted us, he put it on straight away and walked off. When I met Lavi, I was still looking furtively around for Turi, as I was worried I would lose sight of him round the corner of a nearby building.

"Who was that?" asked Lavi, without greeting me first, which was very unlike him.

"A friend of mine," I said, blushing, expecting him to ask me questions that I couldn't answer.

"Why would your friend wear a cape?"

"Since when is it wrong to wear a cape?"

"Since most people who wear capes like that have something to do with magic."

"Would it matter if I knew someone who was interested in magic?"

"I would be worried for you."

"Why?"

"Because of your mysterious origins and unexplained absences."

"I thought you didn't care about that."

"I'm only concerned for your safety."

"You don't have to worry, Lavi, I know what I'm doing."

Like me, Lavi couldn't stop glancing towards the street where Turi had gone to hide.

"Why didn't you introduce us then?"

His jealous tone made me nervous. Lavi had always been overly possessive of me, and although he tried not to let it show, I always saw through him. This was partly thanks to the emotion scanning technique which Atarah had taught me, and partly because I knew him so well.

"He was in a hurry, and he's a loner anyway."

"Is it someone from your past?"

I nodded, unwilling to continue a conversation that led nowhere. I wanted to hurry after Turi, anxious I would lose him again.

"I'm sorry, but I have to go," I said hastily. "I'll see you tonight, all right?" I planted a quick kiss on his cheek, and paused, realising that the friendly rather than romantic gesture was a confession of its own. He glowered.

"Aren't we going the same way home?" His voice was as cold as ice. I panicked, and blurted out the first thing that came to mind.

"I need to buy something…"

Lavi reached for my hand and gave me a proper kiss on the lips. I froze, unable to return the passion. "Please be careful, I wouldn't want to see you in trouble again."

He emphasized the *again*, and I knew what it meant. He knew that I had been in the Establishment for Suspicious Youth, and although I never told him why, he had guessed that my previous behaviour was against the common law. That is why, for Turi's sake, I looked deep into Lavi's eyes, and pleaded with him:

"Let it be, Lavi. If you value our friendship, please let it be."

I freed my hand from his, and set off after Turi. Luckily, he had been waiting for me in the shadow of the building on the corner.

"Are you certain you have the time for this now?" he asked.

I nodded, and clasped his hand.

"Of course, let's hurry, though. My friend Lavi guessed that you had something to do with magic."

"Because of the cape, right?"

I nodded. "These days, the law against magic is tighter than ever. The patrol is all over the city. They pay extra attention to anything out of the ordinary. You might be better off without the cape. Nobody will recognise you anyway, you have changed over the years."

Turi considered it. Then he turned to me.

"Do you love him?"

I blushed and faltered. "I... I don't think so. I like him, he's a good friend, but I can't... I'm not able to... commit to him. Not yet at least." I gave him a nervous glance, unsure whether he knew what it had taken for me to say this.

"Don't be friends with a man who loves you, Seraphina, that's not fair to either one of you."

I wished I could read the strange look he gave me, but he remained a closed book. We continued walking in quiet contemplation from then on, just as we used to when we lived together in the Magic Quarter. As Turi watched the morning light reflect off the buildings, I marvelled at how it coloured his face. Bittersweet nostalgia filled me when I realised how much I missed that face. Still, I was grateful to have him nearby despite the odd effect he had on me, that familiar blend of fear and attraction.

☆

Before Turi and I entered the memorial where the House at the Last Lantern was concealed, we looked around to make sure that we weren't being followed. Hand in hand, we disappeared into the vaulted hall with the portraits of the plague victims.

For the first time in my life, I made out the invisible window beneath the lantern. It was round with a white frame, but it vanished as soon as I tried to make sense of it. It felt as though my senses weren't ready to admit that it truly existed, not until Turi confirmed that what I had seen was real.

"Do you still not trust yourself, Seraphina? You know well enough that your heritage allows you to see things beyond the threshold. You are more gifted than you like to admit."

With one more look over his shoulder, Turi reached into his cape pocket and pulled out a key. I couldn't believe it would be so simple.

"An ordinary key? Is that how you open an invisible house?" He raised a challenging eyebrow, and said:

"If it seems so ordinary, you try to open it." He handed me the key. I frowned and smiled as I stared at the wall, dumbfounded. Finally, he took hold of the key again, and turned it in the air just beneath the lantern.

Out of nowhere, the window I had seen before reappeared on the blank wall before us, along with a simple wooden door. Turi put his arm around my shoulder and led me inside. Then he swiftly closed the door behind us and nudged me forward.

After passing through a long, stone-built corridor filled with bookshelves, we appeared in a room which reminded me of Hieronymus's dwelling in the Golden Lane. There was a single bed, an abundance of tall bookshelves and a table overflowing with books, notebooks and candles. I was surprised to see no window, but Turi explained that this was because the house existed somewhere *in between* the two realms.

"Have you really been shut away in here for all these years?" I wondered as I soaked up the room's studious atmosphere.

"Not really," he said as he guided me past the towers of books. "I went out at night in my disguise."

I moved over to his desk, and read the titles of the books he had been studying most recently – a history of the Magic Quarter, the Secret Thresholds, the Guardians of the Portals, and then a thick notebook, which he had entitled: The Mechanisms of the Merkaba.

"Will you finally tell me more about your research?" I asked, intrigued by the wealth of resources and the thoughts in his diary.

"I'm still not sure if that's a good idea. I have come to agree with Atarah during my many years of solitude. A person should find the truth for herself."

I crossed my arms, feeling forlorn all of a sudden.

"You and Atarah… Always leaving me in the dark…"

"If dark is what you need…" added Turi teasingly before his face turned more serious. I could tell that he was gathering the courage to tell me something important. "Seraphina, I wanted to ask you a favour…"

I didn't like that guilty look and what it signified. He fidgeted a bit, then explained: "I'm going to leave for some time, and I'll need someone to guard this threshold for me while I'm gone."

I couldn't believe it. Not only did he want to leave me again, he had also asked me to accept the burden of a threshold custodian.

"It would be just for a few weeks or so," he added, "and I promise I'll do anything I can to return as soon as possible."

He left me speechless. I watched him in

disappointment, unable to respond.

"Don't worry, Seraphina, I would never ask this of you if it wasn't safe. During the seven years I have spent here, I haven't encountered a single intruder. This threshold is the safest of all. Few people know about it, and nobody really knows how to enter it anymore, except for me and Atarah… Of course, I wouldn't want to underestimate all those nosy, persistent magicians, and in case they show up, I'll leave the metallic disc weapon here for you."

I shook my head. "You know I would never use that."

"You would," he said resolutely, "if it came to the worst, and there was no other way."

I sat on his bed, growing upset, although more with myself than him. Consumed with the affection I felt for him, I forgot what he was really like. He was always focused on some important mission or other things, none of which included me. I was somewhere in the background, hoping that one day I would be the goal.

"Is this the reason you have shown up in my life after all these years?" I asked, weakly.

He dropped down beside me, and held my hands in his.

"No. How could you think that? I *needed* to see you… I always wanted to reunite with you, to become close again." He sighed. "I don't understand why it all had to happen at the same time, but it did. I have come to certain conclusions during the past few days."

He noticed that I had become distant, and was fighting back tears, so he stopped speaking and asked:

"Are you very upset with me?"

"Of course I am," I said, my voice breaking. "I have finally finished school, and many opportunities have opened up for me. If I withdrew from society now, I would risk my air-dancing career. After that damn fall, I was given another, and probably a last, chance to prove myself ready for the stage."

Turi nodded, then shook his head, and smiled.

"I hate myself now... I was being selfish, as always... what was I thinking? Forget about it, Seraphina. I'll find another way to deal with this."

I turned to him with quiet anger. Deep down, I didn't care that he was selfish. I would forgive anything, just to keep him close. I was foolish, and I knew it very well, yet I couldn't help myself.

"Can you at least tell me where you plan on going?"

"To Prague."

I was afraid he would say that. Atarah and I suspected that he would never give up his fascination with the world beyond the threshold, and since he had told me about the mysterious woman on the other side, I sensed trouble.

"Yesterday it all clicked, Seraphina. My years of research have finally paid off. I have come to understand how the Merkaba devices work. They are based on the mechanism and geometry of the real, living Merkaba field, as are our bodies, and the entire world. It's complicated, and as I said, I can't explain it... but, I must see if it works."

"Does Atarah know about it?"

"No. I wanted to tell her, hear her advice, but I've changed my mind. I know she wouldn't approve."

"Can you imagine how disappointed she would be if she knew that you'd lied to her?"

"Well, theoretically, I didn't lie. I only withheld certain information." The rebellious grin on his face sent chills down my spine. Fear for his safety dominated everything else.

"This could be a dangerous game, Turi, I don't like the thought of it one bit."

Turi eased himself onto the pile of bed cushions,

and began reasoning with me.

"Don't worry, I have planned it carefully. As I have befriended Berta, the threshold custodian on the other side, I should pass safely enough, and if my intentions are good…"

"But don't you remember what we were told? How dense and tough that realm is?"

"Berta promised to help me. She said it would be a ground-breaking discovery if I knew how to pass the thresholds. Just as over here, most of the threshold custodians in Prague don't know how to use the Merkaba devices anymore."

"So you shared your findings with her?" I left out 'instead of me', but he must have sensed it.

"No. I wouldn't do that. She knows that I have been researching it, but I didn't tell her about the conclusions I had reached. Like I said, she should find the truth for herself."

He gave me a mischievous smile, and I responded with a scowl. I had a bad feeling about that woman. Then again, I might just have been jealous of her. It was difficult for me to recognise whether it was an intuitive or possessive fear that gripped my heart each time he mentioned her.

The news of Turi's plans made me forget about my daily duties, including my plans with Lavi. I stayed with Turi in the House at the Last Lantern, discussing his departure and what he had learned about Prague. I also told him more about my plans and visions for the future, not leaving out my bond with Lavi. Time ceased to exist in that ethereal building. We rested on the small bed, side by side, re-establishing the relationship we have always had – one that wavered between friendly and romantic.

I longed to keep him close, uniting our bodies and spirits into inseparable perfection. Even though he claimed that he wanted to return soon, travelling to another reality was quite different to being closed in an invisible house a few streets away. I didn't know whether or not I would be able to let him go.

During the years we had lived apart, I had always promised myself that if we were to find each other again, I would tell him what the passing of time had made me realise. Yet, even when the moment came, I still couldn't bring myself to tell him what he meant to me. The intrepid heroine within me kept fighting the strict king who sat on the throne of her pride, almost succeeding, but failing over and over again.

At one point during the conversation, his face moved so close to mine that it terrified me. I didn't know whether to push him away or lean even closer. Our lips almost touched when he whispered: "I'm so glad we are together again, Seraphina." Instead of a kiss, I received another embrace. My head landed on his chest, and rested. Tired from our emotions and from talking, our eyelids slowly became heavy. We fell asleep in each other's arms, as though we were lovers. We used to do that when we were younger as well. It was an old habit, which seemed to have outlasted even the seven years of separation.

✡

I woke up in shock. Not only had I missed my dinner date with Lavi the previous night, I also had an early rehearsal. Luckily for me, we woke before sunrise, so I was able to reach the Air Dance Academy on time. Turi decided to walk with me. Since he was planning to leave in the evening, we wanted to enjoy the time we had left together. He wore regular clothes that day, trying to fit in as I had advised him.

As we neared the academy, we noticed Lavi leaning against the wall by the entrance. He seemed to have been waiting for me, but not in his usual friendly manner. I noticed that Turi had become apprehensive as well, so I was readying myself to bid him farewell.

When I turned to face him, however, I noticed two city guards approaching us. Without thinking, I clasped Turi's hand and hurried him inside the building. Unfortunately, it wasn't safe there either. We spotted another two guards descending the ancient, dark wooden stairs. I squeezed Turi's hand, alarmed. Silence filled the room as we watched them surround us. Soon, Lavi and the guards from outside began closing in on us as well. Lavi pointed at Turi and they gave him a solemn nod. Then, all of a sudden, one of the guards released the metallic disc, the 'kind weapon' as the locals liked to call it. Turi pulled me into a protective embrace, which made the disc miss his head by an inch. It cut into the wooden wardrobe behind us, making it shatter and disintegrate into fine dust.

Turi pulled me into the long corridor on our left. We ran for our lives as another metallic disc exploded a painting on the wall. The labyrinth of academy corridors seemed endless. There was no escape, no clever hiding place. Although I knew the building by heart, I was too alarmed to concentrate on where the nearest exits were. Turi was the one leading the way, and he hardly knew the place.

Finally, we stopped by a large window, weighing up the risk of climbing down. For an instant, I wondered whether I could take Turi and soar with him in the air, but I worried that I wouldn't manage it. In our moment of hesitation, we were startled by a male figure. It was Lavi. He was alone. He must have split up from the guards to have more chance of catching us.

"Stop the guards, Lavi!" I begged him.

"They are here for your friend, Seraphina, not for you. Just let him go."

"Never," I hissed through my teeth, filled with fury. How could he have betrayed me like that, I thought to myself as I held his gaze. How could he be so thoughtless?

Lavi took a step closer, so I covered Turi with my body, letting him know that if he planned to fight him, he would have to go through me first. Lavi paused, and Turi used the moment to reach for his weapon. I stopped his hand. I couldn't let him kill Lavi, despite my anger.

Turi glanced first at me, then at Lavi. They were both deciding what to do next. After a tense pause, Turi placed the weapon in my palm, and with a look at me he told Lavi:

"Take care of her."

Then he gave me a quick kiss on the forehead, and headed for the window. I started after him, but he was fast, and climbed down before I could do anything. I watched as he ran across the street, and jumped on the tram, escaping the city guards by a hair's breadth.

God knows what Lavi had told them about him, I thought to myself, as I had never seen the city guards so aggressive. I sensed Lavi's presence behind me, as I clutched the disc in my hand. It gave me a sense of comfort. After all, I didn't know what to expect from him after the disappointment he had caused me. The weapon's edge cut into my palm and made it bleed, but I didn't care. Levi approached me in a slow, composed way, and his eyes became gentler when they found mine.

"Please give it to me before you hurt yourself." I shook my head, determined to not let go of Turi's only weapon.

"You don't have to be afraid of me," he tried to console me, "I'm here to protect you. I don't think you know who you are dealing with."

"He's not dangerous!"

"How can you be so certain? When you didn't meet me last night, I went to the officials, and described his face. They showed me pictures of wanted criminals, and I recognised him as one of them."

"Then I'm a criminal as well," I said, absentmindedly looking out of the window at the passing trams.

"What has got into you, Seraphina? Why do you care about him so much?" He attempted to reach for my hand, but I flinched away.

"Don't you dare touch me, Lavi! I don't ever want to see you again!" My sharp tone startled him. He stared at me in disbelief.

"You don't mean that."

I turned away, unable to even look at him anymore. "I told you to let it be…" I said softly, feeling lightheaded and weak.

Lavi crouched down, his head in his hands. I scanned his heart, and saw a blur of grey hues with flashes of pink tones, which told of confusion and emotional pain. He must have realised that he had gone too far, that he had jeopardised our friendship and whatever else it could have developed into. It almost looked as though he was about to start crying, which made my heart melt. I caressed his cheek with my hand, noticing my blood dripping onto his shoulder. I tucked the metallic disc into my handbag.

Lavi noticed my injury and silently took my hand in his, examining it. He then pulled out a handkerchief and secured it as a bandage around the wound. As I watched him, I recalled something that Atarah once told me: *every human has a beast inside, but such energy should be tamed lest it become dominant.*

Lavi seemed to have tamed his inner beast, because he let me go in the end. He must have known that he stood no chance when it came to Turi, particularly after he had betrayed my trust. And as for my inner beast, it was calmed by empathy, which had finally won over my initial fury.

☆

Feeling empowered, I went after the person that my whole being called out for. I returned to the House at the Last Lantern, ready to express my affection before it was too late. However, when I noticed the simple key on top of the empty lantern, I sensed that I had lost my chance. Turi must have left it there so that I could keep it safe with me.

Disheartened, I unlocked the ethereal door, and disappeared inside. Except for his cloak, shoes and a few drops of blood on the marble floor, there was no sign of him. The fact that he had set out on his mission barefoot was strange, but I was more concerned by the blood. The thought of him being hurt terrified me to the core.

After a moment of staring into nowhere, thinking about what to do next, I noticed that there was a letter addressed to me on his bed. I felt my knees buckle, and I sank down to read his farewell.

*My dearest Seraphina,*

*I hope you will understand the quick getaway as well as the following plea:*

*I beg you to forget about the favour I asked of you yesterday. You should not come here anymore. I didn't think it through. I have become too accustomed to my loneliness, and have forgotten how people out there think and act, how dangerous it is to be associated with magic in our world. Although the realm on the other side is said to be more reason-based, at least it's open to the practices that interest me. You must promise me to stay safe. Please just take the key and leave. The threshold must wait for my return, and it should remain locked away.*

*Say what you must about me to the city guards and your friends, just remain strong. Your strength is unyielding, Seraphina, I had the honour to witness it again today. In many ways, you are even stronger than Atarah, though you might not agree with me there. However, in my eyes, your strength is in your genuine kindness, and faith in the kindness of others. I'm so glad you haven't changed that about yourself.*

*Please, go on living your dream, and don't worry about me. I shall come back one day.*

*Love you, forever.*


Love you. I kept repeating the two words in my mind over and over. Love you – as a sister, a friend or a lover? I concluded that it didn't really matter. The most important question was whether he was all right on the other side.

I didn't want to follow his advice and return to my life in Pryaya, pretending that nothing had happened. Even my beloved air dancing held no joy for me anymore, not if I knew that he was alone in such a different realm with a woman we knew nothing about.

*No, Turi*, I answered his letter in my mind, *I can't promise you anything. I have to find out how you managed to cross over, and join you in Prague.*

# Chapter XII

# The Hanged Man

In the days that followed Turi's disappearance, I stayed in the House at the Last Lantern, and tried to find how he had discovered the Merkaba mechanism. As he said, the Merkaba was the key, so I started there. I went through his various books and diaries, and first found some information he had been given by Berta. Turi had noted down:

*In Prague's reality, the only text found on the Merkaba is a riddle concealed in Jewish mysticism called the Kabbalah. Some of the Jewish mystics were able to achieve the Merkaba through meditations, incantations, and by using sigils, which are inscribed symbols believed to have magical powers. They worked with the seven archangels, also called the Seven Seraphim, Seven Rays, or Seven Brothers, which translates to the Sat Bhai. That is why the ancient inventors of the Merkaba devices called themselves the Sat Bhai.*

*The path to the Merkaba mystery in those texts is to descend in order to ascend to the highest heavens, the seven palaces of God.*

The phrase *descend to ascend* captured my attention. I kept thinking about what it meant until I found Turi's diary entitled *The Descent*. The diary contained his findings on the geometry and construction of life in both of our realms. I impatiently flipped through the densely-written pages, and focused mainly on the pictures.

First, there was something Turi called the *core*, but mentioned that in Prague's reality it was called the *atom*. The image depicted a ball made of eight other, smaller balls, and three balls that circled around it, resembling the three wheels within wheels or the hexagon pattern. As a comparison, he drew the shape of a hexagram in its three-dimensional form, which was an eight-sided double tetrahedron. Below it, he wrote:

*Just as all numbers begin with zero, so all shapes begin with a circle and create a circular motion. As in all the luminescent shapes, there is no beginning or end, smallest or largest, brightest or darkest. Everything derives from and returns to the same archetypal patterns.*

On the next page, Turi drew the alchemical symbols for the four basic elements, and how they derived from the hexagram.

*The hexagram itself seems to represent the fifth element. After all, what are stars, but balls of light exuding rays?*

Then he drew something he called *The Genes of All Creation*, and noted that in Prague's reality it was called the *Nuclein* or DNA. It was a spiral shape that resembled hexagonal and pentagonal patterns. I wanted to reflect on the two shapes, but found myself intrigued by another diary entitled *The Ascent.*

There, Turi drew the image of a male figure who, depending on the position of his hands and legs, also formed hexagonal and pentagonal shapes. The depiction contained the following comment:

*The physical body is the reflection of the Merkaba as well, as are most of the vehicles people create. Everything is in the same pattern and movement. The wheels within wheels spin over and over again...*

In that diary, I also stumbled across a drawing of our planet, the globe, in a grid of wheels within wheels, which also resembled a combination of hexagonal and pentagonal shapes. Beside it, Turi had written:

*To leave the grid, one has to understand the grid from within and without.*

In my haste, I couldn't concentrate on all that he had written on the subject. I felt as if the pictures themselves would communicate most efficiently, so I kept staring at them. I tried to comprehend why everything seemed to derive from and return to the pentagonal and hexagonal shapes. It was simple yet complex, both logical and magical, and these contradictions made it all the more intriguing. They were all versions of the original pattern. All the shapes communicated with each other. Another one of Turi's notes read:

*The hexagrams and pentagrams can be found in everything. I realise that the two symbols are the gateways to the Merkaba, but Merkaba's true, vast splendour remains a mystery to me. The key to that lock, the key to living instead of dreaming, can be found only in one's heart. If I learn to understand it, then I'll be able to turn stillness into eternity, and eternity into stillness.*

Exhausted from the overload of information and my deep thoughts, I fell asleep on Turi's bed wrapped in the blanket that still smelled of him. I dreamt about the shapes I had seen. They were expanding and shrinking, spiralling and turning in a circular motion. It was the kind of sleep during which you feel as though your spirit has travelled, because before you awake, you find your body limp and distant. When I had fully awoken to my senses, however, I found my whole body was vibrating with a newly found energy.

It was then that I noticed the symbol drawn on the ceiling: two hexagonal shapes with seven circles, six on the outer points and one in the centre. These were interconnected with red lines that resembled two hexagrams on top of each other and blue lines that resembled pentagrams, one pointing up, the other down.

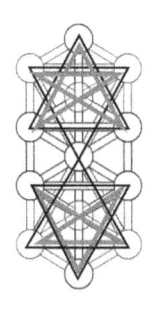

I recognised that symbol. It was drawn on the ceiling in the riverside home of Turi's parents as well. Atarah called it the Tree of Life.

Curious to know more, I returned to Turi's diaries. I found one titled *As Above, So Below* and subtitled *The Tree of Life Riddles.* As soon as I opened it, my gaze fell upon a drawing of circles, interconnected with lines. I studied the picture, trying to figure it out. It seemed incomplete, and it made me wonder whether it could be the riddle mentioned in the title.

I turned the notebook round, and looked at the image upside down. It still didn't make much sense. I kept reversing it, trying to decide what it was that bothered me. The swift movements made the image from above and below merge into one symbol in my mind, and the title *As Above So Below* began to make more sense.

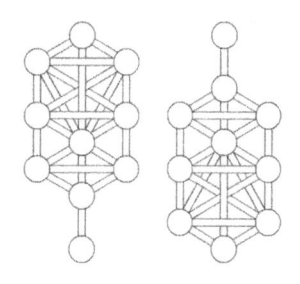

Intrigued, I grabbed a piece of paper and a pen and copied the initial image on one page facing up and on another facing down. Then I positioned the papers over one another and held them up to the light. Finally, I realised why it seemed incomplete. The above and below versions, when combined, resulted in the symbol drawn on the ceiling and at our riverside home – it was the Tree of Life.

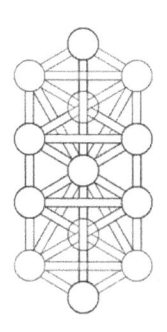

After my initial euphoria, I soon fell into another dilemma. The more I learnt, the more I realised how little I knew. I leafed through the diary some more, and stumbled across a scribble in the corner of one page. It read:

*Just as there is not only one road leading to Pryaya, neither is there a single path to the Merkaba.*

The words preceded a chapter entitled: *The Nordic, Hindi and Kabbalistic Tree of Life.* It was about the similarities between the three cultures in Prague's reality, and their Tree of Life philosophies. Besides the tree, they all had one symbol in common – the hexagram. What they also shared was the idea of descending. They depicted the tree upside down, with its crown in the ground and the roots in the sky. Turi was fascinated with it, and noted down his thoughts on the following page:

*I wonder if it means that our roots are to be found in the heavens, not down here on earth? Could the earthly worlds be the places we go to in order to, metaphorically speaking, branch ourselves? Is it where we learn and expand, but afterwards return home?*

What struck me most was the Nordic *Poetic Edda*, a poem that described the peculiar journey of a god called Odin. In the legend, Odin hung himself from the Tree of Life, also called the *Askur Yggdrasil*, or in some references the *Hagal*, and travelled through different worlds. During his spiritual mission, he also found the runes, an ancient alphabet, which was considered one of the mainstays of the world's creation. Similarly, the Kabbalists regarded the Hebrew letters, which also corresponded to numbers, to be milestones on the journey through the Tree of Life.

I was struck by the illustrations in that chapter. They showed how both alphabets were derived from the hexagonal shapes. The snowflake-like shape was the basis for the runic alphabet, while the hexagram was the basis for all the Hebrew letters. On the last page of the book, Turi noted down his impressions:

*I suppose that knowledge is like an alphabet. Before you learn to read, you see only symbols, but once you become acquainted with these symbols individually as well as their meaning as a whole, then you can learn to read and write, to receive and share information.*

Something within me kept calling out: You already know the truth! But whenever my consciousness tried to grasp it, it faded back into nothingness. Turi had years to pore over the subject in peace and solitude, but I didn't have as much time. Moreover, I was too consumed with worry about him.

As I looked back at the ceiling and at the Tree of Life, and at the two hexagons with seven circles, and the concealed hexagrams and pentagrams within it, I was put in mind of the *Seven Seraphim* and the *Seven Palaces*. I wondered whether they could help me.

I reached into my cape pocket for the picture that I

had been carrying with me ever since Atarah had given it to me. It was the one that my parents blessed for me, the one that depicted the Seven Rays of the Seven Seraphim. I asked them for help, and soon after, an idea entered my mind. I should go to the wild woodlands, and ask Atarah for help. Although I knew she would be unwilling to tell me how the Merkaba devices worked, I had to try to persuade her, as it could be the fastest way to reach Turi.

✡

On my way to the wild woodlands, I mused over Turi's findings. Everything had led to the point at which I gave up – the Tree of Life. I thought back to what Atarah used to tell me about it, how she encouraged me to figure out its mysteries on my own. *The key to the world is the key to your self, and the key to your self is the key to the world,* she used to say.

One windy day, she sat me beneath an old oak tree, and encouraged me to concentrate on its stillness. I embraced the strong, old trunk, aligning my heartbeat with the melodic sound of the creaking wood. It reverberated through me, guiding me to focus on my inner sight, as I was taught to do. Besides the colourful emotions my heart was giving out, I focused on my body, and considered how my veins resembled the tree branches. With that idea, I opened my eyes, and turned to Atarah.

"We resemble trees. Is that what you're trying to teach me?"

She shrugged, and coaxed me back to focusing on the tree. The vision of its twisted, strong roots was encouraging me to fall to the ground, while the solid, powerful trunk was drawing me up to the sky. Somewhere in between heaven and earth, I observed the tree branches moving in the wind, and enjoyed the gentle, constant movement.

All of a sudden, the treetop distorted. It expanded and withdrew, as though taking a deep breath in and out. I considered it normal at first, and marvelled at how the sky behind it seemed to be fluid, like water. Then, my rational mind took over, and I realised that it wasn't possible for a tree to distort like that, neither was it common for the sky to appear fluid. With that thought, fear sneaked in, and I could no longer understand how it could have seemed ordinary to me before. I told Atarah about it, and she said:

"Don't be afraid of such visions, Seraphina, they put our reality into perspective. Consider this instead, my dear: Do we see a tree because it exists or does it exist because we see it? *The shape is not everything, but it holds a key to what everything is.* Everything is connected by vibration, light and sound. If you move, see and listen with an open mind, you will feel how everything in this world is changeable, yet all following the same patterns. As below, so above, as within, so without... The wisdom is all around and inside of us.

"Some religions in Prague's reality believe that God banished us from paradise after Eve ate from the Tree of Life, but the ancient legends in our realm claim that we were the ones who banished God. We became blind to the paradise. It was because we recognised what the Tree of Life was and became our own gods. The consequences were tragic in some cases while in others quite the opposite. Some people dismissed their creator, but others created themselves, with gratitude to their creator.

"However, the majority split from the worlds above and below, from the Earth's core as well as the universe... And ever since, most have been striving to return home. The wise ones knew all along, though, that the key to the world is the key to your self, and the key to your self is the key to the world.

The Tree of Life is within us, in our codes and our bodies, as well as in the worlds which branch from The World."

The World, I repeated in my mind, thinking about the final Tarot trump.

"How many worlds are within the Tree of Life, Atarah?"

"Infinite, Seraphina, infinite…" she was musing over the word *infinite*, I could tell. She did that whenever she repeated a certain word.

"Some of these worlds are completely alien to us, some are connected," she said after a long pause. "It depends whether you exist by the roots, in the trunk or on the branches.

"Our ancestors knew about this, which is why they were able to pass only the thresholds that connected us with the realms vibrating on a similar level. They compared themselves to trees living in an ever-expanding Tree of Life, and that wisdom kept their Merkabas alive."

The memory verified the knowledge I had obtained in the House at the Last Lantern. Everything sprung from the same source, and to the same source it returned. Like the breath, like the light, like the endless pluses and minuses pouring from the initial zero…

Enthusiasm flared within me before the same old questions silenced it: What should I do with the information? What does it mean with regard to the Merkaba and the Merkaba devices?

I felt that I should find the answers *within* rather than *without*. It was probably more about the *state of mind* than the *state of things*, and with that thought, another memory surfaced.

I was standing at my parents' graves with tears in my eyes, being comforted by Atarah.

"Remember what I told you about the Tree of Life? Though they might not be on the same branch with you anymore, trust that they are only a few branches away. Don't ever worry about losing those you love. Just remember that we are all on the same Tree of Life."

The love I felt at that moment felt bittersweet. I sensed their presence and, although I didn't see or hear them, I wondered whether I could have for a moment felt their unity in the ever expanding tree.

With those memories in mind, I asked myself whether it was the mind or the heart that could unlock the secret door to the Tree of Life and the Merkaba, and came up with only one answer – it should be the bridge between the two.

# Chapter XIII

## Death

Before I even reached the riverside cottage, I met Atarah on one of her long, contemplative walks. She welcomed me with a warm, motherly embrace, but she also seemed nervous, which was unusual for her.

"You came at the right time," she said, "I have just had a connection with the Seven Seraphim. They delivered a confusing message... apparently, Turi is in some kind of trouble."

I turned to her, speechless, wondering where to start. I could sense that Atarah was scanning my emotions, and when she was done, she exhaled.

"What happened?"

I took a breath to summon up my courage.

"He crossed over to Prague's reality," I muttered.

Atarah stared into nowhere for a moment. I scanned her heart for a change, and detected distress, disappointment and angst.

"So he has really figured it out on his own... I suppose he must have been ready... or was he? No, he couldn't have been..." she muttered, before turning to me again. "Why did you let him go without consulting me first?"

I was avoiding eye contact, feeling responsible and ashamed.

"It all happened too fast. He assured me that he would be safe because his intentions were pure. I wasn't thinking straight when he told me, we haven't seen each other for so long and... well, it was only after he had gone that I realised I should have done or said something to stop him..." I paused before confirming what she probably knew already: "I'm so worried about him now."

"So you should be," she interrupted, "the price that you pay to pass over is high."

I held my breath in apprehension, my voice barely audible when I asked:

"What do you mean?"

She gave me one of those intense stares she had mastered so well. It never scared me, only encouraged me to take her more seriously.

"When introducing you to the mission of the threshold custodians, I stressed that the mission was to guard the Merkaba devices, not to use them."

"True, but we never understood why."

"Because you considered it a fairy tale."

She thought something over before she continued speaking: "You have to realise that in bygone times, when the Merkaba devices were constructed, people functioned on a different level. They were far more mentally and spiritually advanced than we are today. Some were led astray, that is true, but we have been trying to preserve the work of those who stayed true to their initial aim – connecting realities which co-exist on similar levels of consciousness.

"In the countless realities in and on the Tree of

Life, Prague's was the closest and most familiar to ours. Those who were awakened to their Merkaba used to travel between the two realities even before the Merkaba devices were invented. They exchanged their findings and insights with the locals. Back then it was safe, as they were in completion, in harmony with the Tree of Life. It's quite simple to use the devices and cross over, the problem is losing yourself on the way."

"I don't follow," I said, baffled by all this new information.

Her eyes became gentler, as she realised that she was about to share some painful truths with me.

"Once on the other side, you lose access to your past, to all your memories."

The words struck at my heart. "You have never told me that."

"I know, I'm sorry, but I had to keep it a secret from you. Only threshold custodians learn about this. That's the law." She stroked my arm and continued explaining, "Once someone has passed through the heart monitoring, and they are allowed to cross over, they lose all memory of their past. It's an intentional flaw in the system. That is how our ancestors protected the thresholds, and avoided exposure."

The memory loss was even more worrying than the reality Turi had travelled to. I hadn't imagined that there would be so many obstacles between us from then on. The worst of it, however, was that he had known this all along and decided to leave anyway.

"So Turi knew about this," I stated rather than asked.

"He did, but he believed that the flaw in the system could be overcome by a persistent spirit."

"I can't believe that he risked so much," I whispered, distractedly.

Atarah watched me with a concerned frown, and after a moment said:

"He once told me that he could never forget you, that you would be the first person he would recall."

The words brought me back from my forlorn state of mind. Atarah gave me a sympathetic smile, which made me wonder:

"What exactly did you learn from the Seraphim?"

"Not much."

She shrugged, gazing into the distance, in a way that usually meant she was recalling a vision, feeling, or a celestial message. "Just that some woman is involved, an aggressive woman devoted to her cause. She wants to know how the Merkaba devices work without finding the path on her own."

"Turi told me about her," I admitted, "she's Berta, the air threshold custodian in Prague. Turi seemed to be quite taken with her, though they hardly know each other. I sensed that she was the main reason for his sudden departure."

The news alarmed Atarah even more. "Then it's worse than I thought. She must have been using him for information, you know how clever and well-read Turi is."

"And how gullible," I added.

"We can only hope he hasn't shared his findings with her," said Atarah, and prompted me to follow her.

"Come, Seraphina, we need to talk this through in peace and quiet."

I followed her, trying to recall what Turi had told me about Berta. I had had a bad feeling about her from the start, and grew angry with myself for not telling him so. I wished he had been less impetuous, and given me more time to think it all through.

"Why was he in such a damn hurry?" wondered Atarah, reading my mind as usual.

"It might have been partly because of Lavi," I

admitted. "He had seen us together, and had notified the authorities. They came to capture Turi at the Air Dance Academy."

Atarah's composed face made me anxious. Her stillness always made me more nervous than her rage. It never foretold anything good.

"Have you told Lavi about us?" she asked with a steely edge to her voice.

"No, of course not. I never told anyone, like I promised. Lavi assumed Turi was aligned with magic because he wore the threshold custodian cape. Lavi never knew anything, he was just jealous and imprudent."

"Good," said Atarah with a sigh of relief, "but you can't return to Pryaya now. They might figure out the connection between us all."

This gave me the courage to finally blurt out why I had come to her.

"I can't stay here, not if he's in danger."

Atarah searched my solemn, defiant face, and shook her head, as resolute in her decision as I.

"You know very well that I can't let you follow him."

"You can, and should," I insisted. "We can't leave him alone in a tough, unfamiliar realm with no memories to cling to and a shady woman by his side."

"I may sound cruel now, but I think he deserves it," argued Atarah." He should have been more cautious. I won't let you suffer because of his mistakes."

I couldn't hold my temper when it came to Turi's safety.

"You taught me to think for myself, Atarah. Remember?"

"Of course. So please, do think for yourself, Seraphina," she encouraged. "Take time to consider this. How could you help him without even remembering him? Also, he might not be in as much trouble as you think. I know that you worry about losing him, but what if this trip was meant to be? What if it's his destiny? You know well enough that he lives for his research, he always longed to cross over."

Atarah was right, yet I couldn't imagine letting it go, and simply staying behind, hoping he would return some day. I had tried that before.

"I can't go on living as if nothing happened, Atarah. Although I became used to not seeing him, at least he was always close by. It might be selfish, but I don't want us to be apart anymore."

I searched my mind in despair, trying to come up with a solution. Atarah reached for my hands, conveying her empathy.

"He will come back, my dearest, I can sense it. There must be another way for you to deal with this situation in the meantime."

I shook my head, indomitable.

"Another way? You mean the true Merkaba? You said it could take hundreds of lifetimes before one awakens to it."

"That doesn't have to be, particularly if Merkaba is your destiny."

I locked eyes with her, imploring her to help me.

"Atarah, you know this is not just about me. What if he inadvertently exposes our secret? We need to do something."

She sighed, and her thoughts seemed to trail off. We stood there in silence, trying in vain to come up with a better plan, while the twilight embraced us.

✡

It took some time to convince Atarah to help me, but I managed to in the end. It was thanks to the

Seven Seraphim. After she had asked them for advice, they gave her a sign of luck in the figure of three shooting stars, and thereby blessed the journey I had decided upon.

The following night, Atarah prepared me for the crossing. She wrote a letter, which described my past and future mission, and placed it beside an already prepared set of Tarot cards.

"If everything fails, and all of the thresholds are destroyed, the Merkaba will be your only way back home. Do you remember what I told you about the Tarot's Major Arcana's connection to the Merkaba?" She took the cards out of the paper box, and sorted them into pairs.

"The main theme is a journey from oneness to wholeness. It happens via duality, the two pillars that hold up the threshold. That is why these twenty-two cards work in pairs."

She set the Fool and the Magician cards on top, the High Priestess and the Empress on the left side, the Emperor and the Hierophant on the right. The Lovers and Chariot were placed on the right side below the previous two cards, and the Justice and the Hermit on the left. After the Wheel of Fortune and the Strength cards were placed on the bottom, I realised that Atarah had created a hexagon.

She continued with the rest of the cards, positioning them in pairs in the same way until they formed two hexagons on top of each other:

I realised that their unity resembled Pryaya's symbol of the Tree of Life, and shared my thoughts with Atarah.

"Yes," she nodded with an approving smile, "that is what I'm trying to show you. The duality of the Tarot's Major Arcana has an important connection to the two hexagons in the Tree of Life – one above, one below." She pointed at the cards which separated as well as joined the two hexagons – the Wheel of Fortune and Strength. Then she moved her palm over to the two cards below – the Hanged Man on the left and Death on the right.

"Here is where the biggest change occurs. This is the step during which you embark on the journey to descend in order to ascend."

*Descend to ascend*. The two words reminded me of Turi's research.

"If all goes well," said Atarah, "this is when you should awaken to your past fully, and may begin the journey back to our world."

"You mean that my journey to Prague will correspond to the Tarot?" I guessed, intrigued by the thought.

"Exactly. In one way or another, all journeys in all kindred realities correspond to these twenty-two trumps, including the journey that guides you during your awakening to the Merkaba."

As I observed the two hexagons made up of the twenty-two cards, many things began to coalesce in my mind, and I mused aloud:

"When I was at the House at the Last Lantern, I went through Turi's research, and was surprised to find out that the Merkaba device is connected to the hexagonal shapes, as well as the Tree of Life."

"Yes, my dearest, that is how the machines were constructed," confirmed Atarah. "They align the Tree of Life geometry with that of our codes. Their mechanism reads the sacred codes in your blood, breaks you into tiny light particles, and puts you back together on the other side. You simply prick your feet with a needle, and stand barefoot in the middle."

"Is that it?" I exhaled in disbelief. "Is that the big secret? The mystery which Turi spent seven years of his life studying?"

Atarah nodded, concerned by my reaction. I didn't know whether to laugh or cry. It seemed too easy, too obvious.

"That's why he left his shoes behind," I thought out loud, "and the drops of blood on the floor... I thought he was injured..."

Atarah shrugged. "Sometimes the easiest is the

hardest to find," she said, "mainly when we complicate things in our minds."

"Maybe it's like that with the Merkaba, perhaps we are missing something very simple?"

Atarah agreed. "Most definitely."

Sadness consumed her as she put the cards back into the box. I could tell she was afraid for me, and I understood why. If I were in her shoes, I would also struggle to let me go.

"The Tarot is in case you lose the letter," she said, placing the card box into a scarf bag along with a cup, a branch and a pebble with an engraved Tree of Life. "These objects represent the Tarot suits, as well as the thresholds and their alignment with the basic elements," she explained. "The cup is for the water, the branch for the fire, the pebble for the ground, the scarf for the air and the Tarot for the ether or the Merkaba."

I accepted the gift with deep gratitude. "Thank you, Atarah, you are so kind and thoughtful."

"It's not just a gesture, Seraphina, this will be a crucial treasure to you on the other side. Our subconscious works in miraculous ways. Sometimes a symbol makes us remember more than the spoken word. It's a universal language, one that speaks straight to your heart."

Before she handed me the scarf bag and the letter, she grasped my hands with a serious expression.

"I must warn you about one last thing, Seraphina. It's not only our memories that we lose once we cross over to the other reality. A part of us always dies along the way, a part that may be difficult to retrieve. It could be a part of your personality, your plans, desires, values. Things will never be the same after you set foot upon that device…"

I took a deep breath and gathered my courage.

"So be it. I'm ready."

"Are you one hundred per cent certain about

this?"

She searched my face, hoping to see me waver.

"I am," I affirmed. "I couldn't live with myself if I stayed."

Atarah closed her eyes in disappointment. Although she tried her best to remain positive, I could see that she was scared for me. The parting was difficult for both of us. Our hearts ached at the uncertain future that lay ahead.

I still couldn't believe that I was about to follow such an adventurous path. A few days ago, I had pictured myself as an ordinary citizen in Pryaya, establishing my air-dancing career, perhaps starting a family, but all the dreams that I had been living for had vanished along with Turi. The road ahead had become blank, dark and dangerous, yet still I wanted to walk it. Had I not done it, I would never have forgiven myself. I couldn't help Turi when we were younger, and I had lost touch with him because of it, but now I was ready to set that right.

At the time when night meets the dawn, we walked to the riverbank. The moon was starting a new cycle, so the sky was darker than usual. Atarah deemed it a fortunate sign, which indicated a new beginning, while I secretly worried that it was a dark omen.

The Merkaba device was concealed underneath a pile of sand and mud. We dug it away, and revealed a round shaped stone, which resembled a fluorescent quartz crystal. It was a perfectly crafted technological device, something that would soon tear me apart and, hopefully, put me back together again on the other side. I focused on the engraved Tree of Life symbol, wishing I could keep it in my mind, so that it could be my guidance on the other side.

Atarah handed me a needle that she had blessed under the moonlight, and pricked my feet in a few places.

"Do you think there's any hope that Turi will remember me?" I asked.

"I believe so wholeheartedly, Seraphina, love is stronger than anything." Her voice was tearful, and so were her eyes. Touched by her selfless support, I leaned into her arms. In a tight embrace, we prayed to the Seven Seraphim for each other's safety. We couldn't be certain when we would reunite, or if at all, but neither of us had the strength to think about it.

"In Prague's reality, the threshold may be in the river itself," warned Atarah, "I hope you'll be alert, careful not to lose your belongings."

She pulled herself together, and hurried me over to the Merkaba device. I was surprised at first, but soon understood why. She feared that the longer we lingered on the shore, the more she would feel like stopping me.

I took one last glance at Atarah, our home, the starry sky, and carried onwards, resolutely confronting my fate. For a split second, everything burst into overwhelming, whirling white light and an indescribable sound. The last thing I heard was Atarah's voice, calling out:

"Remember that no matter what happens, you will always have your Merkaba!" *Remember*, I repeated in my mind with complete concentration, you must *remember*.

The next thing I knew, I was standing in the wild waters of Vltava, my mind as blank as an empty sheet of paper.

# Chapter XIV

## Temperance

Somewhere between the Seraphina of Pryaya and the Seraphina of Prague, the new me had awoken. Charged with the newly found information about my past, I turned over one of the Tarot cards from Pryaya, and jotted down what I considered the most important points:

*The hexagonal and pentagonal patterns – the Tree of Life – the Wheel of Fortune – the wheels of the Merkaba – the wheels of Tarot – the journey of the Fool – the journey from oneness to wholeness via duality.*

Then, in more haste, I scribbled:

*Berta – threshold custodian, sought information from Turi, wanted to know how the Merkaba devices worked.*

I felt overwhelmed after the long, adventurous night, and was going to finally lie down when I noticed an unmarked letter on the windowsill. Curious, I opened the window and reached for the simple note, which read:

*Meet me At the White Angel as soon as possible.*

I presumed that the message must have been either from Turi or Oliver, and it sounded urgent, so there was no time to procrastinate. I wrapped myself in Vilma's woollen poncho, and snuck out, trying not to wake her.

As I hurried to the house, I stumbled upon Oliver with a petite, blonde lady by his side. Her furtive, deep brown eyes scrutinized me as I stared at them in consternation. You would think that I would be used to seeing Oliver with one of his female friends by now, but I could tell this one was different. Judging by the look on her face, she felt possessive of him. Then I spotted the familiar, guilty look on Oliver's face, and realised that, for some reason, he had been hiding her from us all along.

"Miss Seraphina. What brings you here so early!" he exclaimed a little theatrically.

"Hello, Oliver," I answered, baffled and uncertain about how to behave. Oliver kept up his casual charm, although I could tell that he was just as uncomfortable with the encounter as I was. Luckily for me, he didn't let the situation become too awkward.

"Let me introduce you, ladies," he said, "Clara, this is Miss Seraphina, my neighbour from the Narrow Street."

"Oh, that shabby old house of yours," she noted with a teasing smile, "the one you use for sleeping off your pub visits?" From the distrustful look she gave me, it was obvious that she knew about Oliver's darker side. I understood. To love a man like him couldn't have been easy.

"And Miss Seraphina, this is Clara, my fiancé." The word *fiancé* came so unexpectedly that my reaction must have shown on my face.

"That's wonderful news," I smiled at them both

while shaking Clara's gloved hand, "congratulations!"

"News? We have been engaged for many years," she said, giving Oliver a bewildered scowl, whose guilt had intensified. He smiled at us both, though, trying his best to cover up his discomfort. I didn't know why it came as such a surprise to me, or why it had upset me. Everything suddenly began to make sense… his odd living arrangements, the strange remarks, and the nervous glances around when we met in public. I supposed he wasn't as sure about the relationship as Clara was.

Wanting to escape the uncomfortable situation I had found myself in, I spluttered, "I… I just came to…"

Just as uneasy, Oliver interrupted me.

"Miss Seraphina, this might be a misunderstanding. It's my fault, I have never explained…"

I held my breath, hoping he would not make it even worse, but thankfully he took a different approach. "See, this is my parents' old apartment. I stay here occasionally, but I live elsewhere now."

"In an apartment we shall both move to after our wedding," added Clara, and we exchanged a polite smile.

It took me a while to grasp why he had lied; he was hiding the fact that he occasionally stayed at the apartment. I guessed it was a love nest, which he used for his other female friends.

"I must have misunderstood indeed," I nodded, unable to hide the irritation in my voice.

"It's quite understandable," said Clara, ostensibly upset yet trying to remain calm. "It's easy to find yourself confused when it comes to Oliver's properties." She stroked his bow tie, making it clear that she had him wrapped around her finger. Oliver turned to me with an apologetic smile. I wasn't looking for his sympathy though. As if I needed to be pitied!

I wanted to come up with a clever response, something that would make me feel better, but my mind went blank. I was painfully aware that I was no good with lies or pretensions. Fortunately, however, someone had come to my rescue.

"Seraphina!"

My heart skipped a beat when I heard the voice. There he was in all his glory, the one I risked everything for, the one I yearned to find all along.

The White Angel statue hovered above him with a joyous smile, reflecting the elation in my heart.

"Turi!"

Having now remembered most of our backstory, and the strong bond we shared, he was no longer just an enigmatic stranger. I hugged him tightly, appreciating the reunion after all the unfortunate separations we had been through.

"I'm so glad you're back," I whispered in his ear. His affectionate embrace made me believe that he felt the same. As usual, everything and everyone became insignificant when Turi was near, so I had forgotten all about Oliver and Clara. It was only when he pulled away and turned to them, that I noticed the puzzled faces.

"Hello. You're Fabian's childhood friend, right?" said Turi with a friendly smile. Oliver nodded, then turned to me, with a raised eyebrow. I realised how strange it must have seemed to him, since last time Turi and I met, we were just strangers.

"Nice to see you again," he said to Turi, and then turned to his fiancé with the words: "We should go, Clara, your parents will worry if we're late."

As Clara and Oliver set off with courteous goodbyes, Turi hurried me inside the house.

"I'm sorry, Seraphina, we have to meet later on. You should go home now."

"Wasn't the note from you?"

"Yes, but I can't talk now." He spoke fast, with occasional glances upstairs.

"I don't understand. Why have you come down to meet me then?"

"I saw you from the window, and came to warn you," he paused, with a mischievous grin. "Well, I also wanted to save you from that uncomfortable situation."

"What do you…" I faltered, as we both knew what he meant. He smirked, and with another nervous glance upstairs, said:

"It's all right, I understand. I'll come to you later on tonight, I promise. Now please go. It's not safe for you to be here."

He patted my arms to comfort me and set off. Watching him leave always stirred something within me, no matter what the reason was. I had been waiting too long and too patiently, so I ran after him.

"Wait! I had so many memories while you were gone."

Turi gestured at me to be quiet, but it was too late. A determined looking woman appeared on the stairs. I recognised that angelic face with piercingly cold eyes. It was Berta.

"Why don't you invite your friend upstairs, Turi?" she suggested as she walked down to meet us. I watched her descend in astonishment. Her grace and allure only increased my anxiety. I didn't have to be a man to understand how easy it would be to fall head over heels for someone like her. I could also imagine, though, why Turi distrusted her even without knowing what I did. There was a dark edge to her charm.

"Hello, I'm Berta."

I shook her outstretched hand, but had a feeling that I shouldn't share my name with her. Turi shot me a warning glance which confirmed my decision.

Berta's eyes narrowed.

"Have we met before?"

Turi responded for me. "I don't think so."

She shook her head, thinking about it.

"Oh, I remember!" she exclaimed. "You're the girl who was curious about the lodge. Oliver's friend." Turi and I exchanged looks. His face clearly showed his panic, particularly when confronted by someone as sharp as Berta.

"So how do you two know each other?" she asked.

"Oliver introduced us," said Turi, brightening with a sudden idea. He cleared his throat, and added shyly, "he recommended the lady's services."

I turned to him in shock, while Berta weighed up whether to believe him or not.

"You mean she's a…" Turi quickly nodded to stop her from elaborating.

"I'm not proud of it, but I sought her out. She was kind enough to wait for her payment." He paused, his voice trembling a bit. "I owe her for one night."

After a moment of studying him, Berta's lips curved into a grin. She was either amused by his efforts at lying or by what he had admitted to. Nonetheless, at least he had come up with an excuse. His face pleaded with me to support the story, so I did and even took revenge by spicing it up a bit.

"You owe me for two nights actually," I said.

Berta reached in her overcoat pocket and pulled out a small, embroidered wallet.

"All right, let's settle this to avoid any more embarrassment. How much do you need?"

I wasn't sure how to respond, having no idea how much a midnight lady's services would cost. Turi nervously blurted out:

"Thirty crowns."

"Thirty?" She gave Turi a reprimanding look. I was taken aback as well. It seemed to be an extortionate price. "We should keep you on a tighter leash, my friend!" she exclaimed playfully while reaching into her wallet.

"Thank you, Berta," said Turi, and stroked her arm. "I'll stop borrowing from you as soon as I settle down."

"Ah, don't mention it, darling," she purred, then turned to me with the words, "Here you go, miss."

She gave me ten crowns instead of thirty. I hesitated whether to accept the money or not. Turi gave me an encouraging nod, so I did.

"Just take your business elsewhere next time." Without even looking my way, Berta returned to Fabian's apartment. She didn't close the door, expecting Turi to follow her. He gave me an apologetic smile, and whispered, "I'll see you soon."

I couldn't bring myself to reply. I remained standing there with the money in my hands, unable to digest this series of surreal encounters.

As I made my way out, the main door swung open. Fabian burst in, heading for the stairs. He didn't see me, as he was upset, absorbed in his thoughts. In a panic, I hid behind the large wardrobe in the hallway, and let him pass by.

After he had barged into the apartment, I realised what must have changed Turi's plan. He and Berta were probably supposed to be away, but had surprised Turi with their sudden return. Deciding to eavesdrop on their conversation, I snuck over to the door, and peeked inside through the keyhole.

I saw Berta standing in the centre of an affluent apartment with her arms crossed, watching Fabian, who was heading straight for the drinks cabinet. He poured himself a glass of brandy, gulped it down in one, and reached for more. Turi looked apprehensive, and even more so when Fabian said:

"I took care of the situation."

Berta embraced him from behind, caressing his

arms for comfort.

"That's good, honey, it was for the best."

He flashed her an accusing, irritated glance.

"I hope so! For all our sakes."

Turi watched him in disbelief, obviously perturbed about something. Fabian gulped more brandy, striding back and forth across the room. He stopped with a look at Turi.

"Stop giving me those judgmental stares. Would you rather have us go down because of his big mouth? It was the right thing to do," he assured himself, "I had no other choice."

Turi shook his head. "They will know who did it. They won't let it be."

Fabian approached him threateningly, but Turi remained calm, keen to avoid a physical confrontation. He was smarter than that. Berta reached for Fabian's hand, and tried to pacify him.

"We must simply act faster than we had planned. Maybe it's a good thing." She placed her hands on his shoulders, gently massaging them. Fabian closed his eyes for a moment then squinted at Turi.

"If only he could remember!"

From the look the two men had exchanged, it was clear that they mistrusted each other. I was trying to understand why, and what they were talking about. Had someone found out about Turi's origin or the Merkaba devices? As I ruminated on it, a gentle voice startled me.

"What are you doing here, miss?"

Absorbed in my spying, I had forgotten all about my surroundings. That's why it came as such a surprise when I beheld an old lady leaning over the handrail on the upper floor. I jumped away from the door, and headed for the stairs.

"Unheard-of rudeness! You, miss, have no manners!" she called after me as I fled from the building, worried about being caught by Fabian or

Berta.

I hurried up Nerudova towards the New World, but sensed that someone was watching me. Hastily, I turned around, and spotted Berta in the upstairs window, half of her face hidden behind a curtain. The vision sent chills down my spine, because I had a feeling that she didn't believe one word of the story Turi had made up to protect me.

☆

On my way home, I noticed Oliver loitering around Vilma's house, deep in thought. He seemed relieved when he spotted me.

"Thank God, Seraphina!" he called out, "I was worried that I would have to wait till evening."

Despite my curiosity, I was too upset to listen to him. "I'm a bit busy now, Oliver, you'll have to excuse me." I headed for Vilma's, planning to wait for Turi there. Oliver walked with me, though, eager to explain his situation.

"I'm sorry I didn't tell you about Clara," he said.

"It's all right. You weren't obliged to."

I continued walking, unwilling to slow down on his account.

"I don't usually talk about her. See, she is.."

I jumped in, unable to cope with his fumbling apologies. "You don't owe me any explanation whatsoever, Oliver."

"I do." He blocked my path resolutely. "For my own peace of mind."

With a frustrated frown, I bent my head in assent. Oliver gave a deep sigh of relief before he began speaking.

"Clara and I have been engaged since we were children. It's an arranged marriage. I like her, even love her in a way, but as you know, I'm not fond of the responsibilities that love brings. I prefer my bachelor way of life. I wish I could change it, I have tried for years, but I suppose there's something seriously wrong with me. I worry that I would torture my wife with scandals and love affairs," he wavered, then corrected himself, "perhaps *lust affairs* would be more fitting, as most of the times, love is not even in the game."

"Please, Oliver," I stopped him, vexed and tired, "this is not necessary. I don't care about your love or lust life."

He moved in front of me and stopped.

"You don't have to care, but I need you to hear this," he said solemnly, boring his eyes into mine, making me focus on him. It could have been my gift for reading emotions or just plain intuition, but either way, I knew he was sincere when he said:

"I had never truly befriended a girl until I met you. You are one of the rare ones. I wanted you to know that, Seraphina. That is why I'm so sorry that I wasn't honest with you earlier. I didn't want to ruin this wonderful connection we have. Particularly not by trying something… Well, something that I would be beaten for by Vilma."

I felt my cheeks flush.

"Thank you for your confession, Oliver, but there's really no need for you to worry. Nothing has changed between us."

"Are you sure about that?"

His eyes felt hypnotic when they searched my face. I nodded.

"All right, good. Now, I'm too intrigued to let this go. Are you romantically involved with the man you were so keen to see last time?"

"I wasn't keen. I was curious."

"Is there a difference?"

Once again, he made me smile.

"Is he decent?" he asked. I shrugged.

"It turned out that we have known each other for a very long time. That's all I can tell you."

"I hope he's better than me."

I tilted my head. "Why are you being so hard on yourself all of a sudden?"

He grinned. "I'm not. I'm as selfish as they come."

I didn't have to agree with that aloud because as always, he read me like an open book.

"Since you have done so much for me, and I am eternally grateful, I'll do you a favour," I said impishly, "I won't tell Vilma about this."

Oliver laughed, and we both stood there for a moment, silently saying goodbye. Somewhere deep inside I felt that it wasn't just one of those 'see you soon' goodbyes, and the thought rattled me. As much as I didn't like to admit that I had feelings for him, I knew I had to make peace with the idea sooner or later. There was no point in fighting it. The more I struggled with it, the worse it became.

So I planted a brisk kiss on his cheek, and strode off, before I tried to kiss him somewhere else. I sensed that he was looking after me, and was tempted to turn around, but once I had crossed the threshold into Vilma's house, the urge slowly subsided. I focused on Turi instead, who I used to struggle against as well. I was finally ready to put things right. There were no more boundaries within, so I hoped that those without would be easy to overcome.

✡

Once in the apartment, I was faced with another surprise. Hieronymus and Vilma were sitting opposite to each other over the kitchen table, holding hands. I had a knack for spotting unlikely couples that day. It couldn't have been a coincidence. Having finally realised that my journey to Prague was guided by all kinds of mysterious signs, I was eager to unravel this one as well.

"I'm sorry for disturbing you," I apologised, "I'll give you two some privacy."

I made for the main door, but Vilma called out:

"We need no privacy here!"

She seemed embarrassed, as did Hieronymus. After an awkward pause, he reached for his hat, saying:

"Please stay, Miss Seraphina. I was readying myself to leave."

"Are you sure? It's no trouble."

He stroked my arm for comfort. "No, I'm quite certain," he affirmed and started to put on his coat. "In fact, I stopped by to see you, Miss Seraphina, but then Vilma and I found ourselves deep in conversation…"

He grinned mischievously beneath his beard. Vilma's cheeks had turned scarlet, which made Hieronymus and I exchange smiles.

"Anyhow," he cleared his throat, "I wanted to ask whether you had had any more insights regarding your research."

"How kind of you to think of me, Hieronymus," I remarked playfully and, on a more serious note, added: "I had some insights indeed, but then I realised it might be best to leave them well alone."

Hieronymus seemed content with the answer. "That's wise, Miss Seraphina. Some things remain hidden in legends and fairy tales for a reason."

Vilma couldn't resist teasing him a bit. "Exactly. Take the wolf from the *Little Red Riding Hood* for instance. Who would want to invite him into their lives?"

"Well, maybe he would surprise you," he replied. "Some things are not as they seem. I once met a completely feral creature who turned out to be not so scary in the end. She has a sharp tongue, but her teeth are becoming weaker."

Vilma glowered. "What do you mean by *weaker*?"

He gave a cheeky grin. "Well, we are not growing any younger, are we?"

Vilma gave him a shove. I sensed that something beautiful had begun for her, and it made me so happy.

"Now shoo," she rushed him off then, "we need a break from this endless prattle of yours."

"Me, prattle? You prattle so much that don't pay attention to who is actually prattling."

I laughed at them both, and called out a cheery goodbye to Hieronymus before Vilma pushed him out of the door. I watched them parting through the window. Hieronymus reached for a kiss, but Vilma kicked him instead. He laughed, and rushed away, his beard shaking like a dusty curtain in the wind.

I chuckled to myself, but the joy faded as soon as I turned away. I felt so lonely all of a sudden. It was as though everyone had someone and I still had no Turi. Vilma noticed my change of mood when she returned.

"What happened?" she asked, concerned. "Are you all right? I hope it has nothing to do with Oliver?" I smiled at her perceptiveness, and shook my head.

"So, the other man? The one you can't talk about?"

I nodded. "It pains me not to be able to talk to my best friend about him, and about all that happened." I looked into her eyes, seeking forgiveness. "I'm sorry that I have been so distant."

"Ah, my dear girl!"

Vilma approached me briskly, and comforted me. "Shall I make us some chicory? It's getting chilly out there, let's sit by the fire."

She scuttled off to the kitchen. "Have you heard

the awful news?"

I shook my head.

"Hieronymus told me there's a big commotion in the Old Town. A man was found dead. They say it was murder."

I went after her, alarmed.

"Do they suspect anyone?" I asked, guessing it had something to do with what Fabian, Berta and Turi were discussing before.

"Yes, someone who was part of some esoteric society... I can't recall the name."

My heart began hammering in my chest. If Turi was associated with the one who did it, he might be in danger as well. I hoped he would come to me as soon as possible.

"Hieronymus said the victim was someone from some unknown esoteric lodge." Vilma emerged from the kitchen with two steaming cups – one silver and the other golden. They reminded me of the ever-struggling dualities. I gazed at them, afraid to lose Turi again. Vilma's knowing eyes saw right through me.

"Oh no, I sense love, hurt..."

"I'm scared for someone," I blurted out. "I wish I could listen to your advice, but I can't tell you anything. Perhaps just that the situation seems more dangerous than ever."

She sat beside me and asked, "What if I guessed? Would that be all right?"

"Let's not tempt fate, Vilma, I would rather have you safe. Why don't we speak about you and Hieronymus instead?"

"Ha!" she exclaimed. "Like there's anything to say about that!"

"Oh, please, the sparks between you two could have set the house on fire."

She shook her head. "I doubt my luck with men will change at this stage of my life."

"Who knows, maybe you have been waiting for a man like him your whole life long?"

"How lucky would I be, eh?" She laughed, and although I almost gave in as well, I smiled disapprovingly.

"He is certainly the most interesting man that I know."

"Well, you don't know many."

She laughed again, and this time I chimed in. After a moment's hesitation, I dared to ask:

"Have you ever been married, Vilma?"

She nodded. "He had many other women on the side, and finally left me for another. I don't like to talk about it, though. A divorced woman is worse than a spinster."

"Well, he doesn't know what he is missing."

She threw her hands up. "In retrospect, I'm happy that he left. It was not a good match. Besides, I'm happier on my own. Dora once told me that true marriage is that which happens within ourselves, and I agree with her. If you haven't balanced your own inner feminine and masculine sides, how can you expect to find harmony in a relationship? Also, I believe that if we find our true selves, we can never be lonely again." She paused. "I'm sorry to be preachy… I never had a daughter whom I could share this with, and I really like the idea."

"It is lovely. And wise."

I was touched that she had compared me to a daughter. I too felt as if she was my Prague's Atarah. Our closeness scared me, as I began to consider the possibility of going back to Pryaya. I knew I would have to make a decision at some point.

What would I say to Vilma, though? How could I leave her without any explanation? Also, she was counting on my help over the next few years. It was then that I noticed the red rose on the table. It filled my heart with comfort. I suspected that if I left,

Hieronymus would gladly take care of her for me. After all, starting a new life with someone in the New World seemed ideal.

☆

Vilma went to bed early that night, but I kept waiting for Turi. So as not to disturb her, I kept to myself in the kitchen like I had the previous night. I looked at the empty cups on the table waiting to be filled again in the morning. It made me think of the objects I had brought with me from Pryaya, and so I reached for them. While turning over the four gifts in my hands, I tried to reach back to the moment when I stood on the Merkaba device. I found it strange that I didn't recall the transition itself. Was it because it was as fast as light, I wondered, or was it a part of the intentional flaw? I wanted to remember. I had an inkling that if I could, I would be a bit closer to knowing how the Merkaba worked.

My eyes shifted to the clock. It was already past eleven. Restlessly, I reached for the Tarot trumps and vigorously shuffled them. While doing so, a card fell out. The Temperance. I observed the image. It depicted two cups, similar to those on the table. At that moment, I recalled what Atarah had told me before I left:

"The main theme is a journey from oneness to wholeness. It happens via duality, that is the main essence, the two pillars that hold the threshold up. That is why these twenty-two cards work in pairs."

On an impulse, I decided to place the cards down in pairs, in the pattern that Atarah taught me. While doing so, I contemplated Pryaya's Tree of Life – two of Prague's Kabbalistic Trees of Life combined – one above, one below. I admired how the two hexagons were united, balanced and in harmony, and wondered what would happen if I arranged the trumps in a circle.

As I did, all of a sudden, there was no first or last card. The end merged with the beginning, reminiscent of the eternal circle of life. The memory of Atarah's voice came to me reassuringly.

"Everything arises from and returns to the circle. That's what the card game is all about. The wheels within wheels keep spinning no matter the space, no matter the time, endlessly."

Curiosity pricked my mind. I supposed I was a part of that card game whether I was aware of it or not.

# Chapter XV

## The Devil

I was almost asleep, meditating on the meaning of the Tarot cards, when a noise from outside startled me. It sounded like stones being thrown against the window pane. I hoped it was Turi, so I quickly threw on Vilma's woollen poncho, and sneaked out into the depth of the night.

The early autumn chill wrapped me in its coldness as I looked up and down both sides of the street. I crossed my arms and walked to the street corner. There was no one, just the still, sleeping houses and restless trees, dark green with a few yellow leaves flickering in the wind. I sensed someone's presence close by, but knew that if it were Turi, he would certainly not hide in the dark.

A whiff of mud and autumn decay indicated that it was going to rain soon. I was about to head back inside when I noticed a female figure approaching me. I scrutinised her features, and recognised Berta. Her stern look and determined, brisk pace alarmed me. I froze on the spot.

"Hello," she said with a smirk.

"Hello," I answered timidly, unsure what to expect from her. The church bells struck three as she neared me and grabbed my hand. Her skin was cool and dry, and her grip felt like a shackle. My first reaction was to free myself, but what she then said stopped me in my tracks.

"Turi sent me. He wants me to bring you to him. He needs to speak with you. Follow me, please…"

My fear turned to curiosity.

"Why didn't he come himself?" As soon as I said it, I remembered that she had me for one of the midnight ladies, so I added: "And can he afford my services this time?"

Berta rolled her eyes. "Please, I know you are not who you pretend to be."

Caught off guard, I became speechless, and before I recovered, she was guiding me to the end of the street. There, I spotted a male figure waiting for us. I hoped it was Turi, but soon realised it was someone else, probably Fabian. That's when my instincts kicked in.

"Where is he?" I asked, unable to hide my growing anxiety. Berta still held on to my arm and said:

"Close by. He can't show his face around here anymore, but you will see him soon, don't worry."

I looked at her, then Fabian, who had begun to approach, and weighed up whether I should trust them or not. Their faces were unreadable, serious.

"Why can't he be seen?" I asked, sensing that it had something to do with the murder, which had happened earlier that day.

"He wants to tell you himself," said Berta, and motioned for me to come along. Despite sensing trouble, I followed them. Their company felt odder with each step. My instincts told me to run off, but worry about Turi suppressed them.

Then, I spotted a cloaked figure in the shadow of a vaulted building. It was my stalker, the earth threshold custodian. I had stopped fearing him since I learned more about his purpose. In fact, I deemed him less threatening than Fabian and Berta. Luckily, they didn't notice him as he pointed in the opposite direction. I assumed that he was either encouraging me to go that way instead, or showing me where Turi really was.

When Berta was a few steps ahead of me I took my chance, and set off in the direction that he had indicated. My Pryaya air-dancing skills must have made me fit, because I outran them easily. I dared not look back, but once I had almost reached Nerudova, I finally turned around.

The street seemed to be deserted, so I wavered about where my next steps should lead. They knew where I lived, so if I returned there, I would put Vilma in danger. If I crossed the street and aimed for Hieronymus's, then he could be the one whose safety was at risk. I decided to just keep going, praying I would meet Turi or the threshold custodian again.

After a moment, footsteps shattered the gentle silence. I caught a glimpse of a shadow looming over the damp, cobbled ground. I recognised Fabian's hat and sped up my pace. He didn't call after me or say anything, which only increased my fear. He was composed, confident, making me feel that my escape was futile.

I continued on my aimless path, looking for more leads, signs or signals. Each time I turned into another lane, he was there behind me. I looked for help on every corner, but didn't see anyone who looked trustworthy enough. Besides a few beggars and drunkards, the Lesser Town was empty.

As I neared the House at the Keys, I wished that Dora was still living in the area, so she could hide me at her apartment. Unfortunately, the buildings were boarded up, closed down due to the first demolition phase. Not far away, however, I spotted a few lit windows. It was a night pub, of the type that Vilma had advised me to avoid, but on this occasion I dashed towards it as though it were a beacon of hope.

An unpleasant odour struck me as soon as I stepped in – it was a blend of alcohol, sweat and smoke. The noisy room was crammed with men of all ages and classes, united in their love of drink and chat. I passed an old harmonica player whose music was more of a chaotic noise, and looked around in haste.

I panicked, trying to come up with an idea of what to do, where to hide.

Initially, nobody seemed to be paying any attention to me, but after a moment, a young man sitting nearby motioned for me to come over. He looked decent – not that drunk, well dressed, and most importantly, there was a big hooded coat on the chair beside him.

I hurried to grab the coat, and wrapped it around myself, hiding my face beneath the hood. The young man laughed at me, revealing his crooked, yellow teeth. Not that decent after all, I thought to myself.

"Is it that cold out there?" his voice was raspy, breath foul, but I caught no danger in his eyes so I asked, softly:

"Could I stay here for a moment, please? Someone is after me."

He embraced me with uncomfortable eagerness.

"Well of course! Would you like some beer?"

Without waiting for an answer, he pressed the cool glass against my lips. I took a sip, just to be polite, but froze at the sound of the door squeaking open.

Apprehensively, I peeked towards the entrance. Fabian strode in, still as hauntingly calm as before. I turned back to the young man, who gaped at me with a wide-open smile, and silently wished I could become invisible.

"How much?" he asked with a leer at my cleavage.

"Excuse me?" I didn't understand at first.

"How much do you charge per hour?"

I stared at him, finally grasping what he meant. Pretending to be a midnight lady seemed to be my fate, I thought to myself with a wry smile. Then, in all seriousness, I weighed up whether or not to play along. I knew that telling him to go to hell would be risky, while giving him a price would encourage him even more. In my peripheral vision, I spied Fabian looking around, diligently seeking me out. Struck by fear, I did the first thing that came to my mind. I embraced the drunk man in return. I remained enveloped by his sweaty vapour until I heard the door squeak again. Then I dared to check the entrance and every corner of the pub. He was gone. I decided that I should wait a moment before I left, to give him a head start.

When the man's hand landed on my collarbone, though, I realised that I had traded one sneaky demon for another. I slapped him recklessly in a rage. Luckily for me, the man was too surprised and drunk to react. I stood up, darted to the window, scanning the street outside. It seemed safe.

I took off the hooded coat, threw it back at its owner, and sneaked out through the sticky door. I couldn't believe my eyes when I spotted Fabian lurking in the shadow of the building opposite like a spider waiting for its prey. He took a step closer and said:

"Stop toying with us, miss, we just want to ask

you a few questions."

His change of purpose made him seem even more suspicious.

Without responding, I turned away, and rushed off at the same speed as before, heading towards the old bridge. For some reason, it seemed like a good idea to me. I thought that below it, I might find a decent hideout. If Fabian weren't so persistent, I would have managed to chase him off long ago, as he was much slower. I had no idea I could run so fast, and realised that I had never tried it in Prague. At times, I even felt as if my feet were rising above the ground, but it must have been just wishful thinking.

I sped along the so-called Devil's Channel, the artificial canal meandering between the houses in the Lesser Town. Vilma told me about the legend surrounding that place. It was named after a devious woman who once lived in the area. Most people considered it just a frightening tale, but judging from my experience, and what Hieronymus had told me, I too believed that sometimes legends were more than just fantasy.

I hid underneath the heavy, stone arch of the bridge to catch my breath. My gaze fell upon one of the small boats rocking in the cold wind. Although it was loaded with wooden boxes, there was still some room in the middle. A spontaneous idea came to me – what if I floated away into the night, and hid underneath the bridge? In haste and without thinking it through further, I proceeded to untie the boat.

I was ready to step aboard when all of a sudden a hand grabbed me and pulled me aside. It was Turi, his lip bloodied, eyes frenzied. He took off his overcoat and tossed it over the boxes in the boat, so that it resembled a hunched figure. He pushed it out onto the water, and let it float away.

Then he bustled me under one of the arched

recesses. We leaned against the wall in tension, awaiting our enemy. From behind the stones, I spotted Fabian and how he had reacted to Turi's trap. He stopped at the riverbank and stared at the boat, clenching his fists. It was evident that he fell for it, and was planning his next move. The street lamp illuminated his angry expression as he untied another boat, jumped inside, and followed the one he thought I was in.

Turi clasped my hand urgently, and we sped through the winding lanes, deeper into the Lesser Town. After a few more steps, we stopped by the entrance to a house, out of breath. As I looked again at his injury, my heart fell.

"What happened? Did Fabian do this to you?"

He nodded. "I had to flee. My suspicion was correct, Seraphina, they never intended to help me. I was so foolish to trust them…"

"I know that something bad had happened. I stayed and eavesdropped after you sent me home." I blurted out, unashamed.

"Then you know," he said, his expression grim.

"I assume," I corrected. Turi looked around, cautious and secretive.

"Fabian murdered someone who knew about the Merkaba devices," he whispered into the night. "I never thought he would go that far. He claims that he was trying to protect us, our mission. What an excuse, right? He's not the one in charge of the thresholds.

"The intentional flaw in the Merkaba devices used to bother me, but now I know how necessary it is. Thank God I couldn't tell them how to use it before I figured out their schemes. I thought I could trust Berta. I had her for a gifted, spiritual person. She claims she channels spirits and angels," he smirked at the thought, "but God knows what she channels instead."

A chill swept through me at the thought. I looked at the river that so eagerly lapped against the shore, and a strange presentiment washed over me.

"Berta suspects that you are more than just," he paused, weighing how to put it.

"A midnight lady?" I finished the sentence for him, my lips twisting into a smile. He half nodded, probably unfamiliar with that title, but smiled back. We stared at each other for a moment. In spite of the desperate situation, I felt the connection we had once shared seep through me. We had become our younger selves again, the boy and girl in a hideout, always on the run.

"I'm so sorry, Seraphina. I shouldn't have approached you back then, I should have protected you from this mess."

"Don't say that. We need each other. I came here for you, after all…"

He gave me a questioning look.

"I remembered why I came here while you were gone. It was because I was worried for you and because I never told you that…" I paused, gathering courage, "…that I loved you."

"I know. I love you too."

His tone was so brisk and casual that it made me wonder whether he had misunderstood me. Perplexed, I searched his dishevelled face, swollen bloody lip, messy hair, then focused on his hands that still clutched mine. I didn't know if I should elaborate, but before I had made up my mind, he continued speaking:

"You may think that you came here for me, Seraphina, but maybe the real reason you came here was to find a better life. You have established yourself so well in this society. Unlike me, you have a gift when it comes to that. On my trip, I remembered how well you were doing back in Pryaya… You were a star."

"Ah," I waved my hand, "that was just for one night, and not even that, thanks to you."

We smiled at each other, and became pensive, gazing down at the wild water. I couldn't decide what to do or say next, trapped in the wonderfully frustrating uncertainty that I had been struggling with ever since we first met.

A gust of strong, cold wind made me recover. I peeked at Turi from beneath my hair, watching his profile, the familiar angles and curves of his face. I longed to lean over and kiss him, but something held me back.

"What should we do now?" he asked.

I shrugged. "We could go over to my friend's place to discuss it in peace?"

"No," he interrupted resolutely. "If you care about your friend, stay away from her just now. Fabian and Berta only know the building where you live, not her, and it should remain that way."

"But what do they want from me?" I wondered. "Wasn't I just bait to lead them to you?"

"Unfortunately not. They suspect that you are from Pryaya as well, and that, unlike me, you remember how to use the Merkaba device."

"Which I do," I confirmed.

"You do?" he turned to me in astonishment. "Why didn't you tell me before?"

His brows were twitching. It was the worried twitch that I knew so well, but had only just remembered.

"I had so many memory dreams last night. It felt like many years, though it was just a few hours. The passing is so simple, Turi, it made me feel like a fool."

"Don't tell me," he stopped me in alarm. "It's for the better that only you know. At least for now..." He thought about it some more and said, "This changes everything... It means that we can go home!"

I weighed up our options and my feelings about it.

"I suppose we could, but since Berta is in charge of the air threshold in this realm, we could only use the earth threshold in the Fifth District or the water threshold."

"Did I share this with you in Pryaya or did you find out on your own?"

"What do you mean?"

"That Berta is the air threshold custodian here in Prague."

"You shared it with me. Atarah and I worried that she might be using you for information."

"It makes sense," he growled to himself. "I found out the truth only recently. I think she didn't tell me because she was afraid I would find out she had killed her colleagues, the other threshold custodians all except for the earth threshold one. I wonder why...

"She also seized the notebook that I crossed over with. She said it contained some important information and later claimed to have lost it. It must have contained all the findings on the Merkaba devices."

"But wouldn't it describe how to cross over as well?"

"I don't remember noting that down. I would never betray the threshold custodian code: You have to figure this out on your own when you are ready."

The thought made me sad. It reminded me of the heartbreak I felt after I learned that he had known about the memory loss and left me all the same. I wanted to tell him, but it wasn't a good moment.

"No matter what we do or where we go from now on, Seraphina," he said after a pause, "we should definitely leave the city. Even if Fabian is caught and imprisoned for the murder, Berta would never stop looking for us. She lives for the idea of travelling to Pryaya, like I used to…"

Turi's words trailed off at the sound of heavy footsteps on the wet cobbles. He instinctively covered me with his body, pressing me against the stone wall. His face was so close to mine that it made me hold my breath. I turned in the same direction as him, and saw a tall, hooded figure making for the narrow street that wound under the bridge, and led to the Old Town. It was the earth threshold custodian.

"He helped me earlier," I said as I looked after him, "I think he's on our side. Maybe we should ask him for advice?"

Turi narrowed his eyes. His body was still covering mine, his breath caressing my lips, making me nervous. I lost myself in the moment, secretly wishing I could stop time. I yearned to fulfil the strange need to absorb him, coalescence with him in body and spirit. The timing was never right, though.

Turi's soft nudge disturbed me from my reverie. He nodded up to the bridge, towards a female figure crossing the river at a brisk pace. It was Berta.

"Something is up," he whispered.

We looked at each other, confused and intrigued. We didn't need to say a word. We both silently agreed that we should follow them, and find out what was going on.

On the way across the river, we passed the pentagram lanterns below the statue of Saint Jan of Nepomuk. I remembered the encounter with the old light-bearer and realised that as then, I sensed that I was on the right path despite the seemingly impenetrable darkness ahead.

With that thought, another memory came to me. It was that of Atarah and I, standing on one of Pryaya's bridges, watching the crepuscular rays fall over the horizon.

"That is why sunlight is so important, Seraphina," she said, "fire is the only element that our bodies lack. We are made of earth, contain water, inhale and exhale air, but where's the fire? It makes you wonder whether the warmth and light of fire represents the spirit…

"Perhaps that is the reason why some fear fire and associate it with hell. Fire is necessary, but in moderation. While some may ignite the inner power of their spirit and burn brightly, others may burn things into ashes, and ultimately burn out… It all comes back to harmony and balance."

She turned to me then, her face beaming.

"Now, the name you were given begins to take on a whole new dimension, don't you think?"

# Chapter XVI

## The Tower

As we approached the Old Town, it began to drizzle. The enigmatic figure of the threshold custodian marched ahead without noticing us. He was either too absorbed in his thoughts, or was aware of us, and decided not to alarm us. We weren't scared of him anymore, as we knew he had the same mission as Turi, and we seemed to have mutual enemies as well.

After he crossed the Rudolf's footbridge, he aimed for the Fifth District. As we traipsed through the narrow lanes, I felt as though we had travelled back in time. I recalled the many times we had snuck in and out of the forbidden Magic Quarter, hatching some secret plan. Like then, Turi held my hand the whole time, keeping me close. It gave me courage and made me believe that no matter what had happened and what was to come, everything would be all right as long as we were together.

The church bells chimed four o'clock in the morning as we entered Josefova, one of the oldest streets in the Fifth District. By now, the place was even wilder than a month ago, before most of the locals had moved out. It had become a dark labyrinth of brothels and seedy pubs. Everything smelled of sewage, rot and decay and the cold, autumn damp didn't help. Despite its decline, it still had that special charm, though. Like in Pryaya, the quarter had magic.

At the corner of Narrow and Jáchymova lanes, we noticed that some of the buildings were already in the process of being torn down, along with fifteen buildings in Maisel Street, which neighboured the Old Town square. It was the first demolition stage. I only managed to catch a glimpse of the ruins, but it was enough for me. I dreaded the thought that what used to be the picturesque entrance to that quarter would soon become a pile of rubble. I agreed with Vilma in that regard, I didn't want to watch the soulful, ancient buildings slowly crumble. Perhaps I was too sensitive, but I thought of them as soulful beings with history and origins, and prayed for their peaceful passing.

I stopped when I saw a thin, medieval house that stood tall in the midst of destruction. I empathised with its emptiness and solitude. I felt the same way when I first entered the quarter – alone and desperate in the middle of a chaotic world I didn't recognise or understand.

"We've lost him," said Turi, as he spun round and scanned the small square we found ourselves in. In its centre stood a well with a cylinder-shaped roof, covered with newspaper clippings and bulletins. Over the latest news, Fabian's portrait was pasted, and above it, a big sign: *Wanted for murder*.

An anxious premonition overwhelmed me. I

sensed that Fabian was close by. My eyes searched the gloomy corners and piles of stone in a futile attempt to locate him. There was no sound except for the raindrops hitting the ground in a monotonous rhythm. Having scrutinised the space back and forth, I was startled to find a composed male figure standing right before us, hidden in the shadow of a lamp. I nudged Turi, encouraging him to look that way.

We were about to run off, but another figure emerged from the arcade behind us and blocked our path. It was Berta, holding the metallic disc, the threshold custodians' weapon.

"Stay still," she ordered with a careful look around, worried about being noticed by those that still lived in the soon-to-be ruins. City people usually didn't wake up earlier than five, but you could never be certain. Everything in the Fifth District was out of the ordinary, particularly on the dawn of its regeneration.

Turi squeezed my hand tight, a warning gesture. I wavered over taking out the weapon I had been given by Oliver – the fancy dagger which I had kept with me ever since – but I was too afraid to use it. I decided that I wouldn't touch it unless I had no other choice.

"There's no point in trying to escape us, Turi," said Berta in a resigned tone, "we all want the same thing anyway. If you behave, nobody gets hurt. We can travel to Pryaya together."

Turi responded with a wry grin.

"What a wonderful idea, Berta. Too bad there's no way to find out how to use the Merkaba device."

"Perhaps she knows," said Berta with a nod at me.

I shook my head.

"I don't know what you're talking about."

"Why are you here then?"

Nervous about remaining quiet for too long, I said

the first thing that came into my head. "We are here to look for clues."

Berta squinted, finally giving me her full attention.

"Don't mess with me, girl, I know perfectly well what you came here for."

Turi hid me with his body, protecting me from Berta's fury.

"You two should leave before they catch you," he said. "Fabian's pictures are all over the town."

"Thank you for reminding us that it was you who blurted out the secret to that idiot in the first place."

"I only hinted at something," responded Turi, "I couldn't have known that he would be insightful enough to put the pieces together."

"Then you should have stopped him," she hissed. "Poor Fabian had to take things into his own hands. After everything he has done for you, you didn't have the decency to help him."

Berta pointed the weapon at my heart then, and commanded:

"Now, either we shall all go to the earth threshold and you will tell us what you know, or I end you right here, right now."

Turi stepped forward and blocked her path. "She has nothing to do with this, Berta. Let her go."

"Actually, you might be the one I let go, Turi. She is more valuable than you now." She pointed the disc at his chest instead.

"You think she would share anything with you after you kill me?"

"Let's see, shall we?"

Her eyes lit up with rage as she moved her hand gracefully, readying herself to use the metallic disc on Turi.

"Wait!" I exclaimed in panic. "I'll tell you everything I know."

A smile of satisfaction spread across Berta's face.

She relaxed her grip, but still kept the weapon pointed at Turi's chest just in case.

"Let's go then," murmured Fabian, grumpy and restless, "before we wake someone up."

He started ahead, and Berta nudged us to follow him. Turi wasn't as intimidated by them as I was, and continued to reason with her.

"This is all pointless and you know it. The threshold custodian will kill you before you set foot on that device."

She gave him a scornful smirk. "I have taken care of him already. He won't be able to stop me this time."

Strange how the tables had turned – suddenly I wasn't scared of, but scared for, the faceless man.

"I suppose you were too blinded by my charms to notice the real me."

I frowned at her comment. The possibility that Turi ever felt something towards that woman pained me. She seemed to be enjoying my bewilderment and turned to me with pretend sympathy.

"Don't worry, miss, we shall all forget everything once we cross the threshold. We may even become friends in Pryaya, who knows?" She gave Turi a playful wink.

"Why are you so keen to cross over if you won't even remember your past?" I asked.

"Whatever the reason was before doesn't matter anymore," said Fabian, "it's all about survival now. Nothing but prison awaits me here. If you help us, I'll make sure that you all pass the threshold unharmed."

He looked into Turi's eyes and gave an earnest nod, "I promise. That you can count on."

The words surprised me. Did he really mean it? What if he was feeding us sweet lies just to achieve his goal? I assumed the second option was more likely.

On the way to the earth threshold, I tried to come up with a way to stop them, but couldn't think of anything, and began to ready myself to leave Prague and start anew in Pryaya. Had Fabian and Berta truly defeated the threshold custodian, and we were all about to cross over, there was only one hope left. Atarah.

✡

The building identical to our home in the Magic Quarter was in an even greater state of disrepair than I had remembered. The tenants, if there were any left, must have still been asleep, as the hallway was completely quiet. I reckoned that most people, apart from Oliver, had relocated, and left the place to fade away before it was torn down. The sadness and resignation of the building seeped into every corner and through every aperture. Our footsteps on the dusty, wooden steps reverberated throughout the space, alerting only a few spiders on their pre-dawn hunt.

Once we reached the basement, Fabian unlocked the cellar door, and Berta motioned to us to follow him inside. He lit up the lantern on the wall, and surveyed every corner of the subterranean space. I still hoped that the threshold custodian would stop them. I knew that, had he been there, he would have to wait and see what they were up to first, that was the general rule. However, there was no sign of him, at least not yet.

"Take care of the door," instructed Berta, and Fabian briskly did as she asked. He turned the key in the lock and secured the door with some planks, creating a solid barricade.

I wondered whether the threshold custodian's weapon could break through. I turned to Turi, seeking an answer in his eyes. He gave me a gentle, sad smile. An idea had crossed my mind as I looked at him. What if I gave him the dagger? He wasn't afraid of weapons, he could use it in case they tried to kill us. I took my chance when Fabian and Berta were distracted, and passed the dagger to Turi. He took hold of it with an inquisitive look. Then, he quickly tucked it beneath his sleeve before they noticed the exchange.

Fabian must have been there before, as he remembered where the Merkaba device was located and headed straight for it after he had finished securing the door. It was in the back corner, which Vilma, Oliver and I had forgotten to check, close to the ancient wardrobe. He swept away the dust on the floor, making us all cough, and revealed the round, alabaster stone with its engravings. Berta commanded me to tell them what I knew.

"Fabian has to go first," she added after a pause. I was partially relieved to hear that, but turned to Turi for confirmation. After all, it was his mission and his heritage that I was going to betray. He was as hesitant and confused as I was, and unable to react. I looked at the door, hoping it would burst open. The threshold custodian was the only person who could stop us from giving up the secret.

"So?" Berta shifted the metallic disc weapon to Turi's head, and I could tell that she was determined to strike. The thought of Turi dying made me blurt out:

"It's in our blood. The key is in our blood."

I looked at the three faces before me – Fabian's eyes were excited, Berta's mistrustful, and Turi's forlorn. Either he was disappointed, guilty about how things had panned out, or he was weighing his options with the dagger.

"Go on!" pressed Berta, impatient to finally learn the truth. Fabian too began to lose his nerve, and roared:

"Speak up, damn it!"

With an apologetic glance at Turi, I said, "Take off your shoes, prick your foot to make it bleed, and then step onto the middle of the symbol, the spot between the two hexagons."

They gaped at me, perplexed.

"Are you trying to trick us? It can't be that simple!" said Berta.

I responded with an indifferent shrug. "That's how it is."

Turi was the only one who understood.

"It makes sense," he mused, for a moment forgetting the situation we were in. He was excited to recall the things he had forgotten about after the shift. "The geometry of our cells and blood communicates with the geometry of the Merkaba devices. They were set up and built that way in order to let us travel in our current body forms. The machine reads the codes, breaks them down, and puts them back together in the other realm. It's a mechanism based on the geometry of the Tree of Life and the Merkaba."

I nodded, glad that he had remembered, but worried about Berta's and Fabian's reaction. If they believed us, then they didn't need us anymore.

"I hope you are right," said Berta, "we don't have time for second chances." She turned to Fabian, and prompted him:

"Go on, do what she said, honey. You have nothing to lose anyway."

I wondered whether she truly cared about him or whether he was just a good test subject to her.

Fabian took off his shoes briskly. Then he reached into his pocket, pulled out a small dagger, and cut into his toe, letting a few drops of blood fall onto the dusty floor. He stole one last glance at Berta, gave her a brave smile, and headed towards the device. Just before his bare foot landed on the round-shaped stone, a blinding flash of light flooded the space.

When we recovered, there was no Fabian, just a cloud of sparkling dust, dying out in the dim light of the lantern. It took me a moment to comprehend that the tiny stars were what was left of him. With that realisation, I turned to Turi, then to Berta, who were both in shock, staring at the empty space before them. None of us knew what to think. Was he on the other side? Were the luminescent particles just some energy he had left behind? Nothing was clear. At least not until we saw a cloaked figure hiding behind the large wardrobe which, when pushed aside, revealed the entrance to a secret passageway. I remembered what Vilma told me about Prague's underground network. The city contained ancient corridors, which linked all the mysterious places, including the Fifth District.

Berta shot the metallic disc at the threshold custodian, but missed him by an inch, and struck the wardrobe instead. It burst into light and cast a shadow on the man, who had dodged back into the tunnel. Before I knew it, Turi was holding the metallic disc with one hand and securing Berta's body with the other, imprisoning her in his arms. The weapon must have bounced back into his hands when he grabbed her.

Berta wasn't ready to give up, though, and bit into his hand. He squeezed her even tighter, but as her teeth bit into his skin with more intensity, he let go. She was after the weapon like a frantic beast. Turi kept fighting her as she twitched and groaned, roared and swore.

In the end, he pushed her away with such a force that she landed in the corner by the entrance, dizzy and weak. Turi tucked the weapon away, grabbed my hand, and pulled me on through the darkness. Berta's weeping reverberated through the tunnel as we followed the only source of light before us – the threshold custodian's lantern. My conscience had caught up with me. I couldn't help feeling sorry for her. Despite everything, mourning the loss of someone you love was something I could relate to.

The threshold custodian waited for us in the gloom of the subterranean passage, still faceless and intimidating, though he had become our new ally.

"Are you all right?" I asked.

"The disc missed you by a hair's breadth," Turi added.

At first, the threshold custodian was still and quiet, but after a moment he said, "My physical body is all right, it's my soul that aches…" His deep, wise voice drifted off before it regained strength. "The connection between Pryaya and Prague is in our hands now, Turi. We need to decide what to do next."

Turi and I exchanged a dumbfounded look while the threshold custodian continued to walk, guiding us out of the labyrinth.

"Since Berta is the only one who possesses a key to the House at the Last Lantern, the last Merkaba device we have access to now is the one at the water threshold."

Turi and I looked at each other in shock.

"You deactivated the earth threshold?" exclaimed Turi in disbelief.

"Yes. Along with Fabian."

I immediately wondered whether Berta was weeping for Fabian or the deactivated threshold. Turi raced to catch up with the threshold custodian, pulling me along with him.

"How could you do that?"

The custodian lowered his head to the cobbled floor. Then he turned to us in a slow, contemplative manner. I searched the void beneath his cape that mirrored the void ahead of us. It made me uncomfortable, but Turi seemed unaffected.

"Out of necessity," he stated, with a glance at Turi. "As you know, the secret is out there."

"Why didn't you stop her?" asked Turi, his voice becoming angry.

"How? The only way to stop Berta would be to end her, and... it's hard to do such a thing... she's one of us..." he stammered, but I sensed that there was more to it. She must have been important to him somehow.

"You deem it better to destroy a miraculous ancient machine?" snapped Turi. I stroked his arm to calm him down.

"It's not just about her, Turi. Thanks to you, more people know about it now, some have even ended up dead. We must protect our mission before it's too late."

Turi scowled. "Why should we trust you?"

The threshold custodian let out a terse laugh.

"Oh, you don't have to. You can give up your mission again like you did when you crossed over and became fooled by her like so many before you."

Was the threshold custodian one of them, I thought to myself? Turi became silent, brooding. He knew well that the custodian was right.

"It's understandable," he went on in a more friendly tone, "she's an enigmatic, persuasive woman, and you hadn't witnessed all the wrong she had done." He paused, thinking something through. Finally, he cleared his throat and said, "I have kept my eye on her since two of the other threshold custodians disappeared. I guessed that she had something to do with it. Now I'm certain. She has always wanted to get rid of her colleagues so she could rule all the thresholds by herself."

"Why would she get rid of everyone except for you?" asked Turi suspiciously.

"I like to think that it was because of our past, but

I suppose she just needed me. I was the only one who had found out how to use the Merkaba devices."

"What do you mean by *our past*?" I asked.

"Let's just say we used to be close, like you two."

He had confirmed my hunch, but Turi was surprised.

"I don't understand. If you were close why doesn't she know how to cross over the thresholds as well?"

"The threshold custodian code is the same everywhere: you should find this out on your own when you are ready. I would have broken the code for her, but I began to fully understand the mechanism of the devices only after she left me for Fabian."

The threshold custodian turned to Turi with sympathy.

"We are of no use to her now. She will cross over, that's inevitable."

"Over the air threshold, I presume," said Turi. "She knows now that nobody guards it on the other side."

"She might do so, but knowing Berta as I do, I think she will seek revenge first. For Fabian. She knows where I'm heading and has more weapons at her disposal."

Anxiety coursed through me at the thought. Turi gave my hand a comforting squeeze.

"So what's your plan?" he asked, finally warming up a bit towards our new companion.

"To reach the water threshold and consult the Sat Bhai about what our next step should be."

"You mean the Masonic lodge?"

Turi's question baffled me before I realised that he probably didn't recall who the Sat Bhai really were yet.

"The lodge members only adopted the name,"

explained the threshold custodian, "the real Sat Bhai translates to Seven Brothers in Hindi. They have also been called the Seven Seraphim, Seven Rays, or Seven Archangels... Our ancestors worked with them, that is why they went by the name."

"He's right," I chipped in, "I remember Atarah sharing this information with me."

The threshold custodian looked nervously behind us, and said, "I should be on my way, with or without you."

He sped up his pace, and I was about to follow, but for some reason, Turi still seemed cautious. He stopped me and whispered, "Do you think we can trust him?"

"I think so," I whispered back. "Although he seemed threatening before, he has never harmed us in any way. And I like the quiet confidence he exudes."

Turi weighed it up. "I suppose you are right..."

We nodded at each other and continued walking behind him, remaining quiet from then on. Turi's face showed sadness. I anticipated that he was mourning Fabian's death. After all, they had started out as friends. I too couldn't shake off the image of his body shattering into pieces. It brought back the faces of the people I saw being killed by Turi and Atarah. I understood why they did it, by then more than ever, yet it still felt wrong.

The church bells began striking five, their muffled peals reaching us even in the tunnel. I concentrated on the sound, and let it guide me to a soothing memory...

It was during the time I was studying at the Air Dance Academy, and was occasionally visiting our riverside home. I was standing on the beach with Atarah, looking out over the valley where Pryaya was nestled. We could see the tallest tower in the city, the one with the golden rooftop that glowed in the night. There was an ancient bell inside, and it chimed so loudly that it carried the sound all across the landscape.

That night, it went on for a whole hour, as it does when someone from the royal family passes away. They had chimed for the Empress and her son, then for the Emperor, and that day, it was for the Emperor who had ruled after him, and who too had become sick.

"I heard a nasty rumour that has spread across the city," I said. "People say that the new Emperor's illness came as a result of his co-operation with the necromancers. One of my classmates told me she had proof that he had sacrificed people in order to be healed. Do you think it could be true?"

"Very possible," agreed Atarah. "After his older brother and his family died from that dreadful plague, he's been terrified of falling ill as well. And since the healing of the white magicians didn't seem to work for his brother's family, he may have assumed that black magic would be more powerful instead." She sighed at the thought, then continued, "If he broke all the strict rules against magic by using its dark side, then he has set an even worse example than his brother. He was not mindful of the magic law – what comes around goes around – and therefore he was destined to fall. Let's just hope that whoever comes to power next will be wiser."

"And less hypocritical," I added. "They forbid magic to common people, but use it themselves in secrecy."

"Because what is forbidden is never forgotten… In Prague's reality, the majority of people don't believe in magic at all. I'm beginning to think it might be better that way," said Atarah. "The dual principles of our realms still keeps us in the balance between dark and light, good and bad. How can we reach harmony and live pure magic if we twist and turn in the same patterns over and over again? The wise ones will continue using magic anyway. They are aware that if their intention is good, it is not to be feared.

"However, most people today are not ready. If their spirits read things in black and white, and they are stuck with their judgments and prejudices, then it is only logical that their magic can't be constructive. What is magic, after all, than a manifestation of a thought?

"That's why we must always remember – and now it's more important than ever – to never tell anyone about the Merkaba devices unless we can really trust them. If the wrong mind begins to tamper with them or spreads the news about their existence to the uninitiated, they would all have to be destroyed."

# Chapter XVII

## The Star

Once we had left the underground passageway, we headed towards the river, past the National Library. There, the threshold custodian stopped near a fountain on a corner of the grand Clam-Gallas palace. It was decorated with a statue which reminded me of a Tarot card called the Star. It too depicted a female figure pouring water from two pitchers. This didn't surprise me, as there was a lot of esoteric art all over Prague.

"It's an allegory of the river Vltava," explained the threshold custodian. I turned to him and realised I was facing a sixty-something-year-old man with long, grey hair and a full beard. His eyes were friendly, and the wisdom they exuded reminded me of Vilma, Atarah and Hieronymus. Turi also seemed glad to finally meet the person behind the intimidating cape. Even he was less suspicious. The threshold custodian smiled beneath his moustache and said:

"I thought it was about time I showed you the true me. I prefer to remain in disguise, caped and hooded. Occasionally, I like to blend in with the crowd, become a common Prague citizen. It doesn't always pay off though. I bet you have had the same experience, Turi." His eyes shifted to his younger colleague.

Turi nodded, intrigued by the comment. "What do you know about our past?"

"Just the bits and pieces I have eavesdropped," he said, and took a careful look around. After he had made sure that the streets were safe, he turned and made for the lane behind him. "Wait here, please, I need to gather up a few things from my apartment."

Once he had disappeared round the corner, Turi let go of my hand and began pacing back and forth.

"Are you all right?" I asked, in a soft voice.

"I will be," he said. "What had to be done was done."

"Yes, but still... Fabian used to be your friend once and so was Berta."

Turi nodded as he silently gazed into the night, in the direction of the Fifth District.

"I'm afraid," I whispered, haunted by the thought of Berta's vindictiveness.

"Don't worry. She won't come after you, she has no reason to. And if she tries anything, she will have to get past me first."

Turi looked away with a sigh while my eyes shifted to the statue above the fountain. Only then did I notice that besides the water, five pentagrams were also pouring from the pitcher.

"Have you noticed the stars?" I asked Turi.

At first, he was confused and looked back to the heavens, but when he realised what I meant, he came closer and observed the statue in more detail.

"Oh yes… the pentagrams," he mused. "After you told us how to use the Merkaba devices, I remembered my research on that topic. Our DNA and bodies are made of the same hexagonal and pentagonal shapes as everything else in this world. I also realised that Atarah had given me clues all along. She told us many times that our bodies were made of stars. Do you remember?"

Before I could answer, the threshold custodian's return interrupted us. He approached holding a bag filled with food and water supplies.

"Let's go, my friends. We have no time to lose."

☆

We followed the threshold custodian, striding on beside the river. We had already passed the old stone bridge and were heading for the water mills that spread out in a southwesterly direction. Leaving the city behind pained me, but mainly made me think of Vilma. I hated myself for abandoning her without a proper farewell. I wanted to tell her how much I appreciated her friendship and longed to express my gratitude for all that she had done for me. I was also aware, however, how hard the parting would have been. It seemed almost impossible to imagine my life without her, as I had become so accustomed to her presence during those few intense months.

"Do you remember where the water threshold is?" asked Turi, waking me from my reverie.

"Not exactly, but I remember that it was not far from the city. I could see Prague's cityscape as I walked towards it. It was where two rivers meet."

"Three, actually," the threshold custodian corrected me, and slowed down to keep pace with us.

"The third river is invisible in this reality. It's the one which runs through Pryaya. Like the river Sarasvati in Prayag."

"I've never heard of Prayag before. Where is it?" asked Turi.

"The Sarasvati is a legendary river in Allahabad, also called Prayag, the place where our ancestors, the followers of the Sat Bhai, originally came from. As here, the third river in Prayag also existed in another realm."

"But unlike here, it was mentioned in local legend," I noted.

"Who knows?" replied the threshold custodian, "many legends have died out, along with their various beliefs and traditions."

I thought back to what Hieronymus and Atarah had told me. "So much was forgotten," I whispered to myself. The threshold custodian gave me a curious look, so I cleared my throat and continued:

"I have always been curious to know why the Sat Bhai brotherhood ventured all the way from India to Europe."

"They had a powerful mission," said the threshold custodian. "They sought out the power places which function as thresholds to other dimensions. They knew that even if the Merkaba devices were to be destroyed, the thresholds would remain, and those who were meant to find them would. Particularly those who had awoken to the Merkaba."

"Do the thresholds connect more worlds?" asked Turi.

"I think so," he answered pensively. "You could study the Tree of Life your whole life and still find new branches that spread higher or roots that grow deeper. I believe that when the right time comes, we shall see more of these worlds. Curiosity is just the beginning."

I liked that thought and pondered over it some

more as I watched the river of fading stars by our side. It made me recall the moment of my shifting.

"Why did you follow me after I crossed over?" I asked the custodian.

He smiled at the question, and said:

"I was curious to know what brought you over, particularly if your intention for the visit was pure. After I put the pieces together and connected you to Turi, my spying became protection." He turned to me, searching my face with an apologetic expression.

"But you wanted me to leave the Fifth District," I asked. "Why?"

"Because of Berta. She often went to spy on the earth threshold, and you were so vulnerable."

"I'm grateful we didn't meet back then," admitted Turi. "I was not yet cautious of Berta. Who knows what could have happened."

"You were there as well," I remembered. "It was the first time I saw you in Prague."

"Really? Why didn't you approach me?"

"I fell over after I saw you leave through the back door."

"You fell? Again?" he said, hinting at the memory of my fall during my first air-dancing performance, "I must really sweep you off your feet, eh?" He gave me a teasing wink.

"Oh, don't flatter yourself!" I exclaimed, though my cheeks must have turned scarlet. The threshold custodian had tactfully walked on ahead, giving us some privacy. Turi secretly grasped my hand, and that time it felt different, because he caressed my fingers, and then intertwined them with his.

✡

The first horse tram of the morning rode past us as we were crossing the Palackého bridge. The riverbank that we had left behind seemed to have slowly come alive, waking to another morning routine. I turned back with nostalgia, wondering whether it was the last time I would see Prague in all its glory. My gaze travelled across the city's panorama and focused on the castle area that crowned the distant hill. Once again, I said goodbye to Vilma in my mind, promising myself that I would try to let her know where I had gone and why once things had calmed down.

A peach light broke through the dark blue and shimmered above the horizon, embracing the rising sun in its colourful hold. Above it, a big star shone brightly. I assumed it was Venus, and the threshold custodian confirmed it.

"It's a good sign to see the morning star," he said. "I hope that fortune is on our side." He paused and then turned to us with a glint in his eye.

"Did you know that as Venus goes around the Sun, it traces out a pentagram when it makes its closest approach to Earth?"

I shook my head, fascinated with the idea of such a heavenly spectacle. It also made me think back to Turi's research, all the pentagonal and hexagonal shapes in our DNA, bodies and the universe.

"Is the pentagram a symbol of Venus, then?" I asked.

"In most cultures, although some associate Venus with the goddess of love, Aphrodite."

"Is she an equivalent of Hathor?" I asked.

The threshold custodian was impressed. "Yes, where have you heard about her?"

"Someone mentioned her in connection to the riddle behind the word *Tarot*. You know, the *rota taro otar tora ator – Hathor*."

"And did this person tell you that like the Tarot, the goddess of love is also connected with the Merkaba?"

"No. How so?"

"Well, most people think that they can unravel the Merkaba mystery using their rational mind, but if their hearts aren't open enough, they'll never understand the fifth, sacred element of the Merkaba. Without that, they may establish all kinds of artificial Merkaba devices, but never embrace the living Merkaba and all its vast possibilities.

"That sacred element is an essence as well as a divine protection. It makes sure that only those with pure, unconditional love in their hearts may activate it. And such hearts belong to those who achieve a state of inner harmony by uniting the bridge between the heart and the mind. The heart is what crowns the mind with a touch of eternity."

His words were almost identical to those that Atarah had once uttered: *"One should learn to connect the bridge between the heart and the mind. Your heart is what crowns the mind with a touch of eternity, and makes you a master of your own life rather than a slave of someone else's."*

I wondered whether they both learnt it from their ancestors, but didn't want to ask. I judged it better to keep Atarah a secret, just in case he turned out not to be trustworthy. Turi must also have been reminiscing because he said:

"I find it curious that in Prague, the Kabbalistic Tree of Life is only half of the one in Pryaya, and seems to show no pentagrams. Do you know why that is?"

"From what I know, it's intentional," the custodian said. "The Jewish mystics were fond of riddles, and wanted their pupils to find the way for themselves. The pentagram must have been concealed for a reason. Perhaps such a powerful symbol couldn't have been exposed openly because like everything in magic, it could be misused. In fact, the pentagram was the original Seal of Solomon, before it was changed to the hexagram. In an ancient text called *The Testament of Solomon*, the pentagram was described as an angelic symbol of power and protection."

"But what about the inverted pentagram? That's considered a symbol of evil isn't it?" asked Turi.

The threshold custodian paused. "Undoubtedly, it has been misused as a symbol of evil, but does that mean that the symbol itself is evil? Of course, symbols are shapes charged with thought energy, the so-called egregore, but they need an intention in order to have an effect. In my opinion, the inverted pentagram simply represents the 'below' in the Tree of Life, therefore, the earth, our roots and heritage. And I see nothing evil about that."

His previous mention of the fifth element made me think of what Vilma had said about the roots of the Jewish Town, and an idea crossed my mind.

"Could the Fifth District represent the fifth element?"

The threshold custodian raised his eyebrow thoughtfully.

"What a compelling thought, Miss Seraphina! It might be... It might very well be. I can see that you have the potential to become a mystic."

"I don't know about that," I blushed. "Turi has always been more interested in magic and esotery."

"I wouldn't agree with that, Seraphina," objected Turi, "I was only obsessed with the science behind the Merkaba devices. For you, however, my findings were the gate to your own inner mysteries. You were more interested in the living Merkaba, and its association with your name and destiny. For some reason, you always had that holy awe but never delved too deeply into it. I remember what you once said to me: *I'd rather that it came to me at the right time. I'm not the inquisitive type like you.* It seems to me, though, that the Seraphina of Prague does like to pursue things, unafraid to explore that part of her spirit."

He winked at me with a gentle smile, and I smiled back, ruminating on it. The morning star had meanwhile disappeared behind the peachy clouds, and the new day had officially begun.

# Chapter XVIII

## The Moon

Later that morning, we reached the headland that united the two rivers in a triangular-shaped meadow. Nearby stood a solitary, wooden hut similar to many other ones we had passed before – just as dishevelled, and left in a state of disrepair. The threshold custodian explained that the nearby village, Lahovice, had been abandoned after a great flood, which destroyed most of the settlement.

"So what do we do now?" asked Turi as he looked out over the horizon with a worried frown.

"Well, I have to make this hut my home now," said the custodian. "With the earth threshold deactivated, and the air threshold in Berta's hands, I will have to remain guarding only this one." He turned to us then. "It's a different story for you, though. You must decide where you want to go from here. I will let you return home if that is what you want. Your intentions are good, I know that, so you wouldn't have to worry about bursting into light dust on the way," he smiled.

Turi and I looked at each other. We both knew that it would be difficult to choose.

"Nonetheless," said the threshold custodian, "I advise you to weigh yours options carefully, because as you know, with each crossing, a part of you dies."

He encouraged us to take a walk and discuss our options. Meanwhile, he promised to keep guard and prepare a simple lunch. We agreed, but instead of talking, we trod the meadows quietly. The question of whether to stay or return home made us both pensive. There were so many things to consider. The bond with Vilma made me want to stay, as well as the fear of forgetting everything again, especially Turi. If it weren't for that, I would be inclined to go back. Deep inside, I had always missed home, despite the wonderful times I had had in Prague.

After a moment's quiet contemplation, Turi said:

"A few days ago, I had a strange dream. I found myself in a town that looked similar to Prague and Pryaya, but was much purer, both in energy and form. Everything was clean, tidy and polished. It was a labyrinth of sand-coloured, ancient-looking buildings. The river's bedrock was sandy as well, and the river itself was turquoise. There were beaches all around, where people were swimming and enjoying themselves.

"I was looking for you in the tiny, narrow streets. I wanted to show you this mesmerising version of our city, which we had never seen before. I found you at last, by the riverside, with your feet in the water. You didn't seem surprised by our surroundings as I was. You said you visit this place often, but the part of you that sleeps is not aware of it.

"We walked through the town, all the way to its end, and found that the river meandered into a valley of white rocks and deep, coniferous forests. That's where we met my parents. I noticed them standing on the edge of the precipice, overlooking the landscape. They said that all will come full circle soon and that we were to start a new journey during the crab moon.

"I asked them what they meant by it, and they said I would know when the time came. I thought that the place was too real to be a dream, and so I pinched myself to see whether I was truly there. I felt the pinch, but no pain. My mother said that was because in that dimension, you feel no pain."

Turi bit back the rest of what he was going to say. Emotion took hold of him. I grasped his hand in mine for comfort.

"That's a beautiful dream," I said. "Do you think it means that we should go back home?"

He shrugged. "I have a feeling that one day we shall explore even more realms than this one..." He picked a dry blade of grass and began to tear it into small pieces.

"How many times are you allowed to cross over before you lose all your memories for good? Is that even possible?" I wondered aloud.

"I don't know. I'm also afraid of losing my memories again, and perhaps never getting them back in the way that I would like."

With that, he locked eyes with me and gave me an encouraging smile. "But this time it would be different. We would cross over together. You would be the first person I saw. And I doubt that I wouldn't recognise you."

Hearing him say that soothed my spirit. I supposed that he was right. Maybe it would even free me from the uncertainty of whether he loved me as a sister or in a more romantic way. There was never a good moment to find out, particularly not then. If we were clear of our past, we could finally find out what we truly meant to one another.

"What worries me more," he continued then, "is that we don't know what we would return to. Who knows what has happened in our realm while we've been gone. I remember that before we left, it was unclear who would end up ruling the empire after another emperor died."

I nodded, recalling the night when Atarah and I discussed it.

"Maybe someone wiser will come to power? Things could change for the better if we had an honest, reliable leader."

"I don't know. I fear that things will have become worse over there."

I had a feeling that he didn't want to go back, so I asked, "Would you rather stay?"

"I really don't know," he said. "I'm just... I'm mainly afraid of losing myself, my mission. What would we do over there?"

"What will we do here?" I countered.

"Well, that depends. If we didn't have to worry about Berta's revenge, we could establish a good life here, don't you think? I mean there must have been a reason why I have wanted to cross over since I was a child. And you seem to like it here too. Wouldn't you be sad about leaving your friends? Unlike me, you were blessed to meet some very good souls. What do you think? You would prefer to go back?"

"I think so. For you, Prague was a dream, for me, it was just a place to go to in order to find you."

He stopped, and looked at me solemnly, then smiled.

"I have just realised that I have never thanked you, Seraphina. I want you to know how much it means to me that you came here to help me."

"You would do the same for me," I said, modestly.

"You're right," he agreed, "and since you came

here because of me, I think it's right that you should decide. I'll be happy either way, as long as we're together."

The fact that we thought the same way lifted my heart. As his eyes travelled over the landscape, I observed his profile, the characteristic tall neck and wide shoulders, suddenly remembering the many times I used to lean on them to fall asleep. One memory in particular became vivid. We were hiding beneath a cliff by the riverside. It was raining, and we sat beside one another, dozing off. I must have been thirteen or fourteen, old enough to realise that I loved him as more than just a friend. It was the first time I had admitted it to myself. I rested my head on his shoulder again, willing the past into the present.

☆

Once the moon had joined the sun in the heavens, we became uneasy. It was very likely that Berta would surprise us with a maleficent night visit. In order to remain alert, we stayed outside by a campfire, wrapped in coats and woollen blankets. Turi kept me close, rubbing my arms to keep me warm. It was because of this contact that I managed to remain more or less calm. I had always felt safe with him, as he had always been so good at taking care of himself. I couldn't imagine that I would ever be able to survive in the wilderness at such a young age as he had, bury my family, and carry my ancestral heritage on as he had done.

The threshold custodian seemed similar in that regard. He kept his hand on the metallic disc weapon, readying himself to strike at any time. Fortunately, the area seemed clear so far.

"Thank God the land here is so flat," said Turi. "We would see her approaching, don't you think?"

The threshold custodian wore a cautious frown, and reacted whenever there was a noise or movement.

"Well, you can never be too careful. I have a feeling she will have been scheming something up, as always."

"Is it wrong of me to hope she had already crossed over?" wondered Turi with a glance towards Prague. "Despite everything she had done, I don't have the heart to wish death upon her."

"I understand. I would feel the same way," I admitted.

"We all hope it's going to be a calm night," said the threshold custodian, "and you two need some peace to decide what to do. Perhaps you should have some rest. The moon is in cancer, it could give you prophetic dreams. I shall keep guard so you can rest your minds. It has been a long and tiring day."

"For you as well," noted Turi, and said, "We should swap over after a few hours."

The threshold custodian shook his head, though, and peered into the dim landscape ahead.

"I won't be able to rest anyway."

A distant dog's howl shattered the silence of the night as if confirming his thought. I had been considering what he had said before – that the moon was in cancer. It reminded me of what Turi's mother had told him in the dream: that all will come full circle soon, and that we were to start a new journey during the crab moon.

✡

Just as we had done as children, Turi and I lay down together. Turi fell asleep right away, but I was restless. I always had trouble sleeping during a full moon, and that night it was more difficult than ever.

Not only had I feared Berta's acrimony, I also couldn't decide which reality I truly belonged to. I wished I could awake to my Merkaba, and be able to travel back and forth whenever I liked.

As I sat by the window, gazing at the moon's radiant halo, I recalled what Atarah used to say:

"Through sunshine and moonshine, the Seven Seraphim exude their wisdom, so stop and listen whenever you feel called."

I tried to focus within and align with the Seven Seraphim as I was taught to do. I knew that they would help me extend the bridge between the girl whose life I was living and my true, eternal self.

With that thought, an unexpected fatigue came over me. I lay beside Turi, and closed my eyes, thinking about the sentence that the threshold custodian and Atarah had uttered: *The bridge between the mind and the heart. The heart is what crowns your mind with eternity.* With the words spinning through my mind, I finally fell asleep and woke up in a dream.

I found myself on a path leading towards a pyramid-shaped island between two rivers. The third river was below me, rushing wildly. The distant church bells began to chime, announcing that the witching hour had begun. Entranced by the moon, I watched as its white light spread colourful rays across the water's surface. They resembled stars, the quiet hopes from above. The chimes faded into the night as I watched the white halo expand and fade, fade and expand. It seemed as if it was breathing. I even thought I heard its soothing rhythm.

With no recollection of how or why I had suddenly become one with the moon, I traced hexagonal and pentagonal shapes within its sphere. Soon, I understood why. The circling, in fact, gave birth to the two shapes, and eventually, the shapes created a tree. The tree trunk was separated by a complexity of branches and roots which spread over a three-dimensional sphere, which again reminded me of the moon.

I tried to pinpoint the centre of that tree within the sphere, but it kept whirling in a continual, cyclical motion. It began to frustrate me, because I knew that I wouldn't rest until I had that spiral under control. A compelling thought then emerged out of my frustration: *Focus on the within in order to comprehend the without.*

Once I began to focus on myself rather than on the moon and its shapes, the movement slowed down. I had found my centre on *the bridge between the heart and the mind.*

"Finally!" I heard familiar, cherubic voices. I realised that I had heard and seen the beings that had spoken to me many times before. They hovered in the air above me, and were similar to those that Ezekiel described in his vision – they had six wings and four faces – a man's, a lion's, an ox's and an eagle's. As their wings flapped, the moon began to emanate rays of seven rainbow colours: red, orange, yellow, green, blue, indigo and purple.

They spoke directly to my mind: "We come when you invite us. We extend your hand where you cannot reach."

"Who are you?" I wondered aloud as I marvelled at their splendour.

"The Cherubim," they replied, "the guardians of space and time. We help the Seraphim, the guardians of divine light, to pass through the grid that humans are trapped in. You already know that, Seraphina. You have aligned with us many times before, even in this lifetime, during which you willingly deactivated your Merkaba field."

"Why on Earth would I do that?" I asked.

Their answer came as an almost inaudible chuckle.

"On Earth indeed, on Earth you deactivated it, in order to find a new way to it." Their voices faded away, and in the stillness, the memories of our conversations came rushing back. I knew that they had been there for me always, but I had not been able to recall them, at least not consciously. I asked the Cherubim and the Seraphim to advise me about what to do and where to go. This time, the Seraphim spoke through the bright, rainbow rays:

"From our perspective, there are numerous possibilities for your future. However, in the here and now, you have to be the one to make the decision. We can't let you see the possibilities your future holds, and we cannot interfere with your free will, but we can give you a glimpse into the future of the two realms, so that you can perceive what might come to be. Would you like to proceed?"

I nodded, and they said, "Firstly, let us show you the future of Prague, as if it were set on the darker path, which it most likely is, now…"

I closed my eyes, and focused on the images they sent me. I watched as the city's regeneration took place, destroying most of the Fifth District, and parts of the Old and Lesser Towns.

At one point, I saw myself walking past piles of bricks and rubble, coughing as the dust reached my throat. I watched as labourers moved towards the western part of the street, and realised where they were headed. They were about to demolish the house in the Narrow Lane – the one that resembled my home in Pryaya's Magic Quarter. The neighbouring buildings were half torn down already, yet still standing proud. Their timeless spirits rose above their wrecked bodies, whispering their long-forgotten ancient secrets.

Then, I noticed a priest and a rabbi walking past each other, heading in the opposite direction. I tried to talk to them, to ask them to stop the men from destroying what used to be my home, but neither one of them reacted. They either pretended not to see me or truly didn't, because it felt as if I wasn't there. My spirit was present, but my body was in flux like time itself.

I shuddered as the white, two-storey, ten-window building received its first blow. The clash of iron and stone made the first stucco wall fall down, along with my tears. Suddenly, a choir of angelic voices could be heard. It was a group of young girls wearing flower crowns, singing a protest song at what was going on. Their defiant stand against the demolition gave me hope that my home would not be lost, after all, only changed…

Later on, I experienced the atmosphere of the new century, the time during which the regeneration had slowly come to an end, as though it had seemed to last longer than was expected.

Prague had changed. The whole city had electricity, and there was a lot more traffic than before. The transportation system was similar to that in Pryaya, and people had begun to live through what they called technical advancement. At first glance, they seemed happy, excited about the future of their modern society, but as time went on, the atmosphere grew darker.

I saw two great wars spread over the whole world in Prague's realm. I saw battles inside people as well as on the battlefields. The most terrifying were those in which groups of people wore austere, dark green uniforms. They were misusing ancient power symbols, and dishonouring the six-pointed star, making it seem shameful. Those people were like monsters, greedy for power, seduced by the darkness. But I could feel that their ill intentions would end up turning against them. Their insignia surrounded them, bracing them like armour. They entered underground tunnels, caves, and deep, swampy forests, calling out for an alliance that felt alien and wrong to me. Their goal was to bring, once again, the expansion of dark magic into the world...

In another vision, I saw the whole world in Prague's reality surrounded by dark clouds. People used weapons not only on each other, but also on animals. The slaughter of animals became indistinguishable from the slaughter of people. It was like a ceaseless wheel of action and reaction, a cycle of repeated mistakes and wrongs that deepened the realm's despair. My heart could no longer handle the strife I was witnessing, and luckily for me, the vision ceased as soon as I willed it to end.

The pure white moonlight cleansed my mind before the colourful rays formed another image. This vision showed the most likely future of Pryaya. As opposed to Prague, the Magic Quarter was still standing, including my home, but the area was dim and murky, as though buried beneath layers of dust and mist that blocked out the sunlight. The city was nestled in a tense silence as I hovered above it, observing everything in a spirit form.

Then, some invisible force pushed me upwards, making me float away from Pryaya. Once above the woodlands, I noticed that the unicorn statue on top of the highest mountain peak was missing its horn while the lion remained untouched.

I drifted across the forested valley floor by the riverside, and overlooked the wilderness. It was busier than usual. Necromancers and witches roamed the deep forests, scheming, making vengeful plans. Like the uniformed people in Prague, these magicians too misused the ancient symbols and made pacts with malicious powers, planning to bring dark magic back. What surprised me most, however, was when I spotted Berta among them...

This insight into the future anguish of the two realms was too much for me to bear. I resisted the visions, made them stop, and returned to my conversation with the Cherubim and the Seraphim.

"As you saw, both Prague and Pryaya will be challenged with dark magic," they said. "That is why, more than ever before, we need you to bring in light. We need our children to stop the spreading darkness and keep the Merkaba mission alive."

"What is the Merkaba mission?" I asked.

"The path to freedom and true godliness."

"But in which realm would we more likely achieve it?"

"We can't tell you," they repeated. "Only your heart knows which path is the right one for you at this moment. Your true self lives in both options. Whatever your heart desires now will be the best for you. The only thing we can advise you is to destroy the last of the Merkaba devices. Our time of peace is over. Perhaps we shall help you build the devices again, but before that, all the visible thresholds need to be inaccessible to the dark powers."

I turned away, disheartened by the news.

"Don't worry, Seraphina," their voices chimed again, "with each beginning something must first come to an end, and each completion makes way for a new seed. The purpose of the threshold custodians won't diminish. Before the chariots were built, their mission was simple – to spread knowledge of white magic, and bring in light. There's still a chance that people will choose otherwise. That is why the more torches they are given, the more likely it is that they will find the way.

"Prague needs to be protected from Pryaya's dark magic war and Pryaya from Prague's physical war. If both worlds met, it would cause a multidimensional disaster. Merkaba should become the only link between the realms in such dark times. In most places around the world, the Merkaba devices have been deactivated already."

With these words, I realised that our decision would be more crucial than we had thought possible. No matter where we decided to live, one of the worlds would remain closed to us, unless we were to awake to our own Merkaba, and be completely free.

"Merkaba is your destiny, Seraphina, so don't you worry. You are almost at the dawn of realising it."

What they said made me think of Atarah and Vilma, my two beloved guides on the road to the Merkaba mystery. I wanted to know about Vilma's future, whether she would be all right during the dark times.

"She will no longer be alive then, Seraphina," the Cherubim reassured. "The dark future is still far enough."

I asked about Atarah then.

"She is a person blessed with sophrosyne, someone who can show you the way beyond the wheels of destiny, and the grid that binds both realms."

"That must mean I should return home and be with her," I mused.

The cherubic voices chuckled again. "Don't keep asking others what you should ask yourself. As we said before, it's about time that you started to listen to your own inner guidance. Others will lead you astray, even if they seem cleverer than you, and even if they mean well."

As their final words faded, I felt myself being pulled back. I re-entered my body, my sleeping self, in hope of a new consciousness.

☆

I woke up beside Turi, shattered by my vision. Turi was already awake. I had woken him, speaking incoherent sentences in my sleep. I told him about the messages I believed I had received from the Cherubim and the Seraphim. Like me, he was unsure what to do, so we both decided to consult with the threshold custodian. We found him where we had left him by the fire. He listened attentively, curious to hear every detail of the dream, and when I finished speaking, he began to share his thoughts:

"The last time I felt a connection with the Sat Bhai, or the Seven Seraphim as you call them, they gave me similar but more confusing guidance. Your dream message seems quite clear, though. I suppose that if such a future were upon us, it would be wise to deactivate the rest of the Merkaba devices. When the right time comes, the wise ones will create new machines, and find new threshold custodians to look after them."

"How do you deactivate a Merkaba device?" asked Turi, as usual, mostly interested in the technicalities.

"It's the same as ending a person," explained the threshold custodian. "The metallic disc of light does it for you. But you have to be firm in your resolve to deactivate the device, or it won't work."

We all remained quiet for a moment, considering our options. Turi was the first to break the silence:

"This makes it even more difficult for us," he turned to me, "because unless we activate our Merkaba, we shall never be able to cross over again. We'll have to remain in one realm for the rest of our lives."

I nodded, silently wishing that someone could make the decision easier for us. Last time it was simple, my driving force was to find Turi, but once I had, I had no idea what I wanted next.

"If I may step in," said the threshold custodian, "I advise you to imagine how you would feel were you never to see either Pryaya's or Prague's reality again. Which place would you miss more?"

Intrigued by the idea, I tried to imagine never visiting Prague again. I felt nostalgic already, picturing its beauty, freedom of expression, and mainly Vilma. Then again, when I remembered the chaos of the regeneration, and the premonition about which way Prague's destiny was taking it, I longed for Pryaya.

Despite the strict rules against magic there, which I had come to view as quite wise, it was generally a more harmonious place to live in. It was my true home, and I felt the need to protect it like a mother would her child. I also missed Atarah, the wild forests at the edge of the river, the lighter gravitational pull, and most of all, the air dancing.

I realised then that never being able to return home would hurt more. With a deep look into Turi's eyes, I admitted to myself and to him:

"If I stay here, I will regret it for the rest of my life. I yearn to see our realm again, while I still have the chance."

Turi nodded with a contented smile. "I feel the same way, and I'm not just saying it because I left the final choice up to you. When I come to think of it, I haven't found the freedom I longed for here either. Also, if the predictions are right, it may become even worse here than it is in our realm. I suppose I can be myself and pursue my interests anywhere. I always have done."

I was so relieved that he agreed with me. I had already pictured us living peacefully in the wild woodlands like we used to. With hindsight, we had certainly been happiest there. What pained me still, however, was leaving Vilma behind without a proper goodbye. She must have been so confused and scared for me. I ached to think about it. There was a solution to that, though, and I turned to the threshold custodian to ask a favour.

"Could I entrust you with a letter for someone?"

The threshold custodian gave me an earnest nod.

"Of course. For Vilma, I suppose? I remember where she lives." He gave me a mischievous look, reminding me how he had stalked me, and how much we had feared him.

"And speaking of letters," he continued, "if you have truly decided to return home, you should write letters to your new selves. You will appreciate the guidance when everything turns blank."

"True, I wish I had done that last time," said Turi. "I was arrogant to believe that it wouldn't affect me. Did you know about the memory loss, Seraphina?"

"Yes, Atarah told me, but the letter I wrote to myself fell into the river when I saw an intimidating, cloaked figure on the shore…" I nodded wryly towards the threshold custodian.

"Well, it's my job to be intimidating, " he said with a smile, but his face fell when he added, "or at least it used to be."

It must have been hard for him to accept that the mission he had lived for was almost over.

✡

After I completed an emotional letter to Vilma, Turi and I wrote a letter to our new selves. I noted down only a few crucial sentences, as I hoped that they would trigger detailed memories with time. The thought made me smile. Strange how for the past three months, I had been desperate to recall my life in Pryaya, and after I had, I wished to memorize the one in Prague instead.

"Will you be all right?" I asked the threshold custodian as we were parting.

"How could I not be?" he said, almost offended, "I'm the last threshold custodian in Prague. I have to be all right."

"Still, please be careful," I urged him, and grasped his hands in mine to strengthen the plea, "you are also a precious messenger now."

He smiled at my comment and nodded.

Turi also said a proper goodbye to him, and thanked him for helping us. Afterwards, he tucked the letters into his coat pocket.

"But, will we remember where the letters are?" I worried.

"Well, isn't it better to put them somewhere safe than to let them fall out of our hands?" He winked at me, trying to lighten the mood.

As the distant church bells began to toll, we approached the meeting of the two rivers. During the short, brisk walk, I looked back at all that I had experienced in Prague, and I prayed to the Cherubim and Seraphim to help me keep these special memories.

Once at the shore, we took off our shoes. The frost seeped through our soles and into our shivering bodies as we pricked our feet with a sharp stone. Then, hand in hand, we stepped into the water and walked further out, our blood mingling with the water.

The ripples soon swallowed our knees, and we noticed the Merkaba device on the bottom among the slippery stones and mud. It wasn't truly visible yet. Its glow would expand only once we had placed our feet on it, but the smooth, white surface and engraved symbols were dimly illuminated in the moonlight. We stood either side of the device.

"One, two…" Turi counted with a gentle nod my way.

"Three, four," I continued, and stole one last glance at the threshold custodian, whose face was focused entirely on us.

Then we both exhaled 'five', and stepped on the device at the same time. At that moment, an explosion hit the shore. A cloud of sparkling dust replaced the threshold custodian, and before I could make sense of what had happened, everything became a blinding flash of light. I couldn't tell whether I was shattering into tiny particles myself or crossing over. There was only that pure, lunar-like radiance, and then – nothing but darkness.

# Chapter XIX

## The Sun

*Memories from Pryaya, November 1896*

I found myself standing in a river, shivering with cold and fear, clutching someone in a strong embrace. The cloudy sky was brightening with the impending dawn, warming up the turquoise river as it snaked through the valley below the misty mountains. On top of the highest peak, I noticed the familiar lion and unicorn statues that glowed with opalescent light. Far in the distance, a city of variously shaped towers and bridges nestled among the hills. A part of me recognised the view, but I didn't recognise that part. I felt split, alienated from who I used to be. I only knew that I *was*.

The man who held me tightly had slowly moved away, and so I looked up to face him. I focused on his features, his wild dark hair, and wise eyes, certain that he was important to me. I couldn't recall what our relationship was, though. Whatever we had experienced before we ended up in that river of clouds seemed like a distant dream. Judging by his confusion, he too remembered me only on some deep, subconscious level.

All of a sudden, a wave of heat came rushing from beneath our feet and we both looked down. We noticed that we were standing on a round-shaped stone radiating white light, and engraved with an unknown yet vaguely familiar symbol. The heat made us both step aside, and as soon as we had, the stone, along with the symbols, blended in with the other rocks and pebbles.

The man before me watched me in silence, his eyes taking in every inch of me. He was hungry for answers and something else, something I didn't understand, at least not until his ardent lips touched mine. I recognised him in the kiss, recalled an attraction that I could not resist.

Before I knew it, we were on the ground, inseparable. There were no reminiscences to reflect upon, no past, only the here and now, and that's what made the moment so beautiful. It felt as though we had finally set ourselves free, letting go of some old limitations that had kept us bound by fear. We didn't mind the cold, moist ground, or the darkness around us. We were our own suns for a while.

☆

The passion that had blossomed between the man and me had fatigued us. My spirit felt fulfilled, satiated, but my body weak. We fell asleep in each other's arms wrapped in the woollen coats we had on. Despite our uncertain situation, our sleep was sound. I dreamt of a reoccurring image, a body bursting into an explosion of melancholic stars. It made me anxious and apprehensive about something or someone. Before the sunlight woke me, a word entered my mind: *Seraphim*.

As I blinked my eyes open, I saw a woman walking towards us. She carried herself gracefully against the rising sun like a celestial being coming down to rescue us. I turned to my resting lover, the irresistibly familiar stranger. He was frowning in his sleep, ostensibly stuck in an uncomfortable nightmare. I shook his arm a bit, and he opened his eyes right away. Alerted, he sat up and spotted the figure who was now spreading her arms to us. A shadow fell behind her, and her face shone through it. Her gentle, tearful eyes spoke right to my heart. I sensed that she was someone dear. Once she had embraced us, squeezing us tight like her long-lost children, I became certain of it.

"I'm so happy! So grateful to have you both back! You can't imagine how intensely I prayed for your return."

She kissed both our foreheads and then hugged us again, even tighter than before. My lover and I stared at one another, trying to remember who she was, but failing. She was aware of our memory loss, though, and as she dried her eyes, she said:

"I'm sorry. I know you must be confused. Come along, I'll try to explain everything." She paused and wavered. "Well, at least that part of the story I know. The rest we shall have to piece back together."

She gestured to the stand of thick bushes and trees ahead. A thatched roof rose above it, grazing the fading blush of dawn. We stood up and wrapped ourselves in our coats, trying to cover up what had happened between us. Although it had seemed perfectly natural before, we both felt awkward since the woman had shown up. She noticed, and it seemed to amuse her.

"I witnessed your arrival last night, but you were so taken with one another, that I decided not to disturb you."

"Arrival? So we have arrived from somewhere?" the man asked.

"Yes, it might be a bit complicated for you to understand at first, but that will improve with time."

The woman led us inside the circular hut, which I recognised as our home. When I turned to the man beside me, I noticed he had a warm feeling about it as well, as he had a light smile on his face. I was keen to know whether we had known each other for long.

Every corner and object inside the hut spoke of contentment and safety. The woman who had introduced herself as Atarah served us with a revitalising honey infusion, and began talking about our backgrounds and origins. We learned our names, Seraphina and Turi, and the whole story, as she knew it, up to the point when we left for Prague, the different reality of Pryaya.

It was hard to grasp everything, mainly the fact that there were many different realms in what she called the Tree of Life. When she pointed at the Tree of Life symbol depicted on the wall, I realised that it was identical to the one engraved on the river stone, which Atarah called the Merkaba device. However, the one in the hut had a figure-of-eight shape snaking up through it, and was crowned with a white ball of light. Atarah explained that it was connected to the so-called DNA, Kundalini, and the Chakra systems, which both Prague and Pryaya realities had in common.

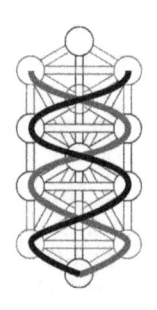

She said that our ancestors worked with its symbolism long before it was forbidden in most empires and cities after the Great Magic War. Those who chose to keep the magic heritage alive were told either to follow the religions chosen by the ruling family, or were banished to the wilderness.

Atarah and Turi's parents were those who chose the latter, even preferred it. However, they were also aware that the path they chose had its risks. Not all magicians worked with magic's creative side. Some preferred its destructive side instead.

"It worries me how many have set out on the dark path," said Atarah, "and they gain more power every day, not only in the wild, but also in the cities. I never understood how, unlike us, they manage to go unnoticed." She paused then continued speaking with a more troubled expression:

"While you were gone, a new emperor came to power. I heard that like his predecessor, he has been tampering with dark magic, under the guise of religion. He plans to build a cult instead of a belief, establish prisons instead of temples. I worry for our future, children."

A soft, female cough disturbed our conversation. We all turned to a woman with dark red hair, who had come from the only private chamber there was. I sensed that we knew her as well, but that was all. My first impression of her was troubling. I wasn't as drawn towards her as I had been to Turi and Atarah. In truth, I distrusted her.

I checked Turi's expression. He seemed neutral but curious. She watched us with a deep, brooding expression whilst massaging her temples.

"Is your head still painful?" asked Atarah. The woman nodded, and approached the table where we were sitting. Atarah offered her a seat and poured her some of the delicious honey drink.

"This should help you with the discomfort. I've heard it can happen, particularly if you cross over from a harsher reality. It takes time before the body adapts to the new realm."

I was confused by what she was saying because Turi and I seemed to feel all right, at least up until the moment when this strange woman had appeared. For some reason, her presence had disrupted the peaceful atmosphere. It felt as though there was an unwelcome intruder in the house.

We scrutinised one another, trying to figure out what our connection was. We hoped that Atarah would explain something, but she watched us with the same unease as we watched each other. For some reason, she preferred to gauge our impressions of one another first, before she said anything.

"What have you been talking about?" asked the woman, still massaging the sensitive spots on her head.

"That the future of these lands doesn't look very bright," explained Atarah, "the thresholds need closer protection than ever now."

"Ah, the thresholds," mused the woman, "I dreamt about them." Her gentle voice wavered. She seemed fragile, both in her manner and in the way she spoke, but it was the kind of fragility which could be used as a weapon. That, at least, I recollected.

"I dreamt that they all disappeared," the woman said. "I searched for them in clouds of mist. Cherubic voices called out to me, trying to guide me back to the light, but I was persistent and continued on and on until I too became that mist."

Atarah ran a comforting hand down her back, saying:

"You might have guessed what was going to happen. I was guided to deactivate the last Merkaba devices. I had already deactivated the air threshold, now I'm deciding whether to deactivate our threshold as well."

We all turned to her, equally as surprised and curious to learn why.

"I couldn't bring myself to deactivate the only link I had to you, though, so I waited and prayed. My patience paid off. However, we should not delay further, children. I trust my guides, and now you have come back, there's no reason to procrastinate, no more time to spare. I shall do it tonight."

"Who guided you to deactivate it?" asked Turi.

"The Seven Seraphim or the Seven Rays, as the magicians like to call them. They give us answers in dreams and visions, sometimes both. They were persistent with this message, and it worried me that I couldn't bring myself to agree."

I found everything she was saying fascinating, but couldn't concentrate as well as I would have liked to in the presence of the red-haired woman. Both Turi and I kept making eye contact with her. The situation was uncertain and tense.

"Will you tell us who this woman is, Atarah?" asked Turi, eventually.

"Well, you should be the one to answer that, Turi," said Atarah with a smile. "You must know each other because you all appeared here around the same time. I saw you two arriving just a moment before this lady."

A suspicious frown creased Turi's forehead.

"How is that possible?" he asked. "We didn't notice anyone else."

"Because you were too taken with each other," reacted the woman, and flashed Turi an acerbic smirk. I could tell she liked him.

"Not that I minded," she added after a short pause, her eyes still locked on his. "I had such an excruciating headache, that I sought out some peace and quiet anyway. Atarah kindly invited me in, and I was resting here until you woke me with this discussion of yours."

"So, you've also lost your memory?"

"Yes, but I seem to remember you, Turi. You were in the dream I spoke of before." She paused, intending to make him guess.

"I hope I wasn't in the mist with you," he said.

"No," she said, "you were in the part that preceded it. We were sitting at a table in a beautiful, sunlit apartment in a city that felt both homelike and foreign to me."

The thought intrigued him. "Was it Prague?"

I sensed worry in his voice, and realised he was coming to the same conclusion as me – that perhaps their connection was similar to the one we shared. Even though on the surface, there was no reason for me to worry, my soul called out to be heard.

"I suppose," answered the woman, and described the first part of her dream. "We were discussing something with great passion, and you were going to warn me about something, or someone..."

With these words, she turned to me. The cold look and the ambiguous choice of words struck me. I fidgeted on my chair, and instinctively moved closer to Turi. She noticed out of the corner of her eye, and smiled, as though mocking me. She seemed to be more confident than I was.

"Someone who knew some important secret," she

continued. "Then there was another man in the room. He was upset."

"Do you know who the man was?" asked Turi, unable to hide his impatience.

"I couldn't see his face, but I had mixed feelings about him. I felt that I both liked and dreaded his presence."

My eyes flickered to Turi's worried face. He held his head as if he too were infected with her pain.

"Have you recalled something, Turi?" asked Atarah, a ray of hope in her eyes.

Turi shook his head. "I almost have. This is so frustrating…"

"Don't worry," said Atara, patting his arm, "I'm sure it will all come to you, or at least some pieces of the riddle. Rather than chasing after the past, let it come to you naturally."

She looked at me then, and I understood her underlying message. Atarah was right, I needed to calm down, and trust what Turi and I felt when we appeared in the water, locked in each other's arms. After all, had he been in love with the red-haired woman, he would have travelled to Pryaya embracing her instead.

As if sensing our silent pact, the woman began to pay more attention to Atarah and me from then on. I could sense her mind was frantic, desperate to remember.

"Have you recalled anything yet?" she asked me.

I shook my head, unwilling to share the strange dream I had had. The red-haired woman's distrustful look made me uncomfortable. She seemed to have seen right through my omission. Atarah tried to remain as friendly as before, though she couldn't hide the wariness in her voice when she spoke to her.

"Since we don't know your name, perhaps we should come up with an alternative for now?"

The woman seemed indifferent to the idea, and

her gaze once again shifted to Turi.

"Why not? I don't mind."

"Does *Berta* sound any good?" asked Atarah.

It was impossible to miss the poignancy of her words. We all exchanged a look, taken aback by Atarah's choice of name. It struck a note within all three of us, I could tell. The woman pursed her lips, readying herself to say something, but changed her mind, and nodded instead. Atarah checked mine and Turi's reactions, and narrowed her eyes, deep in thought.

"All right, Berta it is…"

Then, Atarah's eyes found mine, and we silently agreed that there was something in the air. I couldn't wait to ask her about why she chose that particular name, and what it was she knew about her.

✡

The red-haired woman, or Berta, as Atarah had named her, soon went back to finish her nap, complaining about her worsening headache. Meanwhile, Atarah, Turi and I went to the forest to fetch some wood for the stove. While Turi was dragging the logs back to the hut, Atarah and I stole a moment for a private talk. I told her about the dream I had had, curious to hear her opinion of it.

"The dream could have been a memory," she said, "that's how they usually come back, in visions or dreams. It sounds like you might have witnessed someone being killed by the metallic disc weapon, the one the threshold custodians own. When the disc hits the body, it explodes into tiny stars."

I thought about this, vainly trying to recall the scene in more detail.

"I felt as though he was someone important, but not very close to me. More of an acquaintance."

"It must have been a memory from Prague, as I don't recall ever striking anyone we knew with the weapon."

I shivered at the thought of her killing someone, and couldn't hide my disapproval. She chuckled. "I can see that the trip to Prague hasn't changed you that much."

I tilted my head, not following.

"You always used to be against that part of our mission," she explained.

I returned her smile, then stole a glance at Turi before he disappeared from view. He didn't pay any attention to me, busy with the wood. It shouldn't have worried me, not if he felt the same way as I did, but since he had met Berta, he seemed distant and upset.

"Why did you choose the name *Berta* for that woman?" I finally asked.

"It was a test," she admitted. "Berta is the name of the threshold custodian who lured Turi to Prague. I didn't know what to think of the woman who crossed over right after you. Her heart showed blurry, unclear intentions, and since she seemed to be linked to you, I decided to not use the weapon against her. I thought she could be helpful, the more memories the better, it could make you remember your experiences from Prague faster. However, after I witnessed the strange turmoil she caused between you and Turi, I have begun to wonder whether I made a mistake."

The information about Berta being a threshold custodian resonated with me. I felt an answer clawing its way through my amnesia, yet failed to grasp it.

"I noticed that her name sounded familiar to you," remarked Atarah." Pay more attention to your insights, Seraphina. Your subconscious will communicate to you, give you answers. You have always been very perceptive."

I was curious about the person I used to be and hoped to reunite with her. With that thought, a memory came to me. I was standing in the forest, observing the light and shadow playing between the trees. Then I leapt up in the air, touched the treetops with my fingertips, and swirled back down to continue dancing between the trunks.

I described the recollection to Atarah, and she explained that 'air dancing' was my passion before I left for Prague. She said that I even went to a special academy to study it, and was about to become a professional performer before I met Turi again. The news confused me, especially the concept of air dancing.

"See how we slightly hover above the ground?" said Atarah whilst rising a bit to demonstrate it. "In Prague's reality, beings walk the ground because they are in a denser energy field. Over here, gravity is subtler, and that results in us feeling less heavy. Some learn to float higher and practice different gravity tricks such as the air dancing. You had a great talent for it, Seraphina."

Out of curiosity, I tried to rise as high as she did but failed. I made a few other attempts, without success. Atarah, meanwhile, lowered her body to face me with a sympathetic smile.

"Don't push yourself. It may be more difficult for you now. With each crossing, a part of our personality dies."

"But talents can be revived, right?" I asked.

"Of course," she replied optimistically. "Every part of you can be revived with time. I believe you will reunite with all the Seraphinas you have seemingly lost." She put her arm around me and pulled me closer.

"If the air dancing is an important part of your spirit, then it will come back to you before anything else. Particularly if it's connected to your destiny." She paused and checked my reaction. I was curious to know more, so I prompted her to continue.

"Your destiny is something you have always been drawn to yet afraid of at the same time. The Merkaba mystery. Shortly after you left for Prague, I consulted the Seven Seraphim, wanting to know what your future may hold. They said that if you decided to stay in Prague, you would keep pursuing the Merkaba, but with more obstacles and disappointments.

"However, if you returned, you would awaken to the Merkaba faster through the air dancing. There has always been a powerful connection there, and even what you considered to be mistakes were, in fact, important steps along the path. If they ever slowed you down, it was because you needed to realise something. They also told me that one day you would be the one to keep the connection between the two realms after the destruction of all the Merkaba devices.

"I'm beginning to think that your parents knew this and that it's the real reason why they named you Seraphina. See, the Seraphim angels are the guardians of the Merkaba mystery. They help us remember its purpose. Legend has it that there are three groups of angels who guard the Merkaba – the Cherubim, Ophanim and Seraphim.

"The Cherubim guard its sound as well as its worldly elements and directions. They stabilise us in the realm we choose to experience, but also help us to move beyond it. The Ophanim guard its movement so that we can travel through the different realms in the Tree of Life. And the Seraphim guard its light.

"They all work hand in hand in the process of creation. The Seraphim are like the initial spark – the idea that ignites the spirit. Once the divine idea exists, the Ophanim set it in motion, and the Cherubim help it materialise. The Seraphim are closest to the source, the omnipresence of light, love and creativity. Some say that they exist in another dimension of the sun, others say that they are in the primordial unity, the zero from which everything derives from and returns to, over and over again.

"The more I learn about the Merkaba, the more I begin to comprehend that it's not just about our light body. It's about wholeness, which we achieve if we learn to harmonise the heart and the mind. That's what crowns us with eternity."

The last two sentences struck a note within me. I was sure I had heard those words before. Atarah reached for a nearby stick and began drawing a familiar shape in the mud before us. I soon recognised that it was the symbol I had noticed before in the hut and on the Merkaba device.

"This is the Tree of Life. Turi once unlocked its mystery in regard to the way the Merkaba works, and you had begun to as well. Do you see these two snake-like shapes? They represent the heart and the mind. In their unity, one finds the crown of eternity."

She paused and gave me a benevolent smile. I pored over the image and over her words, as my eyes instinctively turned to the sun, searching for an answer in its radiance.

Suddenly, I experienced a beautiful memory of Atarah and me, bathing in the sunlight, absorbing its energy. I was about six years old, and she held my hand, uniting her own energy and that of the sun into a stream of love, which she then sent through the centre of my palm and into my whole being.

"See the seven rays in your spirit body, Seraphina? Each is attuned to one of the Seven Seraphim. Just as we are able to interpret the colours of someone's emotions, we can also see the colourful wheels in our bodies. Some call them the chakras, the spinning wheels of life, or the wheels within wheels of the Merkaba. Close your eyes, try to focus on them."

I did as she asked and soon began to see the rainbow hues rising up from the core of my spine all the way to my crown.

"Can you see how the two opposing colours create the third? Orange between red and yellow, green between blue and yellow, and indigo between blue and violet? They are the base of more wheels within wheels, and they all derive from and return to the white light."

I imagined the colours spiralling through me as well as through each other, and balanced them from within and without as I was guided to do.

After the memory faded, I saw Atarah differently. She was no longer just a familiar stranger, she was my family, my mentor and my best friend. Although I knew I had loving parents somewhere in another realm, Atarah had replaced them for most of my life. Overwhelmed by this realisation, I embraced her and buried my face into her long, dark grey hair. Then suddenly, another vision entered my mind – the familiar face of a woman in her sixties wearing a colourful, extravagant dress and exuberant flower décor in her hair. I missed her face, but that was all I could remember about her at that moment.

# Chapter XX

## Judgment

The sun had begun to set early that November afternoon, and so we decided to dine and rest before we went on with the farewell ritual and deactivation of the last visible Merkaba device.

I offered to help Atarah prepare the meal while Turi went to chop the wood he had gathered. I couldn't help but watch him through the round kitchen window as I washed the vegetables from Atarah's riverside garden. He, too, occasionally glanced my way, but still seemed rather distant. Atarah was busy stuffing some potatoes with aromatic herbs.

"I wonder whether the food in Prague tastes the same," she said as she decorated the tops with parsley. "I hope you will be able to tell me some day. From what I have heard, they have similar plants over there, though some are quite exotic. Long ago, when one of our ancestors travelled to Prague, he brought back a book with information on the local plants and their healing properties. He then recalled that while he was in Prague, he began to remember our herbs and healing methods, and wrote a secret book about it."

I was curious, but my attention vanished as soon as I noticed Berta approaching Turi.

"I thought she was still asleep," I muttered with a suspicious frown.

I watched as Berta wrapped a cape around her slender figure, and tamed her long, red hair into a ponytail. Her piercing, cool eyes found mine, and I looked away, pretending to not be upset about Turi and her being alone together.

"Turi should remember something about her soon," said Atarah, slicing a big, white onion.

"Before you left, you told me that he was in touch with her. He left after he befriended her through the air threshold machine," she explained as she placed the onion rings in a ceramic bowl.

"There's another machine?"

"Yes. I have never been in charge of that threshold, so I can't describe it very well. From what I've heard, it's a communication device. The air threshold was the only one which allowed the two custodians to be in touch. It's because it was invisible, concealed from the outside world."

She turned to me, hoping that it would trigger some remembrance. It was hopeless, though, as my anxiety seemed to have blocked my mind from everything else but the image of Berta and Turi together. I worried that no matter what had happened between us that morning, and whatever connection we once had, it could be broken because of her.

Atarah poured some oil over the vegetables and tossed some more onion rings on top. Then she flashed me a smile.

"Don't worry, Seraphina, if these onions didn't make us cry, neither will that strange woman. They are as acrid as could be this year."

I smiled back at her and helped her place the ceramic bowl into the oven. She then dried her hands on her apron and began cleaning up the kitchen table. I was going to help her, but she insisted on finishing it on her own. Instead, she sent me to pick some more fresh herbs. We both knew it was just an excuse, though, and exchanged a conspiratorial look.

As I went through the back door, pretending to head for the garden, I hid behind the birches that guarded the door and eavesdropped on their conversation.

"…That's why I didn't tell you more about the warning. I didn't want her to know, just in case…"

"You don't trust her?" asked Turi in surprise.

"Not just her. I trust neither one of them, but for some reason, I trust you, Turi. I feel like you and I have some deep connection."

The words struck like arrows. So that was her strategy, I thought. She wanted to wrap him around her fingers, and make Atarah and me seem untrustworthy.

Turi was quiet for some time, thinking about what she said. It puzzled me and made me wonder whether I might have been wrong about him after all. What if he had changed after he had shifted to Prague, and had turned against me? It could have been that when we appeared in Pryaya, I found myself not in his embrace, but in his captivity. If that were true, however, how would it explain the passion that had been awoken in us?

"I also have a feeling we have known each other for some time," admitted Turi after a short pause.

"You do? I'm so relieved to hear that! I was worried that those two have you wrapped around their fingers," said Berta, her face a picture of innocence.

"Don't worry about that. From the little to nothing I know about myself, I am sure I have always been able to think for myself."

"That's a good quality, Turi. I have an inkling that I am the same way... Have you remembered anything yet?" she asked.

"Just some flashbacks. Sometimes I see you, other times, Seraphina. My feelings are neutral, though. I simply see us together or alone with one another. It's only about the presence."

"I have the same memories," she replied, "nothing fixed, but I have a very bad feeling about deactivating the Merkaba device tonight. I worry that Atarah is planning to manipulate us into something dangerous."

She moved closer to him then, like a predator creeping closer to its prey. "I know you sense it as well. I saw the hesitation in your eyes."

Her sly game outraged me. I was unable to hold my emotions back anymore, and so I strode out of the trees and headed towards them. I caught her look first and held it, unafraid, challenging. Then my eyes shifted to Turi and I noticed him slightly shake his head. I understood that he was warning me. Although I didn't quite understand what about, his tender eyes and the familiar twitch of his brows disarmed me. I swallowed whatever I was going to say, and announced, "Dinner will be ready soon."

Berta squinted her eyes at me, as wary of me as I was of her. I didn't mind. I was finally certain that she was an enemy, and I was determined to find out why.

☆

During dinner, the tension between the four of us grew even worse. I dreaded the insecurity I felt in Berta's presence. I felt the need to assert myself whenever she looked my way. If Atarah hadn't decided to talk about Pryaya's new emperor, and why he had decided to move his residence down south, we would probably have sat there in an uncomfortable silence. Berta kept looking at Turi, and he responded with an occasional nod. It seemed as though they had established their own world already. They ignored me, until I braced myself, and despite Turi's warning asked her:

"Why do you distrust us?"

She turned to me, too taken aback to react, so I continued. "I heard what you said to Turi earlier, and I'm curious as to why you haven't been honest with us all."

I realised that it might have been unwise to confront her so clumsily, but I couldn't help it. I knew at least one thing about myself – I despised lies and deceit.

"I'm sorry if I upset you, Seraphina, I just say what I feel," said Berta after a moment, trying hard to sound casual and composed. I was feeling differently, though, and preferred confrontation over silence.

"Do you, really?" I wondered. "Or are you hiding something from us?"

"Interesting that you would say that," she replied, "as I think that you are the one keeping secrets."

I couldn't believe how eloquently she had turned it around. Unprepared for such a trick, I didn't know how to react, and so Turi stepped in.

"We are all confused, ladies. Accusing and distrusting one another won't solve a thing."

The fact that Turi remained unbiased upset me even more. I wanted him to stand by me, and confront her as well. I turned to Atarah for help. She was scowling at Berta, yet tried to remain calm.

"I think we all need some rest before we do what is most important," she said and locked eyes with me.

"Why don't you all take a nap?" She forced a kind smile. "I'll wake you after my evening meditation with the Seven Seraphim." She stroked my arm, kissed my cheek, and whispered, "Remember to let it flow..."

Then, she turned to Berta and Turi with a casual, 'see you later', and retreated to her private sanctuary, an old shed that she had refurbished after she had moved in to guard the water threshold.

Taking Atarah's advice to heart, I felt ashamed of how I had behaved before. I offered to clear up after dinner as an apology. Turi insisted on helping me, and I happily agreed.

Berta watched us for a while then said, "I'm quite tired. Atarah's right, we should get some rest."

"Of course," said Turi, "the chamber is at your disposal."

It was the chamber that, as we learned from Atarah, Turi and I had shared when we were children. After Berta disappeared behind the door, we carried on clearing up. We were silent and apprehensive in the way we moved around one another. Turi grasped my hand, and whispered, "Let's talk after she falls asleep."

The words, and the way he said them calmed me down. It made me believe that however he had acted before was just an act to keep Berta in the dark about how he truly felt. Like Atarah, he knew that we needed to be cautious of one another. I realised the wisdom of it, and swore to myself to be less reckless from then on, and not let my emotions take hold of me.

After we tidied up, we went our separate ways, planning to wait for Berta to fall asleep. Turi threw some more wood into the stove, and then sat down near to the bookshelf, picking a few books out to read. Meanwhile, I lit up the candelabra by the window and studied the stained glass. It depicted the symbol that was engraved on the Merkaba device and also painted on the opposite wall – the Tree of Life.

Through the bluish tints, the moonlight found its way into the hut. The sight filled me with nostalgia. I reckoned that it must stem from something I had experienced recently, something sad, tragic even. I knew what it was in my heart, but my mind was a different story. I thought back to what Atarah had said before: *the bridge between the heart and mind.*

I turned to Turi, intrigued, but his attention was taken up by the big leather-bound book he held. I didn't want to disturb him, so instead, I reached for something I had been intrigued by ever since I laid my eyes on it – a small box entitled: *Tarot – the Journey to the Merkaba.*

Inside was a deck of cards with familiar images and symbols. Looking at them felt strange. It was as if they spoke to me on some deep, mysterious level. I wondered why the cards were associated with the Merkaba, though.

I took a particular interest in the ones entitled the Magician and Strength, as they had identical hats in a figure-of-eight shape. I was so taken with the symbol that I didn't even notice that Turi had stopped reading. After a moment, he stood up and joined me by the window. He looked at the cards that I was so interested in.

"Does it also seem familiar?" I asked him in a soft tone, anxious not to wake Berta. He examined the cards then shifted his gaze over to the Tree of Life mosaic and then to the Tree of Life painted on the wall.

"It looks a bit like that, don't you think?"

I didn't follow at first, but once I had focused on the two curves sneaking up between the two six-pointed stars, I realised they did indeed resemble the hats of the figures.

"Oh, yes, true," I said, "what do you think it means?"

He shrugged his shoulders. "You would have to ask Atarah about that."

He looked back at the chamber's closed door then leaned over to me and said, "While I was reading, I had a memory of you and me."

"Really? What was it?"

"Our first Winter Solstice in Pryaya."

I tried to remember what he meant.

"Was it a nice memory?"

He nodded.

"Would you tell me about it?"

He wavered, but finally smiled and said, "I would rather let you remember it on your own."

I smiled back, silently wishing I could do just that. The connection we had at that moment gave me the courage to ask:

"That woman," I whispered, "do you trust her more than Atarah and me?"

"No, of course not. I just feel we have some history, that's all."

"Atarah told me you were in touch with a threshold custodian from Prague before you left. Do you think it could be her?"

He shrugged. "Maybe," he paused, thinking it through, "Atarah's advice was smart. We need to be patient. It will all eventually become clear."

"I'm not sure if I can wait. I'm scared."

He gave me a sympathetic look, so I explained:

"Although you are here, right in front of me, I feel like I've lost you. I feel like I have been losing you all my life. I don't need my memories to know what my heart yearns for. It keeps trying to find you, bind you to me, and I seem to fail every time. I might not know our past, but I see the reflection of who I was in you. Which is why I need you on my side…"

He watched me with a caring expression on his face. His eyebrows twitched a bit before his lips curved into a gentle smile.

"I am on your side, Seraphina. I don't know if things changed between us in Prague, and I can't be sure that I didn't let you down or had feelings for that woman at any point. But I can assure you, though, that I too feel bound to you. I feel like I was born loving you. That's the only thing I have been certain of ever since we crossed over."

Those words were all I needed to hear. I felt like grasping them, fixing them in my mind, so that I could read them whenever I had doubts. He pulled me closer and embraced me. As I rested my forehead on his chest, I remembered the many times he had held me like that in the past. It was his way of calming me down. He squeezed me tighter and afterwards pulled away to face me. His eyes showed a blend of shyness and confidence as they wandered across my face.

My lips moved to fill the space that separated us, and paused, timidly inviting him to decide what would happen next. He leaned into the kiss, and whatever had held us back before was gone. No words could soothe me better. The kiss was more than a promise. It sealed something within us both, something we had yearned for since we came to consciousness.

A soft creak disturbed us. Intuitively, we both looked in the direction of the bedchamber. The door was slowly closing. Turi's face inclined to mine as he whispered, "I think she's listening."

Our lips almost met again before he pulled away. I could feel his breath brush against the left side of my face. He planted an intense, painful kiss on my cheek, and then pulled away with a suggestion:

"I know it's chilly out there, but... How about a walk?"

I nodded, and let him pull me up from the chair. Before we left, I glanced at the bedroom door. A strange presentiment came over me. However, I didn't want to pay much attention to it, all I wanted was to be alone with Turi.

He unlocked the door, and as he tucked the key into his coat pocket, he paused in surprise. With a puzzled look at me, he pulled out some papers. They were letters, one addressed to Seraphina and the other to Turi. We opened them and began to read.

One sentence stood out above all the others for me: *Berta killed her colleagues and manipulated Turi to help her on her quest. All she wants is access to Pryaya.*

I turned to Turi in shock. He must have read the same words because he darted towards the chamber. I followed him, but as soon as we opened the door, we noticed that the window was wide open. All that remained of Berta was the mess she had left behind.

✡

We looked for Berta everywhere, but found no trace of her. Atarah guessed that she had remembered something crucial, and escaped out of guilt, shame or self-pity. Either way, Atarah was in an even greater hurry to deactivate the last Merkaba device before any more harm was done.

As the moon rose from behind the clouds and lit up the darkening sky, we joined Atarah by the riverbank. She expressed her gratitude for the mission she had lived for until then, and blessed the new, uncertain one ahead of us.

Turi held me in his arms while Atarah finally released the metallic disc weapon and deactivated the Merkaba device at the water threshold. A short, intense blast of light destroyed the machine, and within a second, the disc bounced back to her hand. It was easy and quick, like the death of the man in my dream. With that thought, I had a sudden recollection of him. He was waving at me, bidding me farewell, when the same weapon as Atarah had used struck him, and he burst into light. The tiny, glittering particles lit up the dark space around him before they fell down like snowflakes, the frozen tears of angels. I wept for him along with them, as I recalled who he was. He was the last threshold custodian in Prague.

Turi noticed my distress, and his eyes prompted me to tell him what was on my mind. I didn't want to, at least not yet, so I just smiled at him through my tears, and shook my head.

We brought our attention back to Atarah who had wrapped the weapon into one of her shiny scarfs and tucked it into her coat. I looked around, worried about Berta, wondering whether she was watching us. I suspected that she was the one who used the weapon against the threshold custodian in Prague and my concern deepened. With no rational explanation, I sensed that the dark times that Atarah had predicted were linked to the darkness in Berta's heart. She was the seed which had begun to sprout, contaminated by bitterness and envy.

That night, however, we still had hopes for a brighter future ahead. Atarah gave Turi and I a tearful look and announced emotionally:

"And so it is done. Thank you for everything dear Seraphim, Cherubim, Ophanim, our beloved ancestors and spirit guides. Please, don't let us go astray on the new journeys we are about to take. May we remain heedful of your warnings, and accept your advice so that we learn to not be fooled yet remain wise fools on our path."

As she spoke, a familiar, cherubic voice entered my mind:

*Assemble all that lights you up and shine on through the darkness.*

With these words, Atarah raised her right hand, waved in the direction of the river, and solemnly pronounced:

"Now all we have left is our Merkaba."

# Chapter XXI

## The World

Dear Vilma,

It took me some time to remember, and I still haven't recalled everything, but I've gathered enough memories to know that I have a very good friend in you. The letter I left for you in Prague could not be delivered, and it pains me because I never meant to leave without a proper farewell. It wasn't fair to you, even though it was the safest option at that time. Many bad things had happened, and I didn't want to risk involving you in the dangerous situation I found myself in. I couldn't share the truth about my home with you back then as I had to keep the thresholds to this realm a secret. However, now all the visible devices which connected our worlds are gone, so there can be no harm done. People would no longer believe that they ever existed anyway.

Although there's no physical way that this letter can reach you, I'll send it anyway, down the Pryaya river that runs invisibly through Prague. You see, we have a High Summer Day tradition here. If you drop a flower made of dried herbs and petals into the river, and allow it to be carried into the sunrise, your wish will come true. This year, I'll send this letter along with a wish that the words reach you despite the barrier between our realms. Whether it is delivered in a dream, a thought, or just in the form of a hunch, it doesn't matter as long as it transmits the following message:

I shall never forget you and shall always hold you dear in my heart.

I hope you are well and happy, perhaps enjoying your days with Hieronymus. I still laugh when I think of the unbalanced harmony between you two. I believe that you were meant for each other. You were right about the *true marriage*, Vilma, that which happens within us. In fact, I found that truth has been there all along, waiting for me to grasp it. Turi used to be my goal, I followed him in spite of my dreams, but the more time I have spent with him, the more I have come to understand what it is that really attracts me to him. He reflects the part of me that I have been searching for – the courage to be as passionate about something as he was. Once I had embraced that, our relationship has become better than ever.

I used to think that we have only one full Tarot cycle per lifetime, but these days I have come to believe that there are many. For me, one such journey happened in Prague. All that I learned and experienced there was important, and is now sealed in the dawn of a new beginning. And the new beginning is the Merkaba. I realise now that the Merkaba mystery was not something that could be solved during my journey to Prague, I was meant to understand that it is my life's purpose. And that's a crucial step, don't you think?

A wise man once told me that the key to the Merkaba lies on the *bridge between the mind and the heart*. I had partly connected the Merkaba with my mind in the past but, until now, not with the heart. That's why the Merkaba symbols and messages seemed so daunting to me when I started to recollect their complexity. They felt empty and spiritless or rather – without a heart.

Atarah, my second mother and friend, says that while Turi's path to the Merkaba leads through science and co-operation with the earthly elements, mine leads through light and movement. That might be why I was named Seraphina, and why I adore dancing. That's another thing you don't know about me, Vilma. I used to be an air dancer in Pryaya. I thought I would never dance like that again, at least not in front of an audience, but then something magical happened.

The other day, as I was swirling between the trees in our woods, I noticed a nightingale watching me. He sang along to the music I heard in my mind. We were in perfect harmony. Then I looked around more carefully, and saw the vista in a new light. I realised that I don't need a theatre to perform. I already had a beautiful open space and the trees, stones, birds and all the other beings of the wilderness were my audience. That awareness was indescribably exhilarating. I have danced with more joy since, and with time, I have had some intriguing ideas for choreography and music.

I wish that some day, when I'm ready, I'll travel back to you, and tell you about all this and much more in person. While for now, the Merkaba remains a mystery, I go on with good faith. It doesn't matter how many more cycles or journeys I have to face. As long as the wheels keep spinning, there's always something new to look forward to.

And so, my friend, this letter is not a farewell, but rather 'until then…'

*The End*

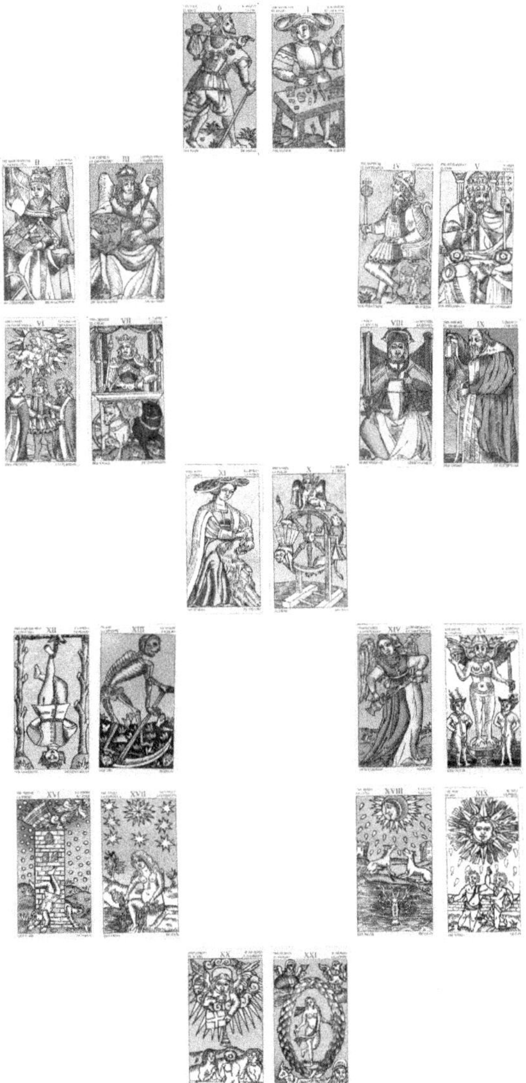

CPSIA information can be obtained
at www.ICGtesting.com
Printed in the USA
LVHW091544120820
663004LV00001B/56